Ex Libris:

______________________

Ann,

Enjoy!

-Colin Wilcox

# Sing For Me

COLIN WILCOX

ISBN-13: 978-0-9885406-0-6

## AUTHOR'S NOTE

Bev was adamant about using the old speech for this story. She loves its precision and rhythms, its nuances. Modlang is fine when talking, of course, but she fires people for using it in writing. It's one of her milder neuroses. I humored it.

# ONE

—VENTURA, CALIFORNIA—

The soccer ball tapped its foot and glared.

"Wake up, snooze boy."

The almost-man thought that was rude, even if this was just a dream, so he opened one eye and glared back.

"Why should I do that?"

The ball slid into a waltz, effortless and graceful. "Because the water goddess will become cranky and obstreperous if you don't," it said.

"Obstrep-a-who?"

"Obstreperous. It's one of those old words, an adult word, and you'll find out what it means for real if you don't hop to it."

The almost-man snorted. "Water goddess. Right. All you need is two functioning brain cells to know there's no such—"

The goddess attacked, icy slaps on warm skin. He jolted awake and levered out of the floating chair, determined to sink his foot into that ball and send it clear to ... the almost-woman. The water goddess. The goddess of crazy yellow dogs and student government, essays and soccer, high spirits and ... curves.

Yeah.

Curves.

She sat cross-legged on the pool deck, smiling and ready to splash him again. He loved that smile, the way it lit those amazing brown eyes, filled them with mischief.

"Okay, what's on your mind?" she said.

He waded toward her and tried to look innocent while he fought a jagged rush of fear. "Huh?"

She raised an eyebrow. "Hello? You wanted to talk? About something? When I got back? Here I am?"

"Uh. Yeah."

*Okay, buddy boy,* he told himself. *Natural and effortless, easy as kicking a ball.*

"Um ... you're back early."

Sludge. Words driven by a watery voice and a thick tongue. He closed his eyes and kicked himself.

"Class was canceled," she said. "Ms. Noguchi was sick and they couldn't find a sub. So what's up?"

He blushed, took a breath and felt the hot glare.

"For the millionth time," she growled, "will you quit worrying about saying something wrong—"

He stopped her with a gentle stroke on a cheek. "I ... uh ... love you."

His face burned but he kept his eyes level, saw the color spread through her cheeks, the panic, the shallow breathing. His chest crackled as it froze.

"Oh, hey, look. I'm sorry if that was—"

She grabbed him and kissed, long and slow, so soft, so warm. "And I love you," she said.

His chest thawed and his heart exploded. No other words for it. "Really?"

"Yes, really."

He stroked her cheek again. She was so beautiful, dappled by the morning sun and playful shadows. Then she stood. He didn't see her hands move, but he saw the clothes fall and the shimmering green bathing suit.

It was modest by the old standards—really just cycling shorts and a sports bra—but daring nowadays. His world shrank, became long athlete's legs, vivid eyes and a full mouth, freckles around a straight nose ... the rest of her.

All of her.

God, yes.

She hesitated for a moment, then slipped into the pool and he reached for her.

"You're more beautiful than ever," he said.

"Of course I am."

He stopped the giggle with a kiss, slow and deep, his tongue searching, twining. This was still a new thing for them, tongues, such a thrill to let their souls collide.

"You're so proud of yourself," she said.

"Of course I am. It feels so good—" He jolted to a stop when his voice cracked, like being twelve again, but maybe she hadn't noticed, except she'd narrowed her eyes.

"Oh, yeah?" she said. "Prove it."

The water sloshed as he lifted her off her feet, savored that tongue. She savored back, then buried her face in the crook of his neck. He let his hands roam downward, gentle caresses of finger and palm. She purred as one of those hands teased at her waist band, slipped under it. Past it.

"You're being naughty," she said.

He purred in agreement, ran his other hand down her back and under the thin cloth, heard the sharp, happy moan. She kissed his neck, then pushed down just enough and kissed one of his nipples, then the other. He shuddered and gasped.

"Oh-my-God-where'd-you-learn-that?"

"I saw my mom do it to my dad. Nice, huh?" Her smile glowed with that happy mischief.

He let his hands wander up and down her back. "Fair's fair," he said. "I should return the favor."

"Oh, you think so?"

"Well..." He pretended to think. "Yeah."

He reached around, groped for the thing that held her top together, realized there wasn't one, saw that look on her face.

"You're so clueless."

More lithe hands, and he caught a flash of green as the top landed on the pool deck. His breath came in ragged waves and his hands shook as they started a frantic journey over her body. She didn't seem to mind. He sank to his knees and lost himself in her for who cares how long, kissing—knowing—with the water cool around his legs and belly, the air filled with sage and the musk of her skin. On an impulse, he stood and nipped at an ear. She moaned, soft and intense. A gentle bite on the neck—a cue from his parents—a kiss for the hollow at the base of her throat. He licked there and heard a gasp, kissed her there again and she shuddered, sharp and hard.

Somewhere above them a seagull cried a long, plaintive note and the caution raced in—this was all too new, too headlong. He'd vowed to never hurt her, especially after they'd become official, but now a part of him was yelling that he was, he would, *knock it off.*

The rest of him savored the musk of her hair and the cool scent of the water.

"Mmm. Wow," she said at last.

"We need to stop," he said.

"Yeah. We do."

She pulled away and he marveled at the flurry of hands, the undulating grace, the shorts landing in the water with a rippling splash.

"Okay," he wheezed. "This is crazy ... Oh-God-you're-so-beautiful-but ... I don't want you getting hurt—"

She held a finger to his lips, stepped into his arms and that *softness*, the wiry hair against his thigh. She giggled as her hands worked, and he felt the tug on his shorts, almost lost his balance as she eased them past that vulnerable part. He shucked them off and kicked them away, prayed this would never end.

"I want..."

"What?" she said. "Let it out. It's okay to just say it. You're safe here."

His eyes took their sweet time, drank in her body as they sauntered up to her face. "I want to buy you a ring," he said in a voice ragged with love and fear and the ache in his groin. "With code, I mean."

Her eyes widened. "I'd ... that'd be ... Yeah! Wow! Yes!" She took a deep breath. "Are you sure?"

"Of course I'm—"

"STOP! CIVIL GUARDS! DON'T MOVE!"

The amplified mechanical voice tore his gaze away, up and to his right. He saw two of them, one thickset and powerful, the other ... oh, God, a woman. They pointed stun guns and wore those riot helmets, the kind that filter out any germ, any virus.

The goddess was livid, her back arched in that proud way. "WHAT THE HELL DO YOU THINK YOU'RE DOING? WE—ARE—*MILITARY*!"

"THAT'S NICE. NOW STEP AWAY FROM EACH OTHER."

The almost-man lost his footing as the goddess pushed him away and advanced on the guards. "GET YOUR FAT CIVIL ASSES OUT OF HERE RIGHT NOW OR MY FATHER—"

He didn't hear the soft *phut* of the stunner, didn't see the dart with its charge, only his goddess, eyes wide and blank as she slumped into the water, arms and legs twitching. His mind jarred loose, lurched forward in a spastic rhythm. The civils were free to leave her like that and give her parents two hours to make arrangements for the corpse in their pool.

"Oh, hey, look," he said. "Please take her out? Please? I started this, okay? It's my fault. I'll do whatever you say, just please don't leave her there."

The first guard yanked his arm and he felt warm concrete under his butt.

"DON'T MOVE."

"I won't. I promise. Please get her? Oh, God, please?"

The first guard looked at a computer. "PROBABLY SHOULD," she said. "DADDY'S IN."

"OFFICER?" the other one said.

"YEAH. A SENIOR."

"WAD OF SECONDHAND ANAL CAVITIES, YOU ASK ME."

The boy knew enough to keep silent while the second guard ambled to the other end of the pool, ambled back with a screen on a long handle, nudged the girl until she was in reach, grabbed her by the hair and dropped her on the concrete, took his time cuffing her hands before he pressed the recovery patch to her neck. But at least her chest was rising and falling.

"Thank you. Oh, God, thank you. I'm sorry. Please, it was my fault—"

"YOU'RE BEING RECORDED. STAY SILENT."

He heard but didn't, more aware of the female guard, so maybe he should do something with his hands, like cover himself. He was about to when a cuff ratcheted tight around his left wrist.

# Sing For Me

WASHINGTON — The Food and Drug Administration today approved the first AIDS vaccine ...

A number of governments and humanitarian agencies have pledged to immunize the areas hardest hit by the virus. The Gates Foundation alone has earmarked $2-billion in aid.

—From a wire story, omissions mine

# TWO

The champagne cork blew past my ear just as the message arrived. Failure to open this link may result in arrest, detention, fines, the usual.

I touched my brooch to let them know I was listening, then groped for a smooth way out of the party. I finally settled on, "Excuse me, but I really need to use the ladies."

I took the back hallway into my office, luxuriated in the quiet for a moment, then waved a hand over the computer. A face appeared—creamy skin and strawberry blond hair, about my age.

"Beverly Anne Wilson?" she said.

"Correct." I put my thumb on the reader, let the laser scan my retina.

"I'm lead officer Sanchez of the Ventura Civil Guard." She transmitted her credentials and the computer verified them. "Ms. Wilson, my partner and I arrested your daughter this morning. Her name is Julie, correct?"

"What for? Why?"

"Is your daughter's name Julie Lynne?"

"Y-yes. What—"

"Birth date August two-five?"

"WHAT HAPPENED?"

My professional side called me an idiot for yelling at a civil. My military side didn't care.

"We found her in your swimming pool. She was with a boy named Richard Daniel Westmoreland. Do you know him?"

"Of course. He's my daughter's—"

"They were both undressed."

From far away I heard my champagne flute crack against the edge of my desk. "Are they..."

"No, ma'am. They're only facing the minor charge, the Class B offense. Ma'am?"

*Minor charge.*

"Ma'am?"

The words lurched and ricocheted.

* * * *

I found myself alone in the Hollywood cliché of interview rooms—two-tone green walls, battered furniture, cameras in every corner, the tangible despair that will probably outlive the building. I sat rubbing my temples and cheeks while an old poem skittered through my mind on crab claws:

*The awful daring of a moment's surrender*
*Which an age of prudence can never retract*

The words shimmered even after the knock on the door. Two officers flanked a well-dressed man. He was a bit taller than I, powerfully built, ruler straight, green eyes vivid with rage.

James Burton Wilson.

Julie's father.

One of history's deeper and wider cavity wads, except I couldn't say that with real weight because he loved our child. He'd been equal parts drill instructor and gentle flame—no face time for her bullshit, but a mentor of endless patience. Julie hadn't spoken to him since he'd moved out.

He marched to a chair across the table, and I saw iron self-control struggling—pounding—to keep his fear in check. He looked past me and into nothing for a moment, then gave my hand a tentative stroke.

"I ... it was my idea to let the kids be alone," he said.

"And I backed you."

"You knew Rick was over?" he said.

"I ... yes. That's what I don't understand."

# THREE

On that morning I'd found myself in the kitchen, trying to laugh at one of those classic dreams. Sometime during the night, I'd tumbled from a ragged sleep into the boardroom at work. Clad in nothing but minty fresh teeth and a fuzzy pink bedroom slipper, my hair the kind of nest any rat would avoid, I'd stood and given the room a winning smile—

"Rotten dog!"

Julie's voice had dragged me back to now. I carried my coffee to the sink and looked out the window at the backyard. It's a beautiful space—an oval swimming pool surrounded by shrubs and fruit trees, made nicely ours by a privacy fence.

On that morning, a playful breeze and the early sun painted laugh lines on the pool surface, wrens and swallows chittered, the scents of primrose and sage crept through the young air.

And my daughter ran around the pool at manic speed.

Julie was a flurry of long legs and baggy shorts, jouncing pony tail and glowing skin, ancient cross trainers, a soccer ball at her feet and a gigantic yellow Lab chasing after.

A twist of emotion raked over me as she flew along, a trill of love and envy. She had such joy in life, such confidence in it. Why could I never be that strong?

Along with that came pride. Despite losing a husband and the usual pains of child rearing, I'd nurtured a level, founded young lady. I'd dangled the values and she'd caught them—how to act, what to say, the correct games to play. She'd get ahead, do better than I.

My emotions roiled until a muffled knock sounded on the fence. Julie kicked the ball into the pool and Harley dove after it with canine abandon. She opened the gate and smiled as the almost-man limped into the yard. He was past six feet, lean and wiry, with blue eyes and a mop of blond hair that no chemical will ever tame.

This was Rick, and after two years of high-school romance, all the clichés still applied. He lit the stars, made the angels weep, you name it. They shared a brief kiss, another, then Julie wrapped her arms around his neck and leaned back.

He glared at her as they toppled into the pool, then stood and said something. Julie's eyes widened, and a moment later two kids were dripping water all over my kitchen.

She breezed past me with an airy, "He needs emergency surgery. I have to change."

I cocked an eye and he blushed, but then he always blushed.

"I went up to head the ball," he said with his usual economy. "Some idiot elbowed me in the back."

"It's seven-forty-one in the morning, Richard, and you already have a game under your belt?" I shouldn't have been surprised. Soccer was his religion, and he was already a demi-god.

"I could always roam the streets unsupervised," he said. "Mind helping with a patch?"

He fished one out of a pocket—he always seemed to need them—started to peel off his shirt, then stopped with a grimace and a stifled cry. Motherhood kicked in, and without thinking I helped him slip it off. Yes, that was an improper, but then he turned around and I caught my breath. The bruise ran from spine to right shoulder, a hypocenter of purple and black with greenish edges. He handed me the pain patch and I rolled it out, pressed it home.

"This will take a while. But this," I gave the patch a kiss, "will help."

Another improper, but I couldn't resist. Seeing his face turn all those shades of red was just too much fun. I helped him into his shirt for the same reasons, then gave him a look.

"Next time, use the eyes in the back of your head."

"I know, I know. Forgot them. At home, I mean, and ... thanks."

Julie breezed in, dressed in the baggy hemps that were all the rage back then. "Shall we?" she said, offering me a dance.

I stepped into her arms and we waltzed to the entryway, with its slanting beams of light and wandering dust motes. It was our new morning thing, one we'd fallen into after Jim left.

She placed her finger in the tester. I did the same, and then the fear paralyzed me.

"Hellllooo..."

My God, the risks I was taking. Who did I think I was, whipping ideas from before the virus—

"Reality, such as it is, calling Beverly Anne..."

I took a breath and smiled.

"You okay?" Julie said.

"Yes, hon. Just keyed up."

In real life I was terrified, but she didn't need to know that. Today could destroy me. Twenty-three years of work, the jobs of three assistants, and my seat in the professional class, all at the mercy of an arrogant runt.

Why the hell had I gone into advertising?

The tester pulled blood through my skin and ran the usual virus check. While it worked I gave myself a final look in the mirror, checked those subtle badges of rank and status—fine wool the perfect shade of business gray, every hair in place (for once, thank God), dye job natural enough, blouse feminine in that understated way, lips a bit thin, nose just not quite ... something.

My daughter bumped me, a gentle thrust of shoulder and hip, and I saw the dancing smile.

"You'll kill them," she said. "You always do."

I hoped so. I'd grown up on the professional tier and I wanted to stay there, give the advantages to my daughter, watch this raptor of a girl bolt from the ledge and fly.

The tester beeped and turned our safety badges green. I pinned mine to my cloak—linen with handmade lace on the collar and cuffs, another badge. Julie pinned hers to a baggy soccer jersey that read 'Pele' on the back in cracked white letters. The sun glinted off a ring on her right hand, a stylized soccer ball, her only concession to girly vanity.

Rick looked away during the process. I'm not sure why testing for the virus is such a private thing. Everyone does it before they enter or leave, and it's not like we frolic naked while we test, but for some reason it's something you just don’t watch unless you're family.

I turned to him when I was done. "Rick, why don't you go float in the pool? The patch will work faster."

# FOUR

I'd congratulated myself on that small piece of love and affirmation, and now it would probably cost me one of my few real friends. Rick's mom and I had bonded over coffee and giggles about puppy love. Diane Westmoreland loved to paint, and she was good enough that I'd tried to entice her into commercial assignments. She was also a master at embarrassing her son and his girlfriend by screaming herself crazy during soccer games.

But now we'd probably nurse our wounded kids as best we could and go our separate ways ... I told myself to stop. *Don't surrender your life to the past tense until it gets there, dearie.*

I also tried to ignore my lover of twenty-three years, and I was busy failing at both when someone lifted me out of my chair.

"Oh, God, sweetie."

This was Jennifer, Jim's older sister, elegant and forceful, striking in the same square-jawed way as her brother. Behind her came a tall man, dressed in wool, handsome in the way of balding guys with prominent noses. He offered the perfect business handshake and I met William J. Selcraig, attorney. Jen said he specialized in representing ... my child.

Who knew the rules.

Who supposedly had her feet on the ground.

"Mr. and Ms. Wilson?" The third voice was dry and official, the strawberry blond hair flecked with gray. Under different circumstances I'd have smiled at Lead Officer Sanchez.

"I'm sure you have questions—"

"Let's start with a simple one," my ex said in a quiet voice. "Was there really a crime?"

Sanchez reached put a computer on the table and said, "Incident footage, Wilson residence." She sounded almost bored, as though she'd dealt with the likes of my ex so often, why even bother to frown?

A quick blue flash and the naked kids hovered over the table, waist deep in the water, growing larger as Sanchez neared the edge of the pool.

Rick said something garbled. Julie's eyes went wide.

"I'd ... that'd be ... Yeah! Wow! Yes—"

Sanchez had enough mercy to stop the video, and in the stifling silence that followed I groped for someone to cling to, anyone, and I looked to my ex. I suppose that was inevitable, residue from those twenty-three years, but any idea of sympathy or help dissolved when I saw the calculating eyes. I'd only seen that look once before, when I'd gone with him on a reserve weekend and watched him win a war game against a superior force.

The lawyer and the cop traded legal-speak about arraignments and charge sheets. Out of the corner of my eye, I saw Jim rest his right hand on the table. If I hadn't known his background, I wouldn't have suspected a thing. The hand was empty, but he was up to something, probably illegal, and that meant our daughter was in more danger, *damn him...*

"My report will say that the boy was at risk of a climax," Sanchez said.

"Oh, really?" Jim said. "And just how do you know? You have some kind of orgasmic divining rod?"

"Would you rather we were too late?"

She had a point. After you're arrested, a tech swabs you with a treated pad. If the pad shows even a minute trace of semen, you have about eighteen months to live.

I knew Jim saw the logic, the transparent reminder that the guards had probably saved his daughter's life, not to mention his career, but that did nothing for the cold gaze.

"Who was observing our back yard?" he said.

"You know I can't tell you that." Sanchez had the same expression I used when Julie was twelve and acting like it. "Do you want to see your daughter?" she said.

"Where do I post bail?" Jim growled.

"You can't, sir."

The cold gaze turned white hot. "You better have a world-class reason for that."

The guard sighed. "It's the law. You know that thing we both swore to uphold? Julie's talking with a psychiatrist—"

"You arrest her and suddenly she's crazy?"

"No, sir. Being arrested in her circumstances hurts like hell."

"And I'm sure you know that firsthand."

I'd have shot my ex at that point, but the guard was perfectly neutral, nicely level. "During training, they gave us a weekend off. They even paid for our mates to join us, gave us hotel rooms. Can you figure out what happened next?" Sanchez let the words hover, gave my ex a frozen smile. "Now, would you like to see your daughter?"

Jim's eyes slid into neutral and he nodded. His hand still hadn't moved.

Sanchez motioned the lawyer and my sister-in-law out of the room. Jennifer glared at that—she could swing more weight than anyone there—but the lawyer touched her arm and inclined his head. She stepped around the table and held on to her brother for a moment, then left without a word.

As my ex watched her go, he slid the hand into a pocket, casually, indifferently, almost a gesture of defeat. I turned away and fought the urge to ask him what he was doing. My simple question would alert the guards, probably keep my daughter safe, show that even though we were military we were cooperating.

"Are you Julie Wilson's parents?"

A bear filled the doorway. Well north of six feet tall, broad and thick. He sported a neat beard and a halo of flyaway white hair. We nodded. He fished a remote out of his pocket, pressed a button, and a shimmering privacy screen covered the walls.

"My name is Alex Johnston. I'm a psychiatrist here. I help youngsters deal with being arrested on sexuality charges—"

Jim stood, the quiet movement and hard focus of a leopard on the hunt. "If my kid needs a shrink, I'm not going to trust some idiot who can only find a state job."

The gentle smile caught me by surprise. "Two years ago, I retired as head of psychiatry at Cedars Sinai. And since resumes seem to be important, Major Wilson, I'm also Colonel Johnston, MCNAF, retired."

Jim froze. "I do *not* intend to make my service or my rank an issue in this—"

"And I'd have your head if you did, major. That's why this conversation is private. I don't want anyone making military status an issue. Ever. Now sit. Please."

Jim complied in body but not spirit. "So why isn't my daughter allowed bail?"

"Because the justice ministry wants to make sure she won't kill herself."

Jim slammed his palms onto the table, a flat, hard slap that nearly jerked me to my feet. "I know her well enough, and that's bullshit, doctor."

Johnston looked at him for a long moment, then another. "Kids in this situation can spiral down at any time, and no one can predict when that will happen."

"And I told you, I know my daughter."

The older man sighed. "If Julie is convicted, she'll be half way to a suicide attempt without my help."

"And you know this how?" Jim said.

"Before I convinced the ministry to let me come on board, half of the kids charged with Class B offenses were attempting suicide, and about half of them succeeded. And even when they didn't they caused permanent damage of some kind—mental, physical. But the telling factor here is that virtually all the kids who tried were the overachievers, the athletes, the top students."

I wheezed, one of those gasping moans that come when something twists too far. I'd lost a husband and now I could lose my daughter? I'd kept it together when my parents died, slogged through my divorce, but when that simple math wafted through the air my core started to crumble, or maybe fade is a better word, and I found myself looking over a jagged edge into ... *oh, God ...*

"Stop."

The voice had force, the quiet projection of something absolute, and it brought me back to myself, and to a white beard and reassuring smile.

"I know this is an emotional time, but I need your attention," he said. "I can steer Julie away from suicide. I'm good at that. But I need to know something." He looked at us with keen, penetrating eyes. "Are you planning to disown your daughter?"

The floor did unnatural things. "What?" I stared at him; he stared back. "You mean ... parents disown their kids because..."

Jim's chair squeaked as he shoved it back, his eyes colder and harder than I'd ever seen them.

"That isn't us." He pointed to himself and to me with rapid, spastic gestures. "Okay, she and I split up, but when it comes to our daughter, that is not us."

"With all due respect, you don't seem too loving at the moment," Johnston said.

My ex shot to his feet. "If you come between Julie and me, I'll go straight through you, mister."

The big man held still and leveled his gaze on my ex. Jim finally sat.

"I served in the same Marine Corps of the North American Federation as you, correct?" Jim nodded. "I'm only going to say this once, major. I'm her warrior now, at least for the next few days, and I will protect her from anyone. Even you. Clear? So you will stand down right now."

My ex complied in body, and hey, maybe even spirit.

The doctor slipped out the door and helped my daughter shuffle into view. She looked at me for a moment, then dropped her eyes. But in that moment I saw wreckage. I'd never seen that kind of shadow in those eyes. She'd walked away from even her worst mistakes exasperated, disgusted, but never beaten. So what was I supposed to do now? What should I say?

When the stress piles up, I focus on details. I took in a faded beige coverall and gray cloth slippers—not her colors *at all*—a restraint belt with metallic cuffs, locked by the usual super magnets and scratched from heavy use, eyes red from what I assumed were tears. I knew nothing of the stunner and wake-up patch.

The doctor pressed a finger to the belt and the cuffs opened. Julie stood with head down for a moment, then turned and made for the door. Jim started toward her; Johnston motioned him back to his chair while he caught

Julie's arm, an elegant little ballet of shame and parental concern.

"Julie." The doctor turned her, held her eyes. "I won't let them hurt you."

Excuse me? Who did he think he was? Who did he think we were? He watched with quiet ferocity as Jim stood tried to embrace her. She shied away and glared at him, distrust vivid on her face, and he dropped his arms but not his gaze. They waged silent war until he spoke.

"I don't care what happened today. I love you, and nothing will change that." He spoke in level tones, tried to reassure.

Julie snorted, shuffled over to a chair and sat facing me.

"I'm sorry," she said in a vacant half voice.

I drew her close. "I know."

She raised her eyes for just a moment, and I still shudder at what I saw—the restless energy of the caged animal, the blank despair of someone who thought herself damned.

"You haven't forgotten that we love you, right?" I said.

Julie shrugged. "They'll keep me here for a while."

"We know," I said.

"After they let me out, um ... I have a roommate. Her name's Kari, and she says I can live with her."

"Of course you ... what did you just say?"

"She finishes her sentence in a couple days and she says there's a spare bed in the post-confinement dorm. I can finish school, get a job—"

My hands found her shoulders and pushed her away.

"Look at me, Julie Lynne." I waited until she focused. "What kind of relationship do we have? We talk, even if it's clumsy. We're honest, we forgive, we move on—"

"But what I did—"

"Yes, what you did. And it's huge, what you did, especially because we trained you not to. But you're my child. Our child." I motioned at Jim. "What happened today won't change that. What happens *after* today won't change that. You will never have to live with some stranger." I cupped her left cheek with my right hand, just so, our oldest gesture. "I meant what I said. You're coming home."

"And if not, you can stay with me—"

Julie threw her father a look that sliced him at the knees.

Silence then, thick with bewildered fear until the doctor stepped in.

"Time to get you settled," he said.

Julie's face paled, but she offered me a tentative hug, fired another plasma charge at her father, then stepped through the door and held her hands out from her sides. We watched in more stunned silence as a guard shackled her and led her away.

"Ms. Wilson? Mr. Wilson?" That reassuring smile drew me out of the trance. "Stay here. Your lawyer needs to talk with you."

Another silence. The whine of the ventilation drove me insane, created a manic need to do something, say something. Anything.

"I pitched a campaign today," I said. "Probably the biggest one I'll ever see."

"Who to?" Jim said.

"Paolo Recchi."

"The clothes guy?"

I nodded.

"That'll be huge."

"It went so well that we threw a ... social. It's not like we landed the account, but we gathered anyway."

Jim put a hand on my arm, and for a moment we were our old selves.

"This must feel so schizophrenic, like such a whipsaw—"

A throat cleared and Will Selcraig entered, took a breath and twisted at a class ring on his right hand.

"The arrest reports contain some mistakes, but you saw the recording—"

"And I've seen you shred that kind of evidence," Jim said.

"Yes. But—"

"Do it again. It's what I'm paying you for."

"But Jim—"

My ex stood and pointed a finger. "I said fight. I don't care what it costs, I want everything you have. Clear?"

"And you'll get it. But fighting isn't your decision."

"What do you mean?"

"Julie's old enough to plead without your consent."

I shook my head. The kid wasn't old enough to vote, but she could toss her life into the composter?

Jim snorted. "Like I'm worried about that?" Without another word, he gathered his coat and marched from the room.

Selcraig turned to me after the door closed. "What will you do if she doesn't fight, Ms. Wilson?"

Fight? Who cared about a fight? My ex had done something with that guard's computer. I wanted to know what, but I didn't dare say a word.

* * * *

Jennifer insisted on driving me home. We took her exotic car and held hands in a numb silence as my tiny commuter trailed behind.

Jim's military status gave us the right to use a lock with keys instead of a computer the civils can override. And on that afternoon my hands shook so badly Jen had to insert and turn for me. For some reason, Julie had left her computer on the table in the entryway, and the message flag undulated over the little cube. Out of habit I waved my hand through the hologram and a young lady faded in—liquid brown eyes and flawless dark skin, intricate braids, an elegant oval face.

"Wilson, Charlie asked me out! I've been dying to tell you all day, so where *is* your slob ass?"

Ke'andra Burke, Julie's best friend since the wise age of five. On any other day I would have celebrated. Instead I used a parental override, deleted the message and went out to the pool. Rick's shorts clogged the filter, Julie's top drifted aimlessly in the shallow end. I retrieved the clothes and sat on the deck.

As the flaccid swimwear left a puddle in my lap, an old memory slithered out, one I'd ignored for twenty years. It hovered, cold and vile, and on its heels came a pounding, nagging guilt.

*Careful. Remember what you really are.*

The dog gave my ear a tentative kiss. Jen took my arm and said something about food.

* * * *

My ex blew into his apartment and threw his jacket on a chair, sat on the jacket and stared out the window. He'd been proud of his life—a military officer without the aid of family connections or patronage, a stellar career and sexy wife, the beautiful daughter. Not bad for a hick from Glacier Provincial Park.

But now ... now the most he could do was shake his head and wonder at his monumental idiocy. He'd grasped at something he thought would make him happier, only to have it crumble to dust, to find that what he'd had was more than enough.

His apartment was a jumble of mismatched furniture and open boxes, even though he'd lived there for eight months. He dove into a box and extracted a crystal tumbler and a bottle of expensive tequila, poured two fingers and slugged it back, poured two more and gave the tumbler an evil look.

"FUCK!"

The crystal shattered against a wall, splattered Agave and shards over half the room. He slumped into the chair.

"Way to go, Wilson. Very mature. Just what your kid needs."

He put his face in his hands and bawled.

# FIVE

The soothing mechanical voice barged in and forced me up. I waved and Selcraig faded in, starched, buttoned down, full throttle.

"I just heard from the court. They'll arraign Julie at two. I need you there a half hour early so we can talk. Dress well but avoid flash. We have one of the best judges in the business, and she likes to see well-kept, supportive parents, okay? Don't mean to be rude, but I need to break off and link Jim."

"Good morning to you, too," I said to the now-blank screen, just before it fuzzed out. "Do you realize what time it is?" I looked at the computer again and saw it was 8:47, hours after my normal wakeup, but what did I expect after a night of chardonnay and reading about the scars justice could leave on my child?

I kicked myself out of bed and into the kitchen. I needed to shower, pick out clothes, and *my* daughter was *not* going to court in one of those ungodly coveralls. I needed to call work, medicate this hangover, and then just what the hell was I supposed to do with myself?

"Coffee," I barked at the machine.

"Right here."

Jen held out a cup with one hand and stirred something with the other.

My jaw flapped. "I thought you went home," I finally said.

"And leave you here alone? I stole your couch."

"You could have used Julie's bed."

"Tried. Couldn't find it."

She was only half joking. A clean room wasn't one of my daughter's strong points. I downed half the coffee, let Jen guide me through breakfast—okay, it was more that I needed her to guide me—and started to feel vaguely intact when the soothing voice intruded again.

"Annie Waldenburg is at the door. She is virus free and requesting entrance."

Still in my nightshirt, I opened the door to our neighbor of twenty-three years. She was a slight woman with well-earned wrinkles, porcelain skin dotted with age spots, flowing gray hair and a vocabulary best described as an unstable nuclear device.

She was also the kind of neighbor you dream of—the one who helped us move in, who took a sneaky look around one evening and got me skinny dipping in the pool, who gave us the rare gift of a farm subscription so our child could eat something other than processed soy beans.

And she was Julie's *grand-maman*, a job she created roughly two seconds after we brought our grub home from the birthing clinic. She'd been a constant stream of love, cookies warm from the oven, and the occasional butt kicking.

True to form, she carried a plate of something sweet and warm covered in a red-checkered cloth, and she looked worried.

"Bev, I don't mean to pry, but is everything okay? The guards were here yesterday, and..."

I sighed, reached for Jen's hand and spilled the story. Annie's face darkened and she set the cookies on the entryway table, beside the computer.

"No matter what happens, don't blame yourself, Bev. Hell, we all know youngsters learn the hard way."

"Did you see anyone snooping around?" I said.

"I was just coming back from a walk on the beach. But really, whoever called the civils was probably trying to look out for the kids, not to mention the rest of us. There was nothing mean-spirited about it."

"How do you know?" Jen growled.

"An old lady's intuition. Give Julie my love, dear, and come over if you need anything—talk, whatever. But really, I'm sure things will terminate well."

She marched away. We stood with our jaws hanging.

* * * *

My ex settled into his office, engaged his own privacy screens and took a cufflink out of his pocket. Except it wasn't a clothing accessory. In the lingo of his weekend job, it was a leech, with enough digital muscle to grab data from any computer within twenty feet, no matter how heavily guarded.

Thing is, anyone can get data. All you have to do is turn the thing on. But if you try to read the data, alarms go off and knickers twist unless you have the right permissions. Or you're good. And my ex was beyond good.

He turned on a muzzle, a device that prevented anything from talking to anything, then plugged the leech into a tiny box. He didn't know what he'd stolen, but his instincts had screamed that the guard was hiding something, and he was determined to see they played fair. He certainly had. For now, at least.

"Computer, did you capture any data?

"Two video files in the ReaLife format, eighty-three arrest records, nine calendar items—"

"Stop," Jim said. "Describe the videos."

"They contain authentication and protection algorithms used by the civil guards and some military units to—"

"Can you play them?"

"Yes."

"Do they contain human genitalia?"

"Yes."

"Obscure that." Yesterday had been more than enough.

"Done," the computer said.

"Play files."

Two screens appeared. The videos ran for a little more than five minutes. He watched them three times, slumped into his chair and tried to unravel the events. To use more of the weekend lingo, his daughter's position had been overrun by superior strength, and when that happens, when it's hopeless, you fight like hell until you can't anymore. Julie certainly would, and so would he, even though it meant he'd go to prison.

He called up his address book and opened a link. The man on the other end was big, blond, cherubic.

"Major Wilson! How are you?"

"You coming in for the next reserve weekend?" Jim said.

"Of course. You're buying the beer."

"I'm going to need a few minutes of your time, colonel."

"Everything okay, Jim?"

"No, Ty. Everything's not."

* * * *

The sleek exotic again, an Italian something-or-whatnot, gliding along the maglev strip toward the Justice Center on Poli street in downtown Ventura.

I broke out of my haze, just enough. "Oh, God, I forgot to link work—"

"Easy," Jen said. "I did it for you."

"You ... *what*? What'd you tell them?"

"I kept it simple. You had an emergency and you'd be back in a couple days."

I took a moment to breathe. "That was probably better than what I'd planned to say."

"Which was?"

"Something career enhancing, such as, 'Oh, hi. My daughter and her boyfriend got a *little* off-rail yesterday, so now I need to go to court in a well-kept and supportive manner.'"

Jen sighed and squeezed my hand some more. "Your neighbor, Annie? That was bizarre."

"She grew up on the tail of the insanity, spent a few years in a hive. I'd be weird about the virus, too."

I shuddered at the thought. Living underground just to stay alive.

"That wasn't just weird, Bev. It was brittle. Angry."

I waved a hand. "She's just upset. She loves Julie to pieces."

Silence, and then I twisted in my seat as the words finally came.

"How can that lawyer fight this thing?"

"Will? He's scary good at what he does," Jen said.

"How do you know?"

"He handled the estate after Gerry died."

That made it my turn to squeeze Jen's hand, to sympathize, but I couldn't. As much as I missed Gerry Bannon, still ached over his loss, I had no time for the memories of constant laughter and a shaved head.

"Oh, come on, Jen. You saw the video. How could anyone decide the kids weren't naked?"

"That may not be the issue."

"It ... what?" I gawped at her, then lowered my voice. "Your honor, the prosecution says those are bare breasts and a gigantic erection, but are they really? If we examine each frame of the video—"

She silenced me with a look, sly and hard. "Your honor, did the police advise the defendants to stay silent?"

"Oh."

"He knows where to hit, Bev."

I caught what felt like my first real breath in days and enjoyed a small spark of hope. I was so busy marveling at it that I barely noticed as the traffic around us congealed into a solid mass.

"Okay, Mabel, what's the holdup?" Jen said.

"The elevated roadway is blocked because of an accident, love, and now all the side streets are jammed full," the car replied. "Something fell off a trailer."

I rolled my eyes. The galactically expensive car had a working-class British accent: *Soomthin' fell offa trayluh.*

"We have to be at the Justice Center by 1:30, Mabel," Jen said.

"Oh, dear. You've a bit of a pinch, then. Data shows almost every side road carrying heavy traffic. The fastest route won't get you there until after two."

"Declare an emergency," I barked.

"Who's this, then?" Mabel said.

I glowered at the dashboard. Just what I needed, a smart-ass computer persona.

"This is Bev, my sister-in-law," Jen said.

"Hello, love!"

"Jen, I am going to use a plasma charge on this wad of a car if it doesn't get us out of here right now!"

Mabel got the hint. The traffic computers opened a narrow lane in the mob of cars, started to back us out, and a human came online.

"This is regional traffic control. What's the nature of your emergency?"

"I have to be at the Justice Center," I stammered. "My daughter has ... a hearing."

* * * *

It's hard to look well-kept and supportive when you burst into a courtroom. What I saw next came in disjointed snips and frags—Julie talking with the lawyer ...

*And God, but that coverall is worse than yesterday's.*

... Jim sitting with his neck hunched and eyes red, clerks bustling with quiet efficiency. The sudden quiet as the judge entered.

"All rise!"

I hated those words, despised them outright. Why should I show respect to people and a system geared to hurt my child? I rose because I was too scared, too conditioned.

The judge wants to stay anonymous, so I'll describe her as a graceful woman in her fifties. The next few minutes slipped away in a blur of formalities—the case number, the lawyers introducing themselves, legal blather and was the charge correct and understood by all? I kept telling myself to breathe, this was just the opening round of a longer fight, one we might even win.

"Mr. Selcraig, are you ready to enter a plea?"

"Yes, your honor. My client stipulates to the charge and pleads guilty."

I groped for Jen's hand while my ex shot to his feet.

"Your honor, this may be out of line, but I'd like to speak," he said.

Julie whirled in her chair and shot fury at him. The judge looked almost as angry.

"Are you related to Miss Wilson?"

"I'm her father. And I don't think she realizes what she's doing."

"Mr. Wilson, part of my job is to make sure Julie understands what she just said. Have you had a chance to discuss your daughter's plea?"

I stood, realized my throat was a pile of wet cotton, but I couldn't see a graceful way to sit down.

"I'm Bev, your honor. And we weren't here to discuss anything because of bad traffic—Julie's mother, I'm her mother—uh ... ma'am, and this is a complete surprise, and..."

I trailed off and choked back tears, heard noises to the effect of recess and found myself in a conference room, sitting between Alex and Jim. I smelled a faint whiff of tequila—the ex was hung over and seething.

A guard led Julie in a moment later, and Jim started in before she was free of the shackles.

"You will not roll over for this—"

"Go yark on a wall—"

"I will not sit here while—"

"James Burton Wilson, you will stop right now or DNA won't help them identify you."

Jen spoke a hair above a whisper. Brother and sister glowered at each other, Jen ice calm and regal, Jim ready to strike. He glared at her, then stormed from the room.

Alex patted me on the shoulder. "Be right back."

"Oh, don't bother," I said through my best fake smile.

He smiled for real. "Bothering's my job."

* * * *

My ex leaned over the sink and finished donating any residual alcohol, looked up and saw the big man offering a cup of water. He took it and rinsed his mouth.

"I understand the urge to fight," Johnston said.

Jim shook his head. "The corps teaches us, what? Never give up. Always faithful. And now ... what's happening to my kid, and she won't let me fight for her?" He stood panting and shaking his head slowly back and forth, hands balled into fists.

"I realize you've known me for about a half hour, but I want you to do two things." It was a direct order and Jim straightened up. "First, call me Alex. Second, get it through your armored skull that this isn't your fight, major. It's Julie's. So, do you want to know what to do?"

* * * *

Jen put her hands on Julie's shoulders. "Alright, niece-of-mine, what's going on?"

Julie's face crumpled. "I saw the vids."

"Feeling ashamed is no reason to plead guilty," Jen said.

"That's not it," Julie said through her tears. "There's more, okay?"

Jen motioned with her hands.

"Mr. Selcraig told me where he'd attack, pick the vids apart. And when he was done, I said that we wouldn't win, would we? And he said I was right, we wouldn't. So if I fight, I'll have to stay here for weeks, and it'll take that much longer for all this to be over. I just want this to be over, okay? I miss Harley, I feel like shit whenever I think about Rick, and I'm tired of seeing all the pain on your face."

"My pain is not your problem," I snapped. "Do you know what they'll do to you? Really know?"

"Of course I do."

I heard far too much teen in that voice, the blithe overachiever just glancing at something horrible, but she turned and drove a fist into the wall as more tears came.

"Dad thinks I'm rolling over," she sobbed. "But I'm not. I'm just trying to stand up. You always say life isn't just about me, right? I have to look outside myself."

"Yes, sweetie, but—"

"I lost sight of that," she said. "And I need to make it right. And I don't know if I can."

"Julie, this the wrong place for idealism," Jen said. "You didn't lose your ideals in the pool."

Julie glared through her tears. "You want to see the video of what I lost? Look, I'm sorry, okay? But I did it, and we won't win." My daughter slumped against the wall and sobbed as she rubbed her bruised knuckles.

Jim and Alex slipped back into the room. Jim was flushed but unwound, for the most part. He approached Julie, hesitated, then reached for her sore hand and spoke in gentle tones edged with tears.

"What have I told you about using your fists?"

"I know. My palm works better..." she flared and jerked her hand away. "I'm not changing my mind, so are you gonna help me or just leave again?"

Jim met the glare with level calm. "Whatever choice you make, I'm behind it, okay? I know you have plenty of reasons to doubt me, but not now."

Julie put her back to the wall and sagged to the floor. He sagged down next to her.

"Mom and Jen think I should fight."

"Me, too. In case you hadn't noticed."

"But I can't," she said. "I can't be in a fight that I won't win. Not today, anyway."

Jim looked at Will. "So ask for a continuance?"

Will found his eyes and held them. "That won't help. We won't find any magic evidence buried somewhere."

Jim turned to Julie, reached for her hands and looked up at Alex. The big man smiled and nodded.

"Okay, then ... look, we love you," he stammered. "I love you." He drew a sharp breath. "Whatever happens in there won't change that. His shoulders slumped and he rolled his eyes. "I knew this wouldn't work."

Julie giggled, probably the first time she'd smiled at him since he'd left, but the little episode chilled me; still far too much of that blithe teen, off on some grand adventure, only now with daddy's blessing.

Except she clutched the lawyer's hand and sobbed as Her Honor's measured voice filled the room.

"Julie Lynne Wilson, you are sentenced as follows."

I tried to remind myself that every age, every society has preyed on itself in some way. It's part of who we are. The inescapable dark side.

"You will spend five days in confinement, where you will undergo intensive therapy."

I tried to be rational—everyone over sixty has lost someone to the virus.

"After you complete that course, you will be confined to house arrest until a condemned sexuality offender is scheduled for execution."

I tried to remind myself that we still feel cornered for good reasons, so we lash out.

"On the day of that execution, you will be taken to the place of that execution and given at least two cycles of non-fatal punishment. This will happen at the same time and in the same manner as the execution, with the extent of punishment to be determined by the prison staff, based on behavioral reports that will be compiled while you're in custody."

I tried to remind myself that at least we have limits on the pain, hard rules and impartial observers to make sure those rules are followed. Thank God for civilian oversight.

"And as a reminder, Julie, if you repeat your crime, you will be tried on capital charges. If you're found guilty, you will be put to death. Do you understand?"

"Yes, ma'am," she croaked.

The gavel fell.

* * * *

An hour later, Her Honor half listened as the bailiff told everyone to sit, then something made her look up, at the boy in the orange coverall. Calm posture, blank face, but she'd never seen such resolve in a pair of eyes. She'd watched a lion take down a gazelle once, and this kid reminded her of that big cat, the same ferocious concentration and purpose.

His lawyer stood and without a trace of humor he requested the charges be dropped.

Against the young lady involved.

Blame should only fall on young mister Westmoreland because he'd started it.

Her Honor winced and fought to stay impassive. She was moved by his attempt to be noble, she said, but Julie had already pled guilty.

The boy's determination plunged into rage, an audible growl and every muscle instantly hard.

"Fine," he barked. "Then I do too. Write it down."

Behind him, his mother leaned into his father and held on in that desperate embrace.

"Richard, let's stop for a moment," Her Honor said. "Stand up and tell me the implications of your plea."

The boy smirked at her and didn't move. "You mean, you don't know?"

"Young man, this court will not tolerate—"

"They didn't explain the whole two-cycles-of-punishment thing in law school? That I'll get more if the dead guy isn't actually dead after that? I'd get my money back if I were you." A smile spread over his face then, sly and hard. "And you're choking on this, aren't you? This is eating you alive, what you have to do to me."

Her Honor caught herself. The system had classified this kid as a Category One, just like his girlfriend—large brain, big talent, recruited by a dozen universities. But the reports had also painted him as shy and remorseful, nothing like the feral thing smirking at her. And he'd read her flawlessly. She'd passed this sentence on dozens of kids, always aware the penalty would leave them writhing in agony and begging for air, saddle them with a lifetime of emotional abscesses they'd struggle to lance. She was deep-down sick of these cases, angry to the point of rage at how the law forced her to mete out so much pain.

But this was also her courtroom, and she couldn't tolerate that kind of behavior. She handed down the same sentence as Julie's, but with indefinite confinement until Rick apologized for his outburst. As she rapped the gavel, she realized she'd given him exactly what he wanted.

ATLANTA — Officials at the Centers for Disease Control announced today that a New York man has died from an aggressive form of the AIDS virus. The death marks the first recorded case of AIDS since 2029.

Dr. Martin Allen, head of epidemiology at the CDC, said the unidentified man contracted what appears to be an offshoot of a strain of HIV called 3-DCR. That strain, which worried health officials when it first appeared in 2005, went from infection to diagnosable AIDS in a short period of time—months instead of years—and proved fatal because it resisted three of the drugs used to treat the disease at the time.

"The virus that killed this man is like a brawny second cousin of the old 3-DCR strain of HIV. It appears to have a much stronger protein coating than the original virus," Allen said.

"We're still running tests, and I don't want to alarm the public, but preliminary findings show that this new strain may be strong enough to survive outside the human body," he said.

When asked about the implications of a physically tougher virus, Allen said, "Worse-case scenario, people could contract HIV, not be aware they're sick, and spread the disease through more casual types of social contact, such as coughing or sneezing. I must emphasize that we don't think this is a danger, and ... we're testing everyone this man came into contact with. We're also taking the standard measures needed to protect the public."

When asked how the man could have contracted AIDS, given the global immunization programs, Allen said, "Vaccines are never perfect, and you can never vaccinate everyone. People need to bear that in mind."

—From the archives of NBC/Pravda, omissions mine

# SIX

The judge gave me one of those arch looks. "You do realize, Ms. Wilson, that it's impolite to sleep while your dog urinates on me?"

I tried to wake up, but I couldn't stop laughing, that helpless wave from the belly that masters you, and in the surreal scape of dreams an understanding flashed between us: Her husband had a thing for fishnet stockings.

"You realize, Ms. Wilson, that I have no choice but to impose the death penalty on your dog?"

I spat out a perfectly logical mouthful of her hair. "Impose all you want," I said as I plucked a strand from between my teeth. "The province doesn't have a budget for dogs."

She gave Harley an evil smile. "Sick 'em."

The dog bounded over and became wet. On my face. Slimy and scratchy and rhythmic, warm doggy breath and he needed a bath and his high whine pushed me out of the dream and into the gray light of early morning.

He licked me again before I could sit up, and I scratched his ears. "Who let you in here? Never mind, I did." Because I'd heard something creak as I'd drifted off to sleep.

"I suppose you want to go out now."

He raced out the door and I followed, down the hall maybe ten feet, and then I froze. I'm not sure what triggered it—the dream, my fear, maybe the morning light on the stair rail or the smell of the house, but my daughter stood right there, almost tangible. She was four, maybe five, dressed in her pajama and standing at rigid attention.

* * * *

"It's red-belly time, Daddy sir!"

At that age, Julie had trouble wrapping her tongue around *reveille*. Her piping voice would roll Jim out of bed, and he'd struggle to keep a straight face while he gave her a stern and serious "inspection."

"Teeth," he'd bark, and Julie would smile as Jim looked close. "Hmm, another tooth on its way. Excellent. Freckles!" Julie would try to hold still while dad counted the smattering around her nose. "One, two, three ... a million! You know what that means?"

"I'm *not* turning into a ladybug, daddy!"

"Bet you are."

"Am not!"

"Are too. Belly button!" Julie would pull up her pajama top and giggle. "Still ticklish. Very good. And why must your belly button always be there, recruit Julie?"

"'Cause it holds navel lint."

"Exactly. Now take us to the chow hall!"

She'd count cadence as they marched down the stairs. "Hup two free four, hup two free four..."

Most of the time, I'd hear a bowl hit the counter, then Julie's voice would drift up the stairs. "Daddy, mom should have chow with us."

"Great idea," Jim would reply. "You go get her while I make the pancakes."

I'd feign sleep while small feet raced up the stairs and the kid tried to sneak in and pounce. She'd be half onto the bed and I'd sit up quick and dig my fingers into her ribs.

"Mommy, mommy, STOP! The pancakes are almost done and I have to help dad!"

She'd race back downstairs, and I'd arrive a couple minutes later to find breakfast unmade and daddy flat on his back, bench pressing his giggling daughter:

down, up ...

"Eleven!"

down, up ...

"'Leventy one!"

"No, hon, twelve."

"Oh, sorry. Twelve!"

down, up ...

"Twelfty one..."

"And just what are you doing to our child, James Burton Wilson?"

He'd give me an innocent look. "Julie presses. They're teaching her how to count."

But counting became routine, so he switched to the catechism.

"If your safety brooch turns red..."

down, up ...

"Stand still and raise my hand."

"And?"

down, up ...

"Do what the ossifer or the soljer tells me."

down, up ...

"And what else?"

"Tell myself that you and mommy love me, and you always will, and never stop telling myself that. Why should I do that, daddy?"

down, up ...

"Because the officer or soldier will give you a patch that will make you go to sleep, and we want you to feel loved if that happens."

down, up ...

"But I'll wake up, won't I?"

*Down.*

"We may not be there right away, and we'll want you to feel loved then, too."

Straight from the approved script. Never mind they heard the real truth from the older kids at school.

The inspections ended one sunny Tuesday when Julie was six. I don't know why I remember it was a Tuesday, but Jim rolled out of bed when he heard Julie's door open.

"Good morning, recruit Julie!"

"That's just baby stuff, dad."

I've never seen a jaw become a rubber band with such speed.

"Did I do something to make you mad, beautiful? Is that why you didn't want to do the morning inspection?"

"Nope. It's just time for me to grow up now."

* * * *

I shook off the memories, let the dog out and told the food center to make coffee. The rich smell began to fill the room as the sky slipped into that fragile early blue and I tried to breathe in some quiet, some calm.

The computer chirped.

"Hi." Julie's eyes shimmered with fear. "Um ... Kari just left."

I groped. *Kari? Oh, God, come on, brain.*

"What ... do you need, sweetie?"

"Could you come? Stay with me, I mean?"

"Of course. As soon as they'll let me in."

"Thanks," she croaked. "They'll let you stay longer."

"Oh, hurry up." The harsh voice came from behind her somewhere.

"And I'm sorry, mom. I really—"

She blipped out and I stood there, wondering why I hadn't poured the coffee and just who the hell was Kari?

I joined the queue of people waiting to see daddy or whoever, stood in the search machine, half listened while the mechno-voice said my image had been flushed and wouldn't be seen by anyone, all valuables to be left at the guard station, and please do not lose my claim check.

The visiting area is forty by ninety feet and painted in that institutional beige. It reeks of the usual anti-viral and something worse—sweat, maybe. It has four long rows of circular tables with integrated benches, all bolted to the floor, and the room is surrounded by a walkway fifteen feet above. The only daylight comes from a thin row of windows above that. In the morning, beams of light slant in, bars almost as real as the ones on my level. A pair of guards manned the walkway and slouched against the rail. Another four paced between the tables.

As I waited for my daughter, a fragment of something came to mind: 'As a rule, jail screws tend to be the recruits who finish in the bottom five percent of any Civil Guard training class.' I don't remember where I read that.

Julie came biting her lip. She burst into tears as I reached for her, and the screws seemed to mob us. Hands pushed, voices commanded us to calm down or the prisoner would be escorted back to her cell, DO IT NOW!

"Oh, there you are!"

I turned to see a woman—late fifties, maybe older. Vibrant energy, musical voice, gorgeous silver hair.

"I've got this one, fellas."

Whoever she was, she had command presence, the same gravity as the big shrink we'd met a few days earlier. She wore a gray uniform cloak, and her badge was strange. The bear shimmered, but it was overlaid with a cross. She parted the screws with a reassuring smile and led us to a door with CHAPLAIN stenciled in crude block letters and another cross above that, this one made of two sticks with the bark still on.

I connected the letters with the cross and my guard snapped into place. *Wonderful. Religion fouls the air yet again.*

Ms. Chaplain shut the door behind us, helped Julie onto a tattered couch that had once been plaid, and I began to form polite sentences: Thanks for the assist, but I can calm my daughter and find a table all by myself. My child doesn't need another layer of shame, and I'm sure we'll achieve hypocrisy without your help.

She handed Julie a box of tissues. "Take all the time you need."

Julie used a handful. "Sorry," she said through hiccupping sobs. "I know I'm not supposed to act weak, and—"

"Why can't my daughter cry?" I said.

"Because her fellow inmates will think she's an easy target for all sorts of sadistic little—"

A rap sounded on the door, brisk and light, almost happy, and the big mind plumber filled the doorway.

"Oh, there you are," he smiled at Julie, then me. "I need to check you out for some healthcare, Julie. Ms. Wilson, you're welcome to come, too."

"You have something up your sleeve, Johnston," the chaplain said.

"Of course I do, dear." He beamed at us some more. "I see you've met my lovely wife?"

"Only sort of," she said. "We haven't had a chance to introduce ourselves, thanks to your mentally challenged sense of timing." She took one of Julie's hands, then one of mine. "I'm Virginia, and even here, it's wonderful to meet you."

I stammered some reply, I think, but mostly I wondered how she could say that with such weight. We aren't easy people—a cynical advertising pro who can't work sane hours, a computer shaman with enough fuck-you to become a military officer without the aid of family connections, and while their daughter prided herself on being nice to everyone, she became feral around a soccer ball.

Perhaps it was the venue—lockups are designed to leave you cowed—but I knew this woman would smile as those flaws became visible, and she'd mean it.

* * * *

I slid into the passenger seat of what looked like a bland municipal hauler. A thick acrylic pane separated us from the cargo hold in back. I switched on the hold's overhead light and saw benches on either side, each with a row of steel rings. I was about to ask the doctor what the rings were for when the rear door opened and Julie clambered in. The reverend followed, and before I could react she'd cuffed my daughter to one of the rings.

I whirled just as the doctor opened the driver's door. "Just what in the blue—"

He held up his hands. "We have to do that or we can't leave. Once we're gone, Virginia will let her go."

We spiraled up from ten stories underground, checkpoint after checkpoint, and I glanced back at my daughter. Despite the cuffs, she'd managed to curl into the chaplain, almost onto her lap, and a thought struck.

*Refugees. God, but they look like refugees.*

We finally stopped at a solid steel wall manned by two screws. They opened the rear door, and one of them leaned in, gave my daughter a predatory leer and ratcheted the cuffs down hard, slammed the door closed and thumped it twice.

The doctor violated the usual boundaries and put a hand on my arm. "Yes, I saw that, and I'm asking you to trust me."

The wall opened and the sunshine blinded me. "Where are we going?" I said through watery eyes.

"We're safeguarding your daughter's health."

We headed east, through town and up a familiar hill. I looked at him through narrowed eyes as the hauler pulled up to our driveway and settled onto its wheels.

"Just what the hell—"

"Do you want people seeing her dressed like that? Trust me, please." He smiled.

I raced through the house and grabbed—light cloak, dress shorts, a blouse she'd "borrowed" from Jen, sandals and ... why not? I grabbed Harley by the collar and told him to be quiet as I rapped the back door. Virginia opened it and nearly jumped out of her skin when the dog bounded past her. I handed her the clothes and slammed the door before she could do anything.

"I've watched you assholes play games with my daughter all morning," I said as I climbed into the cab. "I can, too."

The doctor smiled. "And you're playing well. She's already perking up."

I had to admit he was right. The alpha girl had a thing for doggy kisses, and she'd stopped trying to curl into the chaplain's lap.

"So," I said. "Healthcare."

"Trust me? Please?"

"I will, but only this once. If I don't think you're doing the right thing, I will never stop going to court."

He studied me with those shrewd eyes. "Fair enough. Give me a say-so and I'll back away. No need for court."

That took us to a restaurant on the beach. Julie changed clothes, hopped out of the vehicle, and I had a moment, a small blip of parental something. Joy, perhaps. She was a couple weeks shy of eighteen, but womanhood had laid its claim, giving her the curves I hadn't acquired until I was halfway through college. And in a couple weeks, what they'd do to that body, the fledgling adult inside ... I fought off the rage as Harley jumped out, his tail a furious blur.

"Pee on the tires, boy," I said.

Julie giggled as the Reverend Johnston stepped out and closed the door. "He would but he's empty," the reverend said. "He saw his girl and promptly anointed the floor." She turned to Julie. "What say we go for a run? Be nice to get one in before the hurricane comes."

Julie bit her lip and looked at the doctor. He smiled and nodded. The reverend took a hand and almost pulled her across Spinnaker Drive and onto the sand, the doctor beckoned me and we followed.

"So, what kind of minister are you?" Julie said.

I glared at the back of my daughter's head because she already knew the answer: Useless.

"Presbyterian," Virginia said. "But for now, I'm a chaplain of inmates, which means you ask a guard to call me and I'll come, no matter what time it is, young lady. Clear? The guards have standing orders to contact me."

Old emotion seeped again, told me to make this woman go away and take her faith with her. Except she'd made Julie giggle, and my issues didn't belong here. I tried to shove them away and hope my smile looked unforced.

"I like your hair that way," I said. Instead of her usual pony tail, Julie had clipped the left side back and let the right hang free.

"Oh." She giggled, quick and nervous. "I got my locator this morning. See?"

She pulled the hair back to reveal a small patch of bare skin, freshly shaved and far too white, just above and in front of her right ear. A small bulge squatted in the middle of that patch, maybe a half inch long and still an angry red.

"Stylish, huh? They know where I am to within, like, ten inches?"

Virginia nodded. "Give or take."

I faded—tumbled from career mom to powerlessness. "But I thought they wouldn't do that until you came home."

Julie shrugged, once again the blithe teen. "What's a couple days?"

I struggled for words, wise and parental, but instead I found myself holding her cloak and wondering if the reverend always wore athletic clothes to work. She certainly looked the type. She slipped out of her cloak, handed it to her husband and I saw the bracelet, an elegant thing, braided Celtic knot work done in white gold with an oval setting of rose quartz. I made a note to ask her about it, then promptly forgot.

The pair slipped off sandals and shoes, and I tugged at an old thought about the schizophrenia of it all. Wear a cloak in public or they arrest you, jail you, maybe even give you a job for life in some factory, but not if you're exercising. A gallon of sweat may plaster your clothes to your body, but it also equals modesty.

Without a word they set off at a dead run with Harley trailing, just behind Julie's left hand. She'd always loved to run. After she'd mastered walking, she'd abandoned it in favor of speed because she liked the wind on her face. But this run had an edge, the rush of a trapped animal escaping a snare, manic with adrenaline and fear, so I needed to follow, right? I was the mom. I was supposed to be there when her muscles quit and she needed that hug. I set off and realized the doctor was beside me. I glared at him.

"Healthcare?"

"This is a ... fragile time for your daughter. Fresh air and sunshine don't hurt."

"In other words," I growled, "she's suicidal."

He weighed his reply. "I operate on the assumption that for kids in her position, the idea of suicide is always too close."

"And the beach is better than those wonderful mind benders that I help advertise?"

"In some ways, yes. But mostly, the beach is where we can talk in private. They don't listen out here."

"And just what is it that you don't want the Ventura Civil Guards to hear? I don't need any more of their excrement."

"I want to do something for your daughter that's off-book. I want to try and give her mind and her emotions a place to hide while she's punished."

"What's so wrong with that?"

"The law says Julie must know exactly what it's like to be executed. Condemned prisoners aren't given sedatives or psych reinforcement of any kind, so Julie can't receive any."

"Well then that's easy," I said. "Bend her mind all you want. I won't tell."

He took a deep breath and sighed. "Thank you, but you should know that this is all experimental. It hasn't worked yet. I've refined my techniques—"

"What are they?"

"Hypnosis, basically, and I think I'm getting close, but I have no guarantee it'll work."

I studied him for a moment. "Julie's new friend, the one who left today, she's one of your subjects."

He didn't reply, just gazed down the beach with a smile. "I'd have to say my wife is doing a remarkable job of keeping up."

The heat waves distorted Julie and her priestess as they loped along. Harley nipped at the waves as they broke, one of his other favorite things.

"My daughter isn't eighteen," I said, "so I'm entitled to know about her healthcare. If you want to use her as a lab rat, you will tell me how this young lady fares tonight."

"Certainly," he said. "But don't be in a hurry. She'll need time to recover. And for this to happen, you'll need to ask me for family therapy. It's the only way to get Julie into my office." He pulled a computer from a pocket and I did the same. He sent me a form and I became his patient.

"One other thing." He smiled then. He could slide from commander to grandfather with such ease. "Call me Alex."

Another unspoken boundary violation, one I had no room for. "Your wife said something just before you came into her office."

"Please, call her Virginia."

"Fine. We were talking about sadistic little somethings because my daughter cried when she saw me."

He sighed. "If you show weakness in jail, the other prisoners will play games with you. Steal your food or hair brush, that sort of thing."

"Really? Then you need to know that my daughter meets the corps' standards for advanced self-defense. Thank her father for that one."

His eyes widened. "Oh. That could be bad."

Yes, it could. The jail was already compiling a report on Julie's behavior. Had she cooperated? Was her attitude good when ordered to clean a filthy toilet with her bare hands? That account would follow my daughter to the prison, and officials there would use it to decide how long the pain would last. A fight of any kind would guarantee no mercy.

"I'll do what I can," Johnston said as he put another hand on my arm. This time I didn't mind.

* * * *

Julie and the Reverend had no qualms about dripping sweat and panting for breath while the server showed us to a table. We sat, and suddenly we'd joined hands. I close my eyes closed while Virginia blessed the food. We smiled and chatted like old friends. Julie ordered a chicken and cheddar on rye, then hunted it to extinction in seconds flat. More light talk, she ordered chocolate mousse for dessert, enjoyed a long, sensuous bite, and then she was drowning, snatching at my wrist and hand.

"Uh, mom? I'd like ... I want ... support Kari, um, tonight and ... pray." The last word came out in a whisper.

She wanted to what? How could mumbling at the ceiling do a gnat's footprint worth of good?

"That's fine, dear," I said.

"Look, I know the whole God thing makes you mad, but..."

Being a dialed-in and veteran mom, I said, "Would you like me there, sweetie, or is this something you want to do alone?"

* * * *

I can't reproduce this conversation exactly, but I have the truth:

"Morning,Paul."

"Morning, Sergeant."

"You hear about the Wilson bust, the one in the pool?"

"What about it?"

"They went for it. Pled."

"Really? What'd the judge give 'em?"

"The usual. Five days in the system, home confinement, pain."

Pavel Jankovic probably thought, *Really? That little bitch thinks she'll just go to class and lounge around that pool until she's done? I can fix that.*

# SEVEN

Sixty years ago, while the second AIDS virus was busy wiping out San Diego, a group of married couples fled into what was then the Los Padres National Forest. They had a simple goal—survive the plague and raise their children. They found a small valley with ample water and built log homes.

A decade later, after the coastal cities began to rebuild, officials flew over a tidy little community where no civilization was supposed to be. They approached with caution, those officials, thinking they were up against armed lunatics spoiling for a little revolution. Instead they found a bunch of homesick people hungry for news of the outside world, people busy growing crops and teaching long division, but mostly wondering if they could go home.

They tried, only to find their old lives obliterated—houses destroyed, friends and relatives dead or impossible to find. One of the original settlers wrote in a diary that, "God has taken His knife and excised my past, lopped it off and discarded it like some cancerous limb."

Most of the settlers returned to what they'd built and held on to each other in their grief. The government let them incorporate their patch of earth—never mind it was located on provincial land—and they named it after their leader, Franklin Glendale.

Frank became chief because he'd watched a couple videos on how to build log homes, so boom; you're the mayor and city father, Frank. And because we're grateful, we've named the place after you.

Frank hated the idea. California didn't need a second Glendale, he said, but the other residents shouted him down. The original was still a ghost town, so this would be a fitting memorial. Besides, they had starvation to avoid and kids who hated algebra, so shut up and act mayoral or something.

The place became a curiosity. You could tour the forest and have lunch with people who'd survived the San Diego outbreak. They put on a good spread, organic and grown right there. Cheap, too.

The hole in the woods became a haven for gardeners and people wanting solitude, and then the province came knocking. Greater California needed a home for its new punishment systems—just the things to help keep the virus at bay. Given their history, the locals gave a resounding yes.

Legend has it Frank also coined the most popular nickname for the virus—AIDS Junior. Apparently he had a thing for bad ironic humor. The little glob of RNA had other tags— Curtains, The Ripper, Fade to Infinity, the BBC (Belated Birth Control)—but Frank's nickname stuck, at least here.

I meditated on those bits of history, teased them like a cat with a piece of string as Jen and I drove to the justice center that night.

"Forty years ago, my kid would've been on her way to boot camp. Regardless of any ... *outcome*," I said.

"Forty years ago, you and I would have been frozen somewhere in the salaried classes, enraged that the military brats and the oligarchy shits got a pass while our kids suffered."

"Yeah," I said. "Parliamentary Motion Seventy-Four-Ten. Sexuality punishments shall apply to all persons equally. Increased fairness. Deeper levels of democracy. So comforting."

* * * *

Officer Sanchez met us with a curt nod. Our heels echoed along silent corridors with beige flooring and that dry smell. Through the search machine and don't lose that claim check. She took us by the arm.

"If you behave in an unexpected way," she said, "if anything comes out of a pocket, if voices are raised, really, if you do anything other than talk and pray, the guards will flood the room with pepper gas."

"Uh, but we're just visitors," Jen said.

"That isn't how they feel," Sanchez replied. "This is extra duty for them, and they don't like it."

We nodded.

A single guard slouched against the rail this time. Sanchez motioned us to a table in the middle of the room and pointed at a canister directly over our heads. "The pepper gas will come from there. If it's released, the guards will toss you out of the building and you'll have to seek aid on your own. No emergency services will help you. Your daughter will be here in a moment."

She turned and left without another word. From behind and overhead came the unmistakable *thwup* of someone spitting, followed by the high-pitched crack of something hitting the floor. I started to turn around but Jen put a hand on my arm and shook her head.

"Don't" she murmured. "He's trying to bait us. Ignore it."

"What's he doing?" I mumbled back.

"Let's just say he's eating sunflower seeds."

A door slid open and Julie came, arm and arm with Virginia, smiling and trying to mount some bravery.

"Welcome to jail, courtesy of me. But at least I'm not down in Max A, and I..."

I kissed her forehead and nose. "Jail, schmail. You won't be here for long, right? And what's Max A?"

The kisses did nothing, and she barely stammered the reply.

"Um, it's where you go..."

"It's the maximum security floor," Virginia said. "Where you go if you're facing capital charges."

"It's okay if we ... pray?"

I managed to slough off the ugly new facts. "Julie Lynne, how often have I told you that my take on religion never has to be yours? Don't worry about me."

*Feel free to waste your time.*

She sat next to Virginia and snuggled close. "God will really listen?"

Virginia nodded and what else could my kid expect from a minister? Julie bowed her head and erupted, a hot rush of tears and words—explosions of fear and self-loathing, colored by the constant refrain of why, God, why?

And the crack of sunflower shells hitting the floor.

* * * *

While Julie prayed, a prison matron in a drab uniform stepped into a small alcove. It's a deliberately low-tech place—concrete walls painted off-white. The front of the alcove is dominated by a mirror—she can see out, they can't see in. Below the mirror sits a small panel with a touch pad and a red button. A holo screen hangs on the wall to the left.

Years ago, someone had taped a hand-lettered card to the wall above the mirror: MAIN COURSE, and another to the wall above the holo screen: SNACK. The cards were old and yellowed, but she left them there on the off chance they were good luck charms. This was supposed to be a quick and scientific way to kill—far safer than plunging needles into veins—but she'd seen the process go awry once, and that wheezing horror was enough to keep the cards in place.

She held still while the laser scanned her retina, then flicked on the holo screen—a live feed from the punishment room. She wouldn't dream of calling it a torture chamber. The province has two identical rooms, about ten by fifteen feet, yellow walls and floors of gray ceramic tile. Easier to clean. The "appliances" are also twins, spidery and ugly, made of carbon fiber and gifted with enough robotics to make life easy for the guards.

The matron had just enough time to look out through the mirror and give the killing machine a once-over—nothing looked broken or worn—when the holo screen transmitted movement, the scuffle of shoes on tile, a desperate whimper and frightened breathing. Tonight the system would nosh on a young lady, and this one was pretty. Most of them were just average—plain and brown or yellow or pink, not quite grown—but this one could have starred in those old Alberto Vargas paintings, the ones in the Louvre.

The matron smiled. She loved how the system leveled people. Rich, fat, big brain, whatever, you came in terrified and left broken. Or dead.

More movement, in the mirror this time, and the process is swift and clinical. No cries of 'dead man walking' or that Hollywood stuff. The screws hustled the young man in and the killing device clamped him down. They were about to cover his face when he said, "Wait a minute." They had no reason to wait, they're trained not to, but they hesitated, just long enough, and the prisoner focused on a guard, an elderly man with white hair and the numb demeanor of someone who'd done a horrible job for a long time.

"Your wife is going to watch your granddaughter die here."

The voice sounded almost obscene as it broke the silence, sacrilegious, like a wisecrack during communion.

The guard's professional calm slipped, just for an instant, and he dragged it back into place with a derisive snort.

The matron shook her head and smiled. Nearly all the condemned ranted if they said anything, but this was a first, so cold and convinced. Maybe the approach of death opened their eyes, let them see what we couldn't. Or he was just full of shit.

She glanced at the holo screen and thanked God for school dances. Such a nice source of income. Her husband had gambled away most of their savings on bad stock deals, bless his idiot soul, and the five thousand credits she'd earn from these few minutes of work would send her someplace nice. Thailand, maybe. Ride an elephant or two.

She pressed an icon and the system armed itself with a quiet click. A light flared in the punishment room, a small yellow dot that told the people in *there* that the dinner was ready in *here*, so please step away from the hors d' oeuvre. A guard draped a gray cloth hood over the girl's face and she started that uncontrollable shaking.

Through the mirror again. The other hood was down and the door was closed. That's the signal. You hear that door hiss shut, you're dead. Less than a minute after the main course walked in, the matron pressed a red button. She'd long ago quit marveling at the casual arc of her hand as it ended one life and gouged another. It was no different a motion, no more important, than picking up her handbag.

At first she'd tried to crawl into their heads, intuit what it felt like when she touched them. Did they wink out, or did they explode into ragged shards before the blackness swept in? She finally decided the question didn't matter. The province got its death, she got paid, everyone went home happy. Almost.

She sipped a cup of tea while the process ran, waited while the system reset, pressed the button again. A moment later an error flashed on, blinking and red.

GENERAL PROTECTION FAULT
IN PRIMARY CONTROLLER.
SYSTEM CANNOT BE REARMED.

WASHINGTON — The White House today suspended all air and ground travel between the U.S., Canada, and Mexico in an effort to halt the rapid spread of the new AIDS virus. In a briefing this morning, Press Secretary Katharine Wood said the quarantine measures will be in place for at least four months, possibly longer.

"It's the same situation as the flu pandemic of 2021. People sat tight and the virus burned itself out in a few weeks. The best data we have says that the same approach should work now," Wood said.

When asked if the virus was spreading through the air, like influenza, Wood said health officials have no conclusive evidence.

"It's difficult to tell how the virus is spreading because so many people engage in multi-partner sexual encounters. Scientists at the CDC say that if we'd stop that, they could get a better take on how and why the virus is spreading so rapidly."

When asked if the White House was investigating ways to curb such behavior, Wood laughed and said, "You can't legislate morality."

—Excerpt from the AP archives, omissions mine.

# EIGHT

It's hard to sleep after someone with half your education spits on you while you're trying to pray. It's even harder to sleep after one of them interrupts your goodbye hug, hands your daughter a rag and orders her to clean up the mess.

And when guilt sounds that familiar rhythm—You're still here?—forget it.

The sun peeked above the horizon as I opened my work connection and started the commercial privacy screens. I wasn't engaged in commercial activity, but I didn't care. I connected a small memory bubble to my data store and up came a mask, an algorithm Jim had written. As far as the Net was concerned, I was a low-level housekeeping utility started from a computer in Iceland.

I searched on SANCHEZ, CIVIL GUARD, and found strawberry blonde hair, two kids, a stable marriage, currently earning a third of what I took home. From there I went deeper, into the government data. No dings on her record, solid performance reviews, second highest score on the sergeant's exam. She was ambitious, and that meant a reach that probably exceeded her grasp. I called up another mask and became a routine government audit, just checking the records of one Sanchez, Stacia ... my screen disappeared and the computer froze.

"Hello," I barked. "Retinal scan."

Nothing.

I ran my hand through the keys and made sure they broke the laser beams, all the things you do to restart after a bubble burst—still nothing. I was about to yank the power cell when a message flag began waving and told me to hold in place for an inbound link.

*Shit! Guards!*

I couldn't backtrack the frozen box, yanking the power cell would be an admission of guilt, and me being alone in my office with the privacy screens up would look even worse ... who the hell did I think I was, pretending to be my ex? *Shit, shit, shit ...*

And then Jim was glaring at me.

The spike of fear twisted into anger, that jaw-clenching ferocity. "What the hell?" I growled.

"Do you know what you were doing?" He looked tousled and still half asleep, but he used the quiet voice reserved for Julie when she'd screwed up. "Another two-point-three milliseconds, and the guards would have been all over you. You're running an outdated version of a government eyeball, and the people who carry handcuffs know when it's running. What were you thinking?"

I glared at him until I could breathe again. "I was thinking that I'll be damned before I sit helpless while they spit seeds at our daughter again."

"They ... what?"

I told him the story and he smiled.

"And just what the hell is funny about that?" I growled. "This is your *daughter*, you cavity—"

He held up both hands. "What you just told me confirms that I'm doing the right thing."

"What right thing?" I growled.

"I'm going to set some wheels in motion."

"Wheels ... for God's sakes, Wilson, what the hell are you talking about? What are you planning to do?"

"It's best if you don't know, Bev."

"OH, REALLY? WHY NOT?"

"Because we can't help our daughter if we're both in jail."

"Oh, for ... what did you just say?"

"I'm probably going to lose my career and land in prison."

"AND THAT'S GOING TO HELP OUR DAUGHTER?"

"Bev, we can't help Julie now. And I have to accept that. And so do you."

"Then why are you—"

"Because I need to fight, too."

"And losing everything you've built, that's fighting?"

He thought for a moment, then nodded. "Sometimes, a sacrifice is the most effective weapon."

I looked around to make sure I was alone. "Would this have anything to do with your bullshit at the Justice Center?"

"What do you mean—"

"Don't play your idiot games with me, Wilson. You were up to something when we were talking to that guard. It was all over your face. What was it?"

He smiled, a hard smile that I'd rarely seen and never liked. "I'm sure you'll get the details after I'm arrested. But whatever happens, *do not* try anything with a computer. They have eyeballs on you."

"Why me?"

"Because Julie lives with you. I know it yarks, Bev, but we have to wait. Chances to fight always come up, and when ours does, we'll know it."

"And until then we're the fabled lions in the tall grass?"

"If that helps."

My response came from deep, that innate place of truth. "You can intercourse that one sideways, Wilson."

* * * *

The next day was a Saturday, Jim's reserve weekend.

Colonel Tyler McGowan, Marine Corps of the North American Federation (Reserves), watched as Major Wilson, James B., joined the troops for morning physical training and led them on a ten-kilometer run. He watched some more as Wilson helped with the routine chores of sweeping and dusting, mucking out the heads and polishing brass.

None of that was out of line, but the man carried a wistful sadness that made the alarms scream.

He heard one of the troops say, "What causes you to join us, major?"

"I'm in training for a new mission."

One of the older sergeants piped up. "He's going undercover as the prime minister's chambermaid."

Wilson stood and glowered. "I don't know how you figured that out, but if you breathe a word to anyone, I'll have you both shot."

The laughter was a good place for McGowan to interrupt. "If you'll excuse us, gentlemen, the major needs to leave for camouflage training."

"Camo?" someone said.

"Chambermaids get fired if their makeup isn't perfect."

A chorus of good natured laughter followed them into McGowan's office. Tyler motioned Jim to a seat and studied him for a moment.

"First, I get a link from you and everything is not okay. Then I find you busy doing things normally reserved for junior idiot lieutenants, and all while you're looking ready to cry. Need I say more?"

He watched as Wilson's mind churned its way to a sum, a conclusion.

"I need your advice, sir." He set a small computer on the desk and said, "Play open files."

Two screens flashed on and McGowan was glad the computer ... obscured things.

"WHAT THE HELL DO YOU THINK YOU'RE DOING? WE—ARE—MILITARY!"

Tyler held up his hands, a reflexive move. "Okay, hold it." He wasn't talking to the computer, but Julie froze and hovered.

McGowan closed his eyes and saw the pretty slip of a girl, her head buried under a helmet, eating a melting ice cream cone while she jounced over the desert in her father's assault vehicle.

"Daddy, can I drive?"

And now she wasn't a girl, and he didn't want to remember the young lady that way. He kept his eyes closed and rubbed his forehead.

"Please, Wilson, tell me that you schooled your daughter."

* * * *

Back when my ex was pretending to kill grizzlies with his pocket knife, the government stripped the military of its authority to police civilians. It was a not-so-subtle reminder that democracy was oozing out of the cracks, military rule was done and the Civil Guard had a job for you if you needed one. No family connections necessary.

A few politicians squawked about poor background checks and lousy training for the new recruits, but those voices were small and ignored until an evening in May. A group of newly minted guards, fresh from the academy and proud of their uniforms, celebrated by visiting several bars in Minot, the Air Force town in the province of Colorado.

What happened next still isn't clear. All we really know is the five guards encountered a young airman named Alex Voss, a guy much like them—fresh out of training and working toward something better than a factory. They began to harass him. When he tried to leave, they threw him on the floor, called him a military prick and doused him with Liquid Chrome, the local moonshine.

One of the guards lit a match.

The other airmen in Voss's unit attacked the guard station with plasma charges. Thirty-two people burned to ash in a matter of seconds.

* * * *

"Yes, sir. I drilled respect for the Civil Guard into my daughter from day one. At least, I thought I had."

McGowan took a deep breath and opened his eyes. "Did you talk with the arresting officers?"

"Just the lead. Her name's Sanchez."

"Did she mention Julie's outburst?"

"No. She stopped the video just after we saw the ... bodies."

"Did she mention your rank, or that she knew you were serving?"

Wilson's hands quivered as he shook his head. The guy needed to cry.

"That was deliberate," McGowan said. "She doesn't want any trouble. No one does. And honestly, Jim, your daughter was only trying to defend herself."

"I understand that, Ty, and I appreciate the guard's discretion. But there's ... more." Wilson shot to attention. "Colonel, I respectfully request that you finish watching."

McGowan looked up after the videos finished playing, saw Wilson still at attention, and he understood. The man was falling on his sword, waiting for an old friend to strip him of his career and his freedom. *And I should*, Ty thought.

"When's Julie's trial?" he said.

Wilson shook his head. "She ... pled."

*Come on, cry*, Tyler thought. *We're trained to, for God's sakes*.

"How'd you get a leech into the building—sorry, stupid question."

Wilson had advanced degrees in computer science, and he'd served in special forces. Stealing information was probably the least nasty skill he had.

"I yanked the power cell so the sensors couldn't detect it. Sir."

McGowan sighed. "Why did you bring the damn thing at all?"

"Instinct, sir. And ... that second guard. He didn't even let her ... just marched her out to the car."

The tears finally came.

*There we go*, McGowan thought. *That's what I need to see—an aching daddy, not a furious Marine*. He reached across the desk and dangled the fake cufflink.

"This breaks at least three laws," he said.

"Understood, sir."

"And I can't help your daughter."

"I wouldn't want you to. And there's more."

Ty motioned with his hands and Wilson told him about the spitting, the callous order to clean up.

"I know I just handed you a pile of bovine pastries, Ty, but I couldn't stay silent. This is bigger than me, my career, my kid ... Jesus."

*And we both know you have to fight,* Ty thought. *I certainly would. And we both know what comes next.*

"You're relieved of duty, major, effective now. And do yourself a big favor. Don't leave town. You have a lawyer?"

"Yes, sir."

"Good. You'll need one."

# NINE

Monday. The big day. Julie's five days in lockup were over and the house wouldn't feel so null.

The plaque on the doctor's door read C. Alexander Johnston, MD, Fellow of the Federation Psychiatric Society, the Provincial Board of Medical Supervisors, and pretty much the rest of the alphabet, except his military affiliations. I knocked and heard a commanding, "Come!"

Julie was already on his couch, her feet on the cushions, her chin on her knees, eyes closed. This was a familiar posture. She was putting on her game face—telling herself she could take whatever came and give it back twice as hard—and it scared me. She had to psych herself up to leave jail? I sat beside her and she took my hand in a death grip.

"My window closed, mom."

"Your what?"

"The execution date, Ms. Wilson. The day she's supposed to go to the prison."

Windows. I looked around for something to throw. The good doctor only had pillows, so I resorted to mature adult words.

"What the fuck?"

He didn't twitch. "All executions are on temporary hold because of a glitch. The circuit board in the control panel, the one that starts the ... process, has basically worn out and they can't find a replacement. Mostly because the system is almost forty years old."

I gave him a cynical half smile. "Are we free to go now?"

He held up a hand. "Julie, please explain the rules to your mom."

"I can leave for school at 7:30," she said in a dry voice. "I have to be home by three. If I'm late, I end up back here until I finish my sentence, and it goes on my report."

Ah, yes, the report. Words compiled by strangers in charge of mercy.

Julie looked at me with haunted eyes. "I can use the back yard, but I can't step out the front door."

"And what have we talked about?" Alex said. "Home confinement is truly wretched..."

"But it's better than here, and I'll have the dog and my mom." She tightened her grip on my hand. "And maybe my dad, sometimes."

"And..." Alex fished around in a pocket and handed Julie her soccer ball ring, "this outweighs your mistake, right?" he said. "This will end soon and you'll spend your senior year dominating the pitch."

She gave him a weak smile, but after we shrugged on our wraps she took my arm and hopped up and down in that excited way.

"Go home! French-kiss doggy!"

Three steps into the little waiting area, and the woman stood. Strawberry blonde hair, fit, calm. I told myself to smile.

"Julie," she said. "I'm sorry, but you need to come with me."

No cuffs this time. Just a swift walk to a holding cell.

* * * *

More joy of waiting, helpless while my daughter stood in the body scanner again, posed for new holo-mugs, had her DNA and navel bacteria sampled yet again, and could she please confirm that she was, in fact, Julie Lynne Wilson?

I found myself in the same decaying interview room, only this time Will Selcraig radiated fury and my daughter sat curled in a chair, unseeing.

Sanchez kept her face carefully neutral. "Julie is here because my partner filed a complaint with the Provincial Supreme Court," she said.

I gawped at her, the lawyer, the walls, God, whatever. "Why?"

"He thinks Julie's sentence was too lenient."

"And just what part does he think is merciful?" I said.

"The home confinement," Sanchez said. "He thinks Julie should spend her time here because she tried to use her father's military status to scare us off."

I shot to my feet and my hand raised itself.

"YOU WHAT?"

A hand caught my wrist.

"YOU—STUPID—LITTLE—BITCH!"

Julie didn't move.

"WHAT—DID—WE—TELL—YOU—FROM—DAY—ONE—"

Another hand, on my shoulder this time, turning me around and Sanchez was saying, "Stop, no, ease down. She was just defending herself the only we she could."

I looked past her and tried to bore holes through Will Selcraig. "I will sell everything I own if that's what it takes," I said. "You fight, starting right now, and you never stop."

He gave me a cold smile. "I'll have motions filed by this time tomorrow. But while officer Sanchez is here, I have a few questions."

She eyed me to make sure I was sane, then let go of my cloak.

"When did your partner find out about Julie's sentence?" Selcraig said.

"The day after she pled. It's a routine communication."

"So four, five days ago?"

She drew a breath and nodded. "I know, I know, that was fast. Way too fast."

"What do you mean, fast?" I said.

"Bev, if you file a complaint with the board, they'll take six months to read it and another three or four to decide whether to act on it," Selcraig said. "So obviously he has a serious connection. Do you have any idea who it is?

Sanchez shook her head.

Do you have any idea why he's so angry? Why he's singling Julie out?

"No, but I intend to ask him. And I intend to ask hard."

Selcraig held up a hand. "No. Let anything nasty come from me."

"Excuse me? I can handle my subordinates—"

"Your kids can't." He let that thought come to roost. "Neither can my client. I don't want your partner volunteering for overtime shifts in the cell blocks."

She left, tight with anger, and a moment later I realized why. She owed us.

* * * *

The next day.

"You're here to visit who?" The screw eyed me with bored contempt.

"Julie Wilson," I said.

He consulted the holo-screen on the wall. "Not today, or any time soon."

"Why not?"

"Wilson, Julie L. is in isolation, and you are on the keep-out list. Someone doesn't like you, lady."

"Who?"

"Do I look like some kind of data store? People are waiting behind you."

I put on my best reasonable voice, the one I use with nervous clients. "I understand that. But if you can find out why I'm on this list, maybe I can help fix any problems—"

"Or you can leave before I have you sharing a cell with your little girly."

Will Selcraig added that one to the list of complaints, and six days passed without a word from my daughter. Julie had the right to communicate with her lawyer for as long as she needed to. She also had the right to talk to me for five minutes a day, but it was a right, one stripped away by people unseen and unknown. All I could do was wait in line while the court slogged through its calendar and hopefully remembered that law. When the official seal of the Province of California fuzzed in above my computer, I figured our lawyer was checking in and I waved my hand through the lasers without even looking.

"What's not happening today?"

Silence and more, a palpable rage. I didn't recognize whoever it was. Hair in a near-shave, eyes rimmed and blazing.

"Can I help you?" I said.

"Why the hell did you let her plead guilty?"

My throat twisted. "Rick? Should you be talking to me?"

"Why not? I'm a convict now. Case closed. I can link to the outside world for five whole minutes, and today's your lucky day. So why'd you let her plead guilty? How could you be so fucking stupid? "

My brain lurched and skidded. "Excuse me? I'm not the one who was stupid, you little wad. Just what in God's name were you thinking? I trusted you with my daughter and you endangered her life, her dreams—"

"Why do you think I tried to get her out of it? Why in the hell didn't you just let me go first? I could've gotten her out of this."

His eyes hadn't left my face as I'd exploded, and if anything they held more rage.

"We didn't let her," I snarled back. "She pled against our advice."

The confusion would have been funny if it hadn't carried so much pain. "She what?"

"She stood up and owned her mistake. So how about you grow some balls and do the same? Tell yourself the truth?"

Blank eyes. Lost. "She what?"

"She acted like an adult and told the truth."

"But ... she can't. This dream, I have this dream. SHE CAN'T!"

Part of me groped for words, razors I could launch with cold precision:

> *Oh, yes she can and yes she did, because she's more of a man than you'll ever be.*

But the rest of me was a mom, and I loved this almost-man.

"Rick—"

"Oh, Jesus, God." He dug his hands into his scalp, wrinkled the skin under that glaze of hair.

"Tell me about the dream, Rick."

"Jesus, God."

"Come on, you know me well enough. Tell me the dream. Please? I won't tell a soul. Promise."

He swiveled his head up and his eyes flared again—gird thyself, the truth has crowned and you get to catch what follows. "She's at the prison," he said. "And ... they do it over and over again, and she's screaming. And they laugh at her." He stopped then and the rage faded into that blank stare.

"Does anyone know about this?"

"Sometimes ... I wake up ... I can't breathe."

"Rick, have you told the doctor?"

"Alex? What can he do? Hypnotize me? Drug me? Big fucking deal. He can't help her. Not after what I—"

The Justice Center computers cut us off without warning and ... enough. I was through. I'd leave my job, sell the house and move north, or maybe east to the Maritimes. I'd vacationed there once and met wonderfully genuine people, so I called up my resignation letter. I'd composed it a few days earlier, just in case I was forced to go public with Julie's mistake. Better to leave than be tossed out the door. I was proofreading it yet again and thinking about a simple, honest life in a fish cannery when the message flag waved again. I hesitated long enough to marshal some words. *No, Rick, you can't apologize. But you can make a permanent disappearance.* I waved my hand through the image.

"Mom?"

Lips cracked, eyes dull, she probably hadn't showered in a week. Nothing was more beautiful.

"WHERE HAVE YOU BEEN?"

The eyes hardened. "Jail."

"No, I mean ... I've been trying to talk to you for six days! Where have they been keeping you? Have they hurt you? Are you okay? Why can't I come see you?"

A listless shrug. "I've been in the infirmary, and they won't let me talk to anyone but Will."

"Will ... who?"

She bristled. "My lawyer? To find out why I'm still here? You know, so I can maybe come home?"

"What has he told you?"

"That I have to wait for another hearing."

In other words, please tell me this nightmare isn't true, mom.

"We'll be right there with you," I said. The news didn't sit well and she sagged into her chair.

"Um, have you heard anything about Rick? Is he okay?"

I took a long breath. "No, sweetie. I haven't heard a thing."

Her eyes welled. "Why, mom? Why am I still here?"

"I'm sorry, sweetie. I don't know."

But I found out the next day. The seal materialized and up came a letter, two short sentences and a signature:

> You will meet with me to discuss crucial issues around your daughter's incarceration. Be present at the Ventura Regional Justice Center in conference room 8035 at ten o'clock today.
>
> —Christopher Coughlin.

An oligarch, a member of an old and well-connected political family, oh-so-wealthy and oh-so-quiet, as long as they get their way.

Jim. He needed to know. And Selcraig. I was calling up my address book when windows popped open and they appeared.

"WHO DOES THIS *CAVITY* THINK HE IS?" I roared.

Jim smiled, thoroughly evil. "Ease down, Bev—"

"I WILL NOT EASE DOWN, ORDERING US AROUND LIKE HE'S GOD! PLAYING WITH OUR DAUGHTER'S LIFE!"

"But he's shown himself, Bev. He's visible," Jim said.

I pointed at Will. "YOU CONTACT HIS PEOPLE AND RESCHEDULE THIS FOR NEXT WEEK. AT NINE IN THE EVENING!"

"I wouldn't recommend that," Will said. "I'd go hear him out."

"I DON'T GIVE SHIT WHAT YOU'D DO—"

"But you give one about Julie," Jim said. "And I agree. Let's go hear him."

"Why?" I growled.

"Let's just say I want to preserve the illusion of control."

* * * *

No dingy interview room this time. We had a commanding view of the ocean, leather upholstery, coffee and tea, elegant paintings on textured walls. Will Selcraig led my shackled daughter by the elbow, Jim followed a moment later. Will reminded us that we were paying him to do the talking, so please let him, and the door opened.

Coughlin was medium sized, trim, sandy hair, perfect creases, straight posture, a weak chin and an obvious rod where the light doesn't go. Arrogant and clearly used to having his orders obeyed, he studied Julie with a reptilian smile and my skin crawled.

"As you may have surmised, my name is Christopher Coughlin," he said in a precise, clipped voice. He had the type of cadence I'd heard in my worst college professors, and he spoke to Will as though the rest of us weren't there. "I expect your clients to listen until I'm through. After that, I will entertain questions. I think you and your clients will appreciate what I have to say."

He began to pace the room.

"I'll start by saying I'm a patriot. I love this country, what it stands for, its ways of life, its beauty and vibrancy. I'm also a believer in science, especially genetics. I'm the fourth largest producer of algae-based lubricants in the entire federation, and my business grew in large part because I understand the genetics of oil algae and I know how to modify them, make them more productive.

"In addition to what I've told you, I'm also a man of faith. I can accurately say that my beliefs wrap around my love of country and science, overarch them, give them meaning. I'm a senior deacon at Four Corners Church."

A Consev. The people I loathe the most. From day one, my mother had dragged me to one of their churches, where a banner proclaiming God's love had floated over a sea of condemnation and a pecking order that ate you if you fell out of lockstep.

"Oh, I attended Ashbury Consev up in San Francisco," I said. Why not lull the moron, let him think he was dealing with a gas-head? The corner of my eye caught Jim resting his hand on the table, just like he'd done after Julie's arrest.

"I told your clients to be quiet until I was through," Coughlin said without glancing at me.

"Apologies," Will said.

A long pause while he mulled the offer, and then, "Accepted. Now, I spent most of my childhood in New England, at the best science schools, and they gave me a deep understanding of the human genome, of course, and that's why your clients are here. You see, the younger Ms. Wilson has a remarkable genetic profile, and her mother's is almost as good. To put it in simple terms, they're virtually immune from cancer. Their systems antagonize rapidly growing cells, and that's extremely important to me because I lost my grandmother to cancer. You may have heard of her, Moira Coughlin. She wrote the laws that you violated, young lady." He looked at Julie again and didn't conceal that dark-eyed craving.

Will Selcraig raised a polite hand and Coughlin nodded. "So, you're a believer in eugenics?"

Out of the corner of my eye, I saw Julie working her jaw, her face neutral but her eyes blazing.

"Of course not," Coughlin said. "That was a joke, a pseudo-science. But I do believe we can create a healthier class of people, of leaders, men who can take this society in the right direction. It's something my grandmother drilled into me—that some are appointed by God to lead, to have the strong minds in the strong bodies and not be ashamed to use them."

I stopped myself from shaking my head in stunned awe. The little cavity was sincere. He honestly believed what he was saying.

"So, we've established that I'm well off," Coughlin said, "stable, a man of principle and faith, and that brings me to my point. I'm prepared to offer your clients five hundred thousand credits if they'll give me their daughter in marriage. I'll rescind all objections to their daughter's current sentence, and after she's paid for her mistake and learned her lesson, I'm prepared to become her husband. I have licenses for three children, by the way, and they'll be beautiful. Julie's will be the dominant genes, mine the recessive."

This time, I couldn't stifle the splutter, the disgusted sigh, but Coughlin didn't hear it. New England and the Carolinas never can seem to understand that we don't sell our daughters. It may be commonplace back there, but out here the idea leaves a really loud odor, as we like to say.

"Is that all?" Will said.

My daughter's jaw sped up.

Coughlin smiled. "I'm also prepared to pay your bill, counselor, provided you give me adequate documentation of your time and efforts. Please confer with your clients." He strode to the other side of the table, sat across from Julie and flashed that supercilious, hungry smile.

Will looked at us. Jim leaned around me and looked at Julie. "What do you think, sweetheart?" He was almost ready to laugh.

Without a word, Julie tensed and spat. The wad of phlegm hit Coughlin just below the nose.

"I think we're done here," she said.

TORONTO — The Maritimes and Quebec today voted to approve the so-called Immediate Euthanasia law, which requires police and healthcare workers to kill anyone diagnosed with the new AIDS virus.

"... I know this is an extreme measure," Senator William McIntaggart said, "but we've heard the message ... that people want to stop the spread of this disease. And also, would you rather die while you're coughing blood or go painlessly?"

—From the archives of the
Toronto Globe and Mail,
omissions mine.

# TEN

The exercise of power almost always spins out of control in ways no one can predict. Luther's reformation led to the Thirty Years' War and devastated most of Germany. A long-dead president named Eisenhower insisted on democratic elections in what we now call Indochine and more than a million people died.

But you don't think on that level when you're in the middle of a fight. All we knew was the relief and release of having an outlet for our rage, the joy of lashing out at Coughlin and the injustice he'd engineered. For me it was almost sexual.

Coughlin was still mopping at his face when Selcraig reached across the table with several pieces of folded paper.

"This is a permanent restraining order. You will not contact Julie or her parents, or interfere with their lives in any way." He took another packet from his case and tossed it casually across the table. "And that is a copy of a complaint filed with the Federal Investigative Service. They'll be looking into how and why you used your position on the review board to advance your own ends."

Coughlin fixed us with cold eyes. "I'll destroy you for this."

"Excuse me," Jim said, "but do you have an imagination, Chris?"

That got him. He stood and pointed. "It's Mister Coughlin to you."

Jim rolled his eyes and snorted. "You're six months younger than me, dumbshit, but despite that handicap, I'll bet you have an imagination, and I'll bet you've had some serious fun with my daughter. So now, Chris, now I want you to imagine eating through a tube and shitting through another tube. For the rest of your life, Chris. Because I will make that happen, Chris. And, once you're done imagining the tubes, Chris, I want you to imagine being smart, Chris, smart enough to look beyond your pathetic views of people and life. I know that'll be a stretch, but we're leaving now so that you can start. And if you say one more word, you won't have time to imagine the tubes. They'll become your reality before you can leave that chair."

He reinforced his point by grasping the edge of the conference table and cracking it.

"Have a nice day."

* * * *

Back in his office, Jim reviewed his latest batch of stolen data, opened a link to his sister and invited her for a walk on the beach. They crossed Spinnaker drive and into that area where the Civil Guard doesn't bother to listen, let the surf wash their feet.

He talked. She smiled. He handed her a memory bubble.

Three days later, Christopher Coughlin found himself in Jennifer's office, on a ninety-eighth floor, large and reeking of big money wisely employed. Jennifer didn't offer him a chair, just started talking.

"As you know, we're required by law to ensure that our suppliers and subcontractors use fair labor practices," she said. "We also have standards of our own, and we have some concerns about yours."

"I assume you'll list them?" Coughlin sounded exasperated and bored.

"Of course," Jen said with a breezy wave. "First, about a third of your workforce is prison labor."

"That's perfectly legal—"

"But we don't do business that way. For any reason. Second, nearly eighty percent of your regular employees leave after less than a year, and almost all the rest turn over within two years."

"It's menial labor and a transient workforce—"

"In the past seven years, most of your employees have owned homes within thirty miles of your plant. That makes them locals, not transients."

"Excuse me? They're drudge-class. Most of them barely passed high school and—"

"How do you know? You can't access education records. Not legally, anyway. Also during the past seven years, the province has received fifty-eight complaints about working conditions inside your facilities. At one time, three of your foremen carried clubs or stun guns on the job."

"Someone was—"

"You've made some of your workers stay on the line for more than fourteen hours a day, and two of those workers were twelve years old. It's obvious to me and my in-laws that people don't matter to you; they're really just objects in your eyes. That's why we're canceling your contract, effective now."

Coughlin snorted and gave her a cold smile. "Do you know what I'm going to do? I'm going to go down that hall and talk to Liam. About you."

"You're welcome to, but he'll repeat what I just said and he won't be as nice. This was his idea."

"Well then, since you've been using oldspeak, *underage* and *working conditions*, I'll use it, too. *Altruism*. This is all just wonderfully altruistic, but when the bearings in your wind turbines freeze, Liam will have your neck, and then he'll link me because I'm your only source of supply."

"Really? We didn't just buy a production facility and a dozen algae strains? You don't read the trade news? After we charge off the expenses and staff up with the people you've abused, we'll be saving thirty percent on that particular cost. Now, as you're leaving, I want to see how observant you are."

She pointed at the door. He turned and froze. On the wall behind him, a holo emitter projected an image of Jen and Julie on the gravi-coaster at Disney Universe, laughing hysterically with their arms raised and the wind blowing their hair.

He whirled on Jen, his face a riot of surprise and disdain, fear and shame.

"She's my niece, you sphincter. Now leave without another word."

"I see you're as lacking in moral stone as she is."

Jen pointed at a console on her desk and raised her eyebrows.

"I'll leave when I've spoken my lot," he said. "What's the other old saying? The fruit doesn't fall far from the tree?"

Jen pushed a button.

"That does not intimidate me, *woman*—"

Four burly types came through the door. "He's too stupid to find that big opening in the wall," Jen said. "The one he just came through."

One of the burly types motioned toward the door.

"I'll give the orders here," Coughlin sneered. "I'm a senior member of the Judicial Oversight Board for this province." The old speech again, each syllable delivered with imperious precision.

The burly type snorted, produced a shimmering badge and returned the old speech in kind. "How nice for you. You can discuss it with your fellow board members after you make bail. The law requires me to notify them."

While the burly types led Coughlin through the lobby in handcuffs, Jen linked her brother.

"This won't stop him," she said.

"Not yet," Jim replied. "Just wait."

"That's the problem, little brother. Until you work whatever dark magic, he's going to take it out on Julie."

"He'd be a fool to do that, Jen. He got a notice this morning. Big Uncle's looking at him, so he has to shine his shoes and sit up straight. He won't lift a finger against any of us."

* * * *

Rey Juarez listened with anger, then incredulity, and finally with a helpless belly laugh.

"Good for her!" He pointed to just below his nose. "Right there? Really?"

"Pinpoint," I said. "So ... your offer to help?"

"I meant it, Bev."

"Can I ask why?"

"Because they put my nephew through that ... process about a decade ago."

I wheezed a quiet, "Oh."

That's why he hadn't fired me. He should have, by all rights. I wouldn't have trusted the biggest break of my career to the mother of a convict.

"So what do you have?" he said.

A week later, the Net's largest muck channels ran stories about the grandson of a crusading legislator. The pieces included video testimonies from workers who'd been beaten for not arriving thirty minutes before their shifts began, images of unsafe and outdated machines that had killed a dozen people so far, and records that showed Coughlin had paid no fines or made any changes as a result of those deaths.

The FIS expanded its investigation. And like I said, it felt good.

# ELEVEN

"Oh, hey. Sorry to interrupt your lunch, Ms. Wilson, but is Julie okay? I've been linking her for at least a week and it's like she's been vaporized or something."

She wore colors I could only dream of, glaring yellow with orange trim. Beautiful on her, hideous on the rest of us. I caught my breath.

"Kee, is your mom around?"

"Yeah, she's ... this is bad, isn't it?"

"Can you go get her, please?"

She squared her shoulders and struggle to dial up her bravery. "They're going to die, aren't they?"

"Ke'andra Marie Burke, what did I just ask you to do?"

She disappeared and I rubbed my face, heard the keening sob and the piping urgency of my five-year-old.

"Mom, mom, this is Ke'andra and she skinned her knee rilly bad!"

Julie's new friend had lustrous dark skin. The bloody white and pink of the gouge looked almost pornographic next to it. I applied the dermal patch and gave her a hug.

"What happened, sweetheart?"

"We were surfing," she said between hiccupping sobs. "Like the surfers do at the beach and stuff."

"What were you surfing on?"

"The stair rail. It was fun."

*"Bev?"*

"Does your mom let you do that?"

Her eyes shifted to the floor. "Prolly not."

*"Bev..."*

"What's your mom's name?"

"Priscilla, but everyone calls her Buddy and she likes you better if you call her Buddy."

*"BEV!"*

I shook myself and saw Buddy, here and now, smiling and concerned. She's a weekend warrior like my ex, a teacher of poetry and literature the rest of the time. Calm and reflective, she's a perfect foil for a daughter who only achieves tranquility when sedated.

But perhaps that was changing. Ke'andra looked at me with quiet gravity and said, "They're going to die. Rick's gone silent, too."

"No, Ke'andra. But they did commit a Class B."

She bit her lip, then shot fire at her mother and me. "She promised. She said she'd be careful. Rick, too. They promised us."

She swiped at the screen and the link broke.

* * * *

While Ke'andra and I talked, Alex sat down with Rick.

"Do you have a plan for when you get out?" Alex said.

"Yeah. Teach English somewhere off-continent. I've already found openings in Greenland and Botswana."

"So, drop off the grid?"

"Beats paying taxes to our beloved federation."

"You'll be in a much better frame of mind if you apologize to the judge and go home."

"Fuck her," Rick spat back. "I told her the truth. Are we done here?"

"Not really." Alex opened a drawer and threw Rick some clothes. "Put those on."

Rick caught them, started when he saw they were his clothes, and then he felt the slow crawl of fear.

"What's this?"

"Your mom brought them."

"She..."

"You're going home anyway."

Rick flared. "No apology. Ever."

"You've made that clear. Now will you just get dressed?"

"What made the lord high bitch change her mind?" Rick said as he tossed the coverall onto the couch.

"The obvious. If you're here, you just have to shave your head and slug me when I'm not looking. If you're home, you have to face your parents, your friends, your guilt. And Julie. To say nothing of her parents. You can run away after you're done, but not before."

Rick was half into a pair of sweat pants. He let go and slumped onto the back of the couch, stared into nothing while he absorbed the new truth.

"I was that easy to figure out?"

"Most people are, from the outside. It's not so easy to see from the inside."

"Can I ask a question?" Rick said.

"Of course."

"Why didn't you hit me back?"

Alex smiled. "Because that would have given you a cachet in this place that you don't need. It would have made you a man in the eyes of people who don't have the smallest idea of what manhood really means."

"I'm sorry. For the black eye, I mean."

"Thanks for the apology, but if you really want to make amends, go home and don't run away."

Rick felt the shaking spread from his hands to the rest of him, so bad that Alex had to help slip on the tattered old soccer jersey.

"I..."

"I know," Alex said. "You're frightened. And the worst part is waiting right outside that door. But remember that they love you and they haven't disowned you. So try to hug them back."

* * * *

Life in the tattered remains of the Wilson household took on a new rhythm—work punctuated by a happy five minutes, lite meals at local cafes, easy on the wine, no working after ten.

Then came school.

We'd always had a special breakfast on the first day, followed by The Parade—a line of cars with one or more students perched on hoods, slowly crawling the last block toward the school's entrance.

I was trying not to think about that when the message arrived, loud and persistent, heralded by the official seal. I would, without fail, report to the Golden State Academy, where I would be given the schoolwork for Wilson-comma-Julie L. And then I would, without fail, report to the Ventura Regional Justice Center and turn that work in for completion by Wilson, Julie L. I would then, without fail, retrieve the completed work by no later than three that afternoon, and so on. I would do this until Julie was no longer incarcerated.

Failure to comply would result in a fine of one thousand credits per day, and *the bastards*. They'd stolen my mornings, my time to breathe and feel whole.

I took manual control of my car, stormed past the line of blaring horns and yelling kids, blocked part of the drive aisle and blew past the cheery youngsters wishing me good morning. The slight, balding man stopped me two feet later. Dan Connery doesn't seem like much at first, but you don't run a school without a lot of steel and a keen take on people, and he understood me well enough to usher me into his office.

"You got an official communication this morning," he said. "I know because I received a copy. I've also received a summary of Julie's case, and I am furious—"

I shot out of my chair. "You don't have the right—"

"—at the system. What they're doing to Julie is obscene."

One of the usual student cubes sat on his desk, and he tossed it to me. "That has all of her work for the year. She can go as fast as she wants to, and you don't need to come here again. The records will show that you picked up and dropped off right on schedule."

I held up my hands and sagged into the chair. "That's forgery, Dan. I can't ask you to cross the line for my kid."

"I'm not. The machine simply transmits her work once you're past the Justice Center's firewalls. It saves you some travel, that's all."

I shot him a look and he shot one back.

"Okay, I'm not just kicking at the boundaries for Julie. I'm doing it for every other kid whose mom or dad has had to come in every day for two or three months. Nothing in the law prevents me from loading up that computer or setting it to transmit. I got the idea this morning, and I wish I'd had it years ago." He smiled then, predatory. "I also added a bunch of tutors and avatars."

"Who?" I couldn't resist.

"Einstein, Dickens, Poe. She'll get a kick out of him. He was a total ass, so she can tell him off whenever she wants. It'll be good therapy."

"Thank you, Dan. I ... they ... wouldn't even let me celebrate her birthday. I tried to visit and they refused."

"Why?"

"I don't know. They told me to leave or she'd face consequences. I'm amazed we even get our five minutes over the computer."

"You have a lawyer, right?"

"And he's carpeted the system with motions and petitions, so now we sit and wait."

The usual followed—he was sorry, call if I needed help, Julie was a great kid, I'd find a nice surprise on the computer.

The words bounced off.

* * * *

"You're late."

I gave the guard my best smile. "The principal needed to talk, and—"

She snatched the cube from me and placed it in the scanner. A moment later, the barrier opened and she gawped.

"That isn't right. You're on the keep-out list. She pulled up another screen, read it, then made eyes. "Well you were on the keep-out a minute ago, but the education ministry says you and your kid need face time. Come on."

She escorted me to that cavernous visiting area, locked the door behind me and I knew a surge of fear—I was alone in the place where that screw had spit at me—then realized it was empty because visitors wouldn't arrive for another two hours. Julie and Virginia came through a moment later, and I saw hunched shoulders and cracked lips, but I got a body-slam hug and it felt so good to just hold on.

"Did you bring it?"

I hesitated, then gave her the tangible reminder of what she was missing. She took it and bit her lip.

"Can you stay for a while?" she said. "Just a bit? I need to do something hard."

"Until they throw me out," I said. "What's going on?"

Julie snatched at my hand, and our footsteps echoed in the cavernous room as she led me to a table. "Health education module five," she barked at the computer. "Legal consequences videos."

"Hang on, wait," I said. "Are you sure this is wise? Now? Here? Today?"

"The good doctor seems to think so," Virginia said. "And I've promised to be here, so let's do this thing."

Julie started the videos and they were just like I remembered—the early version of the standard death machine, the girl smiling at someone off camera, the timer running while she becomes the first person to die for violating the federation's shiny new chastity laws. A quick cut, and her terrified boyfriend follows. Two young people, still in that vague space between adolescence and adulthood. Five of the longest minutes anyone can ever know.

I'd forgotten about the sound, though. I'd remembered voices and wheezing breath, but that may have been my classmates gagging, or maybe the soundtrack had been cut since I was in high school. Either way, silence gave the piece a raw power, eradicated disbelief and any form of mental escape.

Julie sagged into me as it ended. "I'm sorry, mom."

"And you're forgiven, sweetie." Sometimes, you just need to hear it again.

"I've been so afraid of watching those."

Virginia reached across the table and cupped Julie's face, exactly like I do. "What's next, dear?"

"Do you think ... do you think they went to heaven?" Julie said.

"What's next, dear?"

My daughter came to herself and gave us a shy smile, so unlike her. "A quiet room and no guards, lots of time to learn. You'll come back?" she said to me. "This afternoon?"

"Of course. I'm required—"

"Thanks."

* * * *

On that morning, the transition from jail to the manicured frenzy of an ad agency was a gut-wrenching free-fall. Alice down an endless hole.

I'd gone into advertising because it's an essential industry, a key to rebuilding the global economy and getting the world back to its old state, and I was one of the geniuses tasked with Making It Happen. So, on behalf of Paolo Recchi and Making It Happen, I'd flagrantly stolen an ad campaign from the 1960s. The good artists borrow and the great ones steal, right?

I'd robbed the grave of a long-dead auto maker called Volkswagen. They'd put a small image of their car down in the lower-right corner of an otherwise blank page. The caption had read, "Think Small."

Now that corner held Recchi's clothes, laid out flat in black and white, and the caption read, "Think You."

Sheer genius.

If it flew we'd put L.A. back on the advertising map, and we'd get rich. In my crazier moments I'd told myself the money would even bring contentment. But on that morning, all those things seemed juvenile.

I had more than two hundred messages waiting, and I found myself scanning and deleting with cold fury. I was so deep into my holy war on the insignificant that I didn't notice my boss settle onto a chair next to me.

"Everything okay?"

I finished jumping out of my skin, sighed and looked around to make sure we were alone.

"I got to see her for the first time since she was re-arrested, and her eyes were blank, Rey. She's barely here. And then we watched those videos."

"You mean..."

"Yes, *those* videos, and her eyes were even more blank afterward. But aside from that, I'm just fine."

Rey took a swipe at the current taboos and reaffirmed what it means to be human—he put a hand on my arm. That's why I'll work for the guy until I'm dead. For free if I have to.

"I saw the same thing in my nephew," he said. "But that light comes back, Bev. It may be a different color, but it's there. And in happier news, have you heard about Coughlin?"

I shook my head.

"Someone inside his organization leaked a huge data bubble, and it confirms what we'd heard. He used armed foremen to keep workers in line. I guess the data included sales receipts for clubs and stunners, so Big Uncle is taking a hard look."

"Score one for the little people," I snorted. "It won't help Julie at all."

"You mean they won't let her out?"

"She stays put until the provincial supremes hear the case, and I doubt even God knows when that'll be."

He studied me for a moment. "You have these wonderful bags under your eyes."

Rey would starve as a comedian, but his humor works on me. "Thanks," I said as I dissolved into helpless laughter. I felt so much lighter that I didn't really mind when the official seal faded in above my computer.

"Should I leave?" he said between chuckles.

"No, no. It could be good news."

So I read and the laughter stopped. Once again I was compelled, and so was Julie.

"What is it?" Rey said.

"I've just become an egg donor."

# TWELVE

I jerked to my feet out of habit, not respect. The judge was a man this time, and as we sat I made sure my fingers were hopelessly tangled with Julie's.

"Okay, Mr. Selcraig. What's so urgent?"

"My clients have been summoned to donate their ovarian follicles to one of the national cancer studies," Will said.

"And that's urgent?"

Will ticked through our encounter with Coughlin, and then he dropped a bomb.

"Coughlin is the majority shareholder in Santana Genetics, which in turn is one of the contract companies doing the DNA extraction for the study. But Santana Genetics also has a subsidiary called SoCal Fertility, which specializes in using surrogate mothers to produce children for infertile couples.

"Coughlin isn't married, he has no heir, but he does have licenses for three children, and it's entirely possible that he wants Julie Wilson's eggs for the purpose of creating his own offspring."

"Do you have any evidence that this is what Mr. Coughlin is trying to do?" the judge said. "Any direct link between him and this order to donate? Any evidence that shows he intends to use the eggs for something other than a cancer drug?"

"Nothing direct, but the circumstances are compelling," Will said.

"Are you aware that this effort has been going on for years, and it's made some big strides in fighting several cancers?"

Julie tensed and I pinned her arm to the chair.

"I am," Will replied. "But until recently, the study has used DNA extracted from blood, not human ovum. So why do they want to invade the bodies of Ms. Wilson and her daughter? Why can't they just take blood?"

"Point noted. Do you have anything further?"

"Ms. Wilson and Julie had medical scans earlier today, and the results show that they'll both have ripe ovarian follicles in roughly four days. That isn't enough time for me or the FIS to investigate Coughlin's connections to this matter, and so we're requesting a delay."

Will sat. The judge made notes, then looked at us and smiled. "I'll have a ruling for you in three days."

* * * *

I sat outside the judge's chambers while a guard shackled my daughter for the trip to her cell or study room or wherever.

"I could *so* use a latte," she sighed.

"Well then *so* get one," the guard said.

"What do you mean?" Julie said.

She looked at us like we were from Mars. "There's a coffee counter in the visiting area? And it's visiting hours?"

"There is?" I said.

"Of course there is. You've never seen it?"

"We've never been allowed a visit during regular hours," Julie said.

The guard consulted her computer and rolled her eyes. "You're not on the keep-out, so go get a fix. I'll get your daughter through the gates."

Julie stood in line behind me because that's what you do. No cutting or doubling up, nothing to spark someone's temper. The counter sat behind a thick pane of something indestructible. The girl behind the counter moved with practiced speed. She was one of those beach-perfect blonds, all high cheekbones and sleek curves under a workaday wrap. She didn't smile.

"What can I get you?" she said in a musically raspy voice.

"Double-tall soy latte, extra hot."

"Will that be all?"

Julie peeked around my right shoulder. "No. You have to make another one and then come hug me, seester."

The girl's eyes went wide. "Shit! Holy rat-bastard shit!"

"Nice to see you—"

"Why are you still here?" the girl barked. "You should be home. I was gonna surprise you, come for a visit."

"Long story," Julie said. "Sit with us?"

"Uh ... yeah. I'll fix your ... yeah."

She entered through a heavy steel door next to the latte stand, carried our coffees with easy grace and ignored the stares from lonely people in ugly coveralls. *The classic ice queen*, I thought. *Just like me at her age*.

Another small ballet followed—Julie hugging her and then guzzling half her latte while the girl offered me a smile and a tentative hand.

"Hello, I'm—"

"Mom, this is Kari Edstrom. Your new eldest daughter."

She punctuated the introduction with a belch, and Kari shot her a look.

"Now I know why you're still here."

Julie snorted and began the narrative; Kari darkened as the facts slid by.

"Jizzheads," she said when Julie finished. "Useless pile of daddy-fucking jizzheads."

Okay, maybe not the ice queen.

Julie shot the world an evil smile. "Speaking of dads, mine showed me how to rip someone's ear off, and if they compel me I will. And I don't give a shit if that goes on my report."

"Oh, yes you do," Kari said. "They cut my punishment by seventy percent, and you know what? Even if they're that nice, every little piece of you is going to care, Julie. Besides, the extraction doesn't even hurt. You go to sleep, you wake up."

"You mean ... they did you, too?" I said.

"They do everyone," she said. "Just gotta have the right profile."

"Okay, why?" I said.

"Who cares? Knowing wouldn't have made me feel any better, although I did get a laugh when it was over."

"What happened?" Julie said.

"They had to junk mine. After they were done I mentioned I was dyslexic, and they were like, 'You are? Why didn't you tell us?' And I was like, 'Why didn't you ask?' Jizzhead cretins."

"So no little Karis running around in nine months?" Julie said. "Maybe that's what I'll do, tell them I'm dyslexic or insane."

Kari glared at her. "They check for that now. But really, Jules, it's a few hours where you're not here, you get a nap out of the deal, and they give you this really nice mood stabilizer. For a couple days, you're bulletproof."

"Don't care," Julie snapped. "They don't get me twice. First caregiver who comes within reach loses an ear, and I don't give an airborne sex act if she's the sweetest granny on the planet."

Kari looked at me. "Is my younger sister really this stupid? Can you talk some sense into her?"

But what does the rational parent say? You're grounded? Promise to behave or I'll tell the guards? Maybe prayer would help: Dear God, please let them shackle her permanently. But even then, they'd write up any curses or bad attitude. I came back to now and saw two faces, one that didn't care and the other hoping for wisdom. And I had none. And I had to try anyway.

"Julie, that training was all about self-control, self-defense—"

"And I'm not defending myself here? Hello—"

"We all have to do things we hate," I hissed at her, "choose between—"

"VISITING HOURS ARE OVER. PRISONERS TO THE WALL WITH HANDS RAISED, VISITORS TO THE EXIT GATE."

My jaw dropped and my daughter laughed. "Yes, mom, they use the same voice as our doorbell. I almost died the first time I heard it." She stood and raised her hands. "And yes, I know I have a choice, mom. I get to choose between right and left ears. See ya tomorrow."

No chance to hug. No chance to steer her away from an idea that was almost suicidal. I stood and moved against a small flood of gray coveralls. Kari shot fire at a guard who smiled at her.

"Look at me one more time and I report you, jizzhead."

He flinched, gawped, turned away, and the crowd swept me toward the gate.

* * * *

Claim check, belongings, and how could I have been so proud of this handbag? When had something like that ever mattered?

I stood in the sharp afternoon sun and the tears came, hot and thick, and I told myself to stop with the melodrama, I was in public.

"Oh, there you are. Alex told me about your hearing ... okay, why don't you come with me?"

Virginia took my arm and me and I was back in her office. She listened, and then she also defied the taboo. It felt so good to have my neck rubbed.

"You know we force our kids because we love them, right?

"Of course," I said. "But how do I force this?"

Hers was a sad smile.

* * * *

My computer chimed and Jessica Rabbit faded in. She's one of my favorite old cartoon characters, and a sort of code. Only someone who knows me sends that image, so a familiar wanted to talk, and it wasn't likely to be a happy conversation. I hesitated, opened the link and Kari appeared.

"Have they ruled yet?" she said.

"No, dear. We don't expect to hear anything until later today."

"Um, okay. Sorry to bother you."

"Kari, it's sweet of you to be concerned. Are you free for lunch? I'll treat."

In other words, we're both terrified, so how about some chocolate?

I founder her waiting by the employee entrance, coated with the shame of I don't deserve, and it took the threat of liverwurst to make her admit she loved South Asian food. We settled in to Tikka Masala and Balti Gosht, and I didn't have to say a word. She just spilled.

"My boyfriend was from Venezuela. Eduardo de las Vegas y Campos. Eddie of the valleys and countryside. He was the only guy who didn't stare at my boobs. So we kiss and hold hands, go to games and all that. It was fun, you know? I felt like I could finally just be me."

"Were your parents okay with it?" I said.

"My dad ... who knows. He's so wrapped in his career. Mr. airline pilot."

"What about your mom?"

"She died when I was eleven. So I guess Eddie was also *there*, you know? Someone to talk to and hold. Just ... so nice." She eyed me for a moment. "I suppose you want details."

"No," I said. "Not unless you want to share them."

"We went to the prom," she said. "What else? It was the usual deal. We split a hotel room with three other couples so we could change, right? And the hotel would monitor the room to make sure it was ladies only, then men only and all that.

"We have a great time, and then we're back in the room alone, just us, and I still don't know why. We kiss, and then he takes me into this part of the room where we can't see the security cameras, and we kiss some more, and he asks me if he can ... kiss my boobs." She unconsciously crossed her arms over the offending anatomy. "And then I was in cuffs. There were hidden cameras everywhere.

"So now I make coffee, enjoy the luxuries of post-confinement housing and worry about my new sister."

"You mean, your dad..."

"Disowned me? Not really. But he wants me on my own. Says it's good for me."

"And it is," I said. "You go to school, start a career—"

"I'm dyslexic," she snorted. "I can barely read. Who'll want me?"

My reaction was quick and visceral, across the table for her hands. "I do, dear. I do."

I knew my motives were mixed, but then they almost always were.

* * * *

The ruling came at 4:01. The judge had contacted the government drone in charge of the study and been assured that any tissues were used to culture a targeted cancer drug, not make babies. And no, he'd never heard of one Christopher Coughlin. For those reasons, the extraction would proceed. I could opt out by paying a fine; Julie had no such luxury.

* * * *

The jail infirmary surprised me. It's as sleek as any hospital, cheery and spotless, none of the rage and despair that permeate the rest of that place. The doctor was one of those people you can only classify as odorless and tasteless.

"Sweetie, I'm going to go first," I said. "I want you to watch and see that this isn't hard."

"Sure, mom." Her smile made it plain. Ears were still on the menu and she was hungry.

But someone pressed a sedative to my neck and life became a flood of promise and joy. The table was comfortable and the towels they draped over me were so warm that it just made sense to smile at the little cones on my abdomen, with their thin tubes running out the top and those fine needles inside...

"Do you feel anything, Ms. Wilson?"

"Huh?"

[a stretch of gray]

"Any pain now?"

"What? Oh. Uh...

[an easy, soothing arc of time]

"Three good eggs so far, two to go."

[blackness]

"And there we are. Welcome back."

The delicious haze bled away so quickly, and that was so unfair.

"Come on, let's sit you up."

"Nnnooo. Please? Just a couple more minutes? Feels so good..."

"Well, I suppose we can let you rest while we start on your daughter."

Daughter. Julie. Important. Something about ... I looked over and saw her eyeing the doctor like a snake with an unsuspecting mouse. The drugs evaporated in a hurry as I sat up and reached.

"Sweetie, when was the last time I told you I loved you? Really told you?" I said.

She shrugged. What did that matter now?

I took her chin in my hands and kissed her forehead. "I love you so much, and I'm so sorry for all this."

My thumbnail peeled away a cover. My right index finger caressed her cheek. The patch Alex had glued to the tip did its work, and Julie's eyes went from diamond to blank to closed.

# THIRTEEN

She sat in a far corner of the visiting area, under those shafts of light, chin on her knees. The screw locked the door behind me, and even though I knew we'd be alone I threw nervous glances at the balcony.

She gave me a half smile as I put the computer on the table and kissed the nearest cheek.

"Feeling okay? Nice to have it done," I said.

"Bastard cavity rags. Couldn't even look at me when they put me under."

I had no idea how it would set her free, but I gave her the truth. "It wasn't them, sweetie. It was me. I did it."

I remember a sudden blur, the hollow crack of the computer against my left cheek, another blur through my haze of tears, a sharper crack as she heaved the little cube against the floor.

I reminded myself that it wasn't about me.

I reminded myself that I'd vowed to raise my child with more grace and less alcohol, to never be my mother.

But the hollow smack of my palm against her cheek, echoing around that cavernous space ... so satisfying.

"You idiot bitch. You're more than smart enough to figure this one out."

She stood, blinking away the tears. "And I have," she snarled. "Don't talk to me again. Ever." She turned on her heels and walked away.

I gathered my handbag, finally realized I should pick up the broken computer, rap on the door. The guard opened it and went on full alert.

"What happened t' you?"

"Oh, I tripped over my cloak and hit a table." The lie came easily. I'd used it before. "I'm afraid I also broke the computer, so I'll need to get a new one. Seriously, ma'am, I'm okay, just embarrassed."

"Ought getta look-at."

"I will, ma'am. I'm just glad nobody saw me."

* * * *

"I hit her, Jim."

"I probably would have, too." He looked so haunted as he rolled the bruise patch over my cheek.

"Alex told me that he's seen them give full punishment twice, and it left the kid destroyed each time. No spirit, no will to live. I couldn't let her hurt that doctor, and she would have. But I still feel so damned," I said.

"Well, you're not. You did the right thing in an impossible situation. So ... please don't do what you're doing now." He smoothed the patch with a gentle finger. "Don't stuff the emotion. Please?"

That had been one of our chronic fights: Why can't you just let it out now? Why do you have to glare and stay cold for the next six days?

I'd made some honest efforts to fix that, but it's hard to let go of a tool you've used since childhood. Keeping the lid screwed down was the safest way to weave between a control-freak lush of a mother and a distant father with an explosive temper. That kind of self-imposed cage is hard to leave. It's safe there.

"Can I make a suggestion?" he said. "I have a ... gift, I guess. Something to help you vent. I can just set it out by the pool later today."

I nodded and realized I was going numb. Venting was a good idea.

"And why don't you take the morning off?" he said. "I'll stop by school, get a new computer."

"I'm not sure you can. The directive says that I pay a fine if I don't show up."

"I'm sorry," he said, and he kissed me, a gentle brush on the forehead.

I was half way to the school when I realized he wasn't just empathizing about the morning.

* * * *

"I'll pay for the computer, Dan."

"No. You won't."

"Yes. *I will.*"

He gave me that look, the teacher using much patience on the idiot student. "We get them for free."

"Oh."

He handed me a freshly uploaded machine. I thanked him, started for the car and found myself wandering the halls instead. Why hurry to another bruise? That, and I was probably grieving, trying to claim what I was missing. I'd looked forward to this year, to chaperoning dances and watching Rick blush, to the bake sales and the school play. And yes, I'd even looked forward to sitting on those rock hard benches while my daughter and her boyfriend wowed the college scouts.

I passed the health education unit and saw the windows blacked out. Maybe the kids were watching the videos Julie had already seen. Other doors—Bill Cayetano diagramming a sentence, Donna Li challenging her sophomores to think about the implications of the Master Charter's second clause.

And then the choir echoed down the empty corridor.

Soccer and voice had no trouble getting Julie out of bed in the morning. She only had a workaday alto, but she loved to use it, and as my feet carried me toward the room I heard Clara Rayner telling her charges to bring the volume up, to not worry about overwhelming the solo.

"So, on one, two—"

Voices struck a chord in a minor key.

The smoky contralto exploded, pure whiskey-and-cigarettes, setting fire to an old spiritual.

*When I'm gone, when I'm gone, I'm gone, gone*
*O mother, don't you weep when I am gone*
*For I'm going to Heaven above*
*Going to the God I love*
*O mother, don't you weep when I am gone*

I stood, frozen by the wave of sound and the joy in that voice, the heart, the palpable love of tone and cadence, of life. *Sing for me*, I thought. *Please, God, sing for me.*

*O mother meet me there*
*Mother meet me in the air*
*O mother, don't you weep when I am gone*

I wanted so badly to enter that room and see who owned that incredible gift, to drown in that flood of music—*sing for me*—but parents didn't do that.

And the day was full.

And I was late.

* * * *

The guard scanned the new computer and looked puzzled. "Says here I'm supposed to deliver this to the chaplain."

"May I ask why?" I said.

"Prisoner don't wanna see nobody. You, her father, nobody."

"Fine." I managed a smile. "I'll pick it up at three."

I arrived a few minutes late, hoping she'd reached forgiveness. This time the guard was an older man, gruff and tired. His computer flashed a message and he shook his head. "Chaplain has you flagged. Come on."

She met us outside her office and smiled at him. "Oh, thanks, Steve. Here, I owe you." She handed him a credit disk, one that I recognized—issued by the Justice Center and good for a free latte. All I could think was, Dear God, please inspire Kari to poison the milk.

"What's going on?" I said as I sagged onto the ratty couch.

"Julie has the right to ask for more study time, so she entered a request and it was granted." she said. "That means her computer can stay here. They'll transmit her work a couple times a day."

"And she doesn't have to talk to me," I said.

"She'll figure it out, Bev. She'll forgive."

I blew off the rest of work, went home and changed into tattered gardening clothes, went out to scratch the dog and pull weeds. Jim's gift stood by the pool. He'd set up his old punching bag in a shady corner of the yard, a heavy leather satchel hanging from a stand.

"Oh, how thoughtful," I said to Harley. "A heavy thing that helps you practice violence. Such a nice ex-master, don't you think?"

A pair of those wrist brace/boxing glove things dangled from the chain that held the bag. I put them on, tried to remember what Jim had tried to teach and I'd tried to ignore.

"Let's see. Plant the feet ... from the hip..."

I threw an experimental punch. The next one was harder, more satisfying. I tried a combination of rights and lefts, a kick, and wasn't I supposed to growl when I threw the blow? Yeah, from the diaphragm, keep your feet planted and then it was chaos—flailing arms and feet, no balance, no control, growls that became screams that became tears and suddenly

I was too tired to breathe. I leaned into the bag until I'd recovered my wind, then I turned toward the street.

"DAMN YOU, WILSON! YOU KNOW I HATE GETTING SWEATY!"

* * * *

I'd cleaned up the remains of a light meal and poured a second glass of wine when he linked.

"I was maybe a bit thoughtless," he said. "I put the bag up and got half way back to my office when I realized you hate exercising. Sorry about that. Want me to come get it?"

Jim is another one of those comedians who shouldn't even try, but it worked. "James Burton Wilson, you are so full of shit."

* * * *

The message arrived two days later.

Wilson, Julie L. had applied for post-release housing and an entry level job that accommodated her class schedule. No action was required on my part; this was a courtesy communication. In other words, if they did release her she wasn't coming home.

I called an estate agent and put the house on the market. If I had to walk out my front door alone, I wanted a different door.

* * * *

With life reduced to work, feeding the dog and flailing at a heavy bag, I found myself asleep by seven or eight and up at three or four, using the quiet to sketch ideas. The work was edgy and dark, an echo of the posters that advertised punk rock bands way back when. I was hard at it one morning when the message flag lit up and displayed a dripping paintbrush.

Diane Westmoreland. The conversation I most wanted and most feared.

She was only leaving a message, but I was desperate to talk so I opened the link. Her eyes widened and whatever she was saying derailed, crumpled against the surprise of seeing me.

"Oh," she said. "I wasn't trying to ... I'm sorry if I woke you."

"I was up, Di. Sleep is a bit scarce."

"Same with us, too. Look, I wasn't trying to avoid you, I just wanted to thank you, and I couldn't sleep, so I thought I'd leave a message."

"Thank me?" I said.

"For talking to Rick. He..."

She sobbed, high and keening, and her chest heaved as a load of tears began to spill. I still pause when I think of the ways we cried during that time. We had no choice, really. We faced a system with no regard for humanity or dignity, one that after a certain point has no reverse gear or stop button. Rage does no good because you can't unload it on the system, only on yourself and those you love. The media do no good because they don't care, and even when they do, it's hard to separate the story from the hype and the noise. Legislators do no good because the machinery of death is too hot to touch. Bombs are useless because the system rebuilds and comes roaring back, angry and thus more potent than ever. All we could do was cry.

"Rick and I didn't really ... talk," I said.

"Oh, I know," she said as she blew her nose. "He was a complete wad, and he's been dying for a chance to apologize. It's been driving him over the wall."

"That, and Julie hasn't been at school," I said.

"Well, yeah. But Bev, that isn't why I tried to leave a message. I wanted to know how you are."

I recited the litany of events and Diane's exhaustion seemed to grow, a dark ivy spreading along her face and through her eyes.

"My son can wait," she said. "You don't need to deal with him now."

"No," I said. "I want a chance to actually do something."

What happened next would have left me in hysterics if it hadn't been tinted with so much pain. At seven that morning, the computer emitted a cute little *dweep*, Rick's tone, and the terrified almost-man faded in.

"I'd like to apologize, if I can, but I don't want to do it over a link. Can we ... face-to-face?"

"Where do you suggest?"

"Uh ... school?"

Dan Connery graciously lent us a quiet room across from his office. Rick hustled in, dressed to the nines, and thrust a bouquet of orchids toward me at something approaching the speed of light.

"Ma'am. The flowers. They're for you. And I'll understand if you want me to just go, but I had to at least try, you know?"

"Try what?" I said.

"To apologize. That I'm sorry."

"Yes, Richard Daniel, you can apologize. And yes, Richard Daniel, your apology is accepted. And yes, you're forgiven." I studied him for a moment and I *knew*. "That really yarks, doesn't it? Forgiveness is exactly what you don't want."

"Yes, ma'am. It's the hardest ... thing. I told myself to be careful, you know? To just leave after I said it."

"Said what?" I asked.

"That I loved her. I just felt so proud, you know? I'd been so afraid to say that, but I did, and then it all got out of hand. I was telling myself to just walk away, but I wasn't man enough."

I groaned and threw him a look. "Which means, of course, that she wasn't woman enough." That thought ricocheted around the room and into the void.

"And then I decided to really do the fear, you know? I ... asked her."

"Asked her what?" I said.

"If I could buy her a ring. With code, you know?"

My world shrank to just his words and my breath, the intense focus that comes when the mugger pulls a knife or the client puts hard eyes on your idea.

"Oh, geez. I'm sorry. Uh, ma'am. I thought you knew."

I scrabbled for gracious words and a quick way to the door. The only route I could see was another boundary violation, so I made it a good one—I kissed his forehead, his eyes, his cheeks, and he suddenly looked so old, so worn and spent.

"Rick, did you hear me, really hear me, when I said you were forgiven?"

"I ... yeah. Thanks."

"Good. Now your day is full and so is mine. I hate to cut this short, but I need to go."

Rick turned a corner, and even though I bolted down the hall, the tears fought their way out before I made it to my car.

A ring. With code.

I'd celebrated my eighteenth birthday by going to the courthouse with one Michael Gordon. We'd left wearing "adult" rings, with computer chips that certified we were legal. Over my mother's hurricane of threats and protests, we spent the summer at his parents' beach house, playing at adulthood—cheap wine and clumsy romps in the midnight surf, inedible attempts at grilled food.

The official name is a provisional union. Two people get the hots for each other and find the nearest courthouse or automated kiosk. No property changes hands, and the ethos is firm— you let each other go as gently as you can when the lust cools. It's a bit like the old Scottish tradition of handfasting, where you stay together for a year and a day, then marry or part ways.

Shiny/happy on the surface, but I scratched that shell when I was about twelve, just enough to see the monster beneath. The system makes it easier to trace plague vectors and know who to euthanize. But it doesn't answer the age-old question of why so many people get into trouble. All it can do is make you stare at the age-old answer—when you're under the boardwalk and the buttons are coming open, you just don't think.

Around here we call them convenience marriages.

The day before he'd left for college, we sat on the beach, bathed in a soft wind and the smell of the ocean, the sunset an absolute riot, and he'd taken my hands.

"Are we really forever? Let's be honest here."

I kissed him. "No, we're not."

The memories usually brought a smile, but not on that day. Instead I sat in my car, pounded the steering wheel and tried to fend off two ugly needles of emotion, starting with jealousy. If he hadn't asked Julie to marry him, I'd have offered myself, taken him into my home and my bed, showed him how to make my body sing. That spun into rage. The shy kid had reached so far, only to find himself in shackles.

I drove home and flailed at the bag without bothering to change, screw any wrinkles or damage, and I only stopped when Di linked in.

"How'd it go? Did my contribution to the gene pool say the right things?"

"Oh, yes, along with world-class flowers."

She studied me for a moment. "So how come you look so awful?"

"Because it would have been fun to have Rick living here, his sense of humor, the calm that he somehow creates in Julie."

I decided to avoid the part about having him in my bed. I can be smart sometimes.

"I can maybe help you feel better," Di said. "I hope this isn't out of line, but I told Scott about what you've been through, and he wants the name of the doctor who did your extractions."

"Why?"

"He wants to go after her license."

"Bennington," I said without hesitation. "Can he really do that?"

"Why don't I have him link you? And Bev? Thank you for loving my son."

*I wish I could*, I thought. "He makes it easy," I said.

I expected to hear from Scott in roughly three days because he has that kind of schedule, so I was a bit startled when he appeared about two minutes later.

"How can you go after that doctor's license?" I said.

"You know the rule about first doing no harm?"

"Yes." I wasn't liking this.

"They took your eggs because they can use older machines to extract the DNA. That's the only reason. If they take your blood, they have to use modern equipment. So they go after eggs instead and make more money." He gave me a nasty smile. "Go talk to your lawyer."

WASHINGTON – The Supreme Court today upheld New York's controversial chastity law, which classifies sexuality offenders as bio-terrorists.

The ruling was aimed specifically at the so-called ultra-ravers, those thought to be most responsible for spreading the second AIDS virus.

Writing for the majority, Chief Justice Morena Vitale said, "The medical studies have made it clear that the current health and social crises have been largely fomented by the behavior of what some call the 'Rave Crowd' or 'Party Class'...

"This behavior has resulted in millions of dead, widespread economic hardship, and a crumbling of cultural norms...

"In the past, countries have not hesitated to condemn terrorists, which, by logical extension, includes bio-terrorists. Any group or class of people that willfully spreads a contagion that kills in the tens of millions can be considered a terrorist organization, no matter how loosely affiliated its members may be...

"Some have said that it's impossible to legislate morality. Measure 419 is not an attempt to do so. It merely opens the door for the prosecution of those who willfully endanger the lives of innocents.

Frankly, this court thinks Measure 419 may be too little, too late."

—Excerpt from a New York Times article, omissions mine

# FOURTEEN

You'd think that a lovingly restored older home with pool, sweeping view, the latest kitchen, and the All Federation Grandmother next door would attract a horde of buyers.

Not so much, to resurrect an old phrase.

The house collected dust for three weeks until my estate agent politely asked me to disappear for a couple hours on a Saturday. With nothing better to do, I invited Kari to lunch. She ignored a cheery, "Have a good one" from the guard and gave me long hug.

"You really don't like the screws," I said.

"I get tired of being smiled at."

"So why do you keep your job?" I said.

"Because it's the only thing I can find, and I can file reports on them. If I file three and they decide my complaints are warranted, the stupid jizzhead is gone."

"Oh, really?" I told her about the sunflower seeds and she smiled.

"That's Randy. Total idiot."

"Can you write him up for me?"

"No, but I will if he even looks at me. Do you mind if I change? I had a milk disaster this morning."

I followed her past a sign that said POST CONFINEMENT HOUSING and found myself in a long room filled with bunk beds and small locked chests.

"Home sweet home," she said. "The people are nice and the rent is ... what it is, I guess."

"It ... what?" I spluttered. "Rent? For this?"

"Five hundred a month."

"And how much do they pay you to make coffee?"

"Eight hundred."

"Oh, hell no." I seized her elbow. "Come with me."

"Where are we going?"

"Home."

I marched her out of the car and past a startled agent. "Sorry," I said. "But my life circumstances have changed and the house is off the market." I pointed to the door. "Effective now. Thanks for trying."

I took Kari's elbow again and marched her into Julie's room.

"Okay, it's dusty and I should have made the bed weeks ago. She'll probably kill you if you move a single trophy, but since she's refusing to come home, I don't think she'll notice and I certainly won't care. Rent is two hundred, plus you have to do some of the dishes and feed the dog."

"Dog?"

She fell in love with Harley because that's what he did, and then she looked around the yard.

"Can I work in the garden?"

"Of course, dear."

"There's this gardener, up at the prison. Her name's Sachi, and she had me work with her all day, do this little bonsai tree. It was such a nice way to pass the time, quiet and ... real, I guess."

"Well, then you go feel connected."

She took me by the arm, one of those spastic gestures. "Promise me something? When you're up there, go talk to her. Sachi. She'll help you forget where you are and you'll need that. Please? Say you will?"

I promised, and I remembered my dictum to Alex, that I wanted a full report on this girl before he worked his voodoo on Julie. I didn't need one. The wreckage was obvious and any voodoo was just fine.

That night, I got lost in one of my techno-romances until I felt the nerves at my door and saw the ferocious blush, almost as bad as Rick's.

"What is it, dear?"

"My mom used to rub my neck, and..."

My mixed motives and I followed her into what I already thought of as her room, despite the trophies, and she purred as I worked at the knots.

"I've wanted someone to do that for so long," she said. "When I was at the prison, I asked a guard if she would, and she said yes, but then she just stopped. Got up and left. I asked where she was going and she said she was off shift, have a nice evening. I couldn't believe it. They were going to hurt me, and she's all, 'Have a nice day.'"

I put my mixed motives on sabbatical. "Are you taking anything for sleep?" I said.

"That hasn't been too bad. I've been doing trauma stuff with Alex."

"Stuff?"

"It's like hypnosis, makes me fight through all the emotion. It's really hard, but it lets me function. Suicide's a long ways away now."

My hands stopped. "Suicide?"

"They had me on watch, like, an hour after I was arrested or something. I was so numbed out. I remember sitting on a floor somewhere, and someone was asking me if I could feel my face, and I was all like, 'Who needs a face?'"

"Did you have a plan?" In other words, did she have one now? If so, I'd have to idiot-proof the house.

"It was ... logical, you know? I'd pay for my mistake, I wouldn't have to worry about a job, my dad wouldn't have to deal with his screw-up kid, and mom was waiting. I couldn't lose."

"So, you didn't have a plan?"

"Oh, I had two. My dad had some tri-fents left over from an injury, and if they were gone, I was going to take myself to a frat party, get drunk, dance some idiot into a room and strip. Waive my appeals, no more worries about my future, the big whammy's painless and mom's waiting."

I caught my breath. The first plan may have failed because someone could have found her, but the second was an armored guarantee. The common rooms in frat and sorority houses all have surveillance, and the police would have arrived in seconds, probably before the girl was fully undressed.

She shook her head and smiled. "Obviously, I wasn't all here."

"But you're all here now," I said. "I mean, your head's on the pillow, your feet are attached, butt's in place. Shoulder blades, too."

I rubbed some more and she giggled. "That feels so good. If you see me going all wiggy, you won't ... toss me?"

I chuckled. "Tomorrow, dear, we're going to buy flowers, get you connected to the earth, and I'm going to teach you a dance called the Flail."

"A dance?"

"You wear fighting gloves, and you do it whenever you get wiggy."

* * * *

A couple days later, my work computer emitted a generic noise and the message flag said that one Leif Edstrom wanted to chat. I accepted and a man with blond hair faded in. Rather handsome.

"Are you Bev Wilson?" he said in a stiff voice.

"Modern technology makes that a virtual certainty—"

"You've taken in my daughter?"

"Yes, I h—"

"I don't approve."

"Why not, if I may get a word in—"

"She needs to be on her own."

I bristled. "What she needs is some hope. A school that can teach her to read. A chance at a real job. A way to feel like a decent person. She doesn't need to give more than sixty percent of her pay back to the province and live in a ratty dorm with twelve other people. And you know what would really help? A father who says he loves her."

"She's heard that."

"Really? How often?"

"Ten minutes ago," he said in softer tones. "And I'm looking for schools."

"Well you just keep doing that." I flicked at the screen and broke the link.

* * * *

The next three weeks ran by in a flurry of rubbed necks, flower beds that got nicer and a quiet young lady chopping vegetables beside me.

Then Rey  knocked on my office door, slumped into a chair and nearly broke down.

"My daughter," he said.

"What—"

"She had her first kiss. Last night."

Silent minutes crawled by, because how can you find words for the roils of fear and joy that come with living in our time, of knowing that romance can kill your child and you have to let go anyway?

"Was it sweet?" I finally said.

He smiled. "The noises ... I had to stop myself from laughing. They were watching some romance vid, my daughter was crying, and he was sort of cooing at her. I poked my head around the door and he was stroking her face, and..."

"All proper and in bounds," I said.

"Yeah. I thought my nephew's experience had prepared me for it, you know? But ... my daughter." He closed his eyes and sighed. "Jesus."

It wasn't an oath.

"Were you around for Julie's first kiss?" he said.

"I was."

"Were you as terrified as I am?"

"No. Maybe I should have been, but no. I let myself laugh."

* * * *

I was frosting a cake for a bake sale and listening to the growls and scuffles of Harley Ball. My tingly mom-sense was on the alert for blood and permanent physical damage, not romance.

"Ha! Bite me, Goofus!" Julie had stolen the ball.

"Yeah, right. Harley's on your side. He cheats."

Rick's shoes squeaked as he sprinted after his tormentor. She yelped, I heard a huge splash, and I looked out the kitchen window to find them in the pool, Julie splashing Rick, cold murder in her eyes.

"I DON'T LIKE YOU ANYMORE FOR A WHILE! Throw me in because I smoked you!"

"Excuse me? I was just hot." He splashed back and waded toward her. "Besides, you're ... I mean ... I wouldn't care if you smoked ... you're so beautiful," he stammered.

I held my breath. Rick looked at his feet, his face crawling with love and rank terror. He offered Julie his hands first, then his arms and she stepped into them with a nervous giggle as he took aim, closed his eyes and got her smack on the chin. Round two was far more successful—clumsy and shy and then not clumsy anymore.

I managed to stifle the laughter and let them savor each other for a while, then headed outside and dangled my legs in the pool.

"Hey, gang, come here." They whirled in surprise and blushed as they came, Julie wanting to kill me and Rick wanting to just die. I wrapped my arms around them. "I think it's wonderful that you feel this way about each other. So there's something we need to do, right?"

* * * *

"You had them sign a dating contract?" Rey said.

"I know, I know. The idiot things don't work. I shouldn't have bothered."

"Don't be too hard on yourself. I did the same thing last night."

And I knew why. You need to feel like you're doing something, even if you know it's useless.

We sat for a few moments, and then the official seal appeared and waved, made noises and demanded obeisance.

"I think I'll let this one go to storage, review it later," I said.

"Better not. It might be good news."

I chuckled, opened the link and gawped at my sobbing, terrified daughter.

"Mama? We got our windows."

Mama.

The word was bad enough. She hadn't used that term since she was four, and even then she only used it when she was sick or frightened.

"When, sweetheart?"

"December. January. God, mama."

"What? December or January? When is it, sweetheart?"

"Rick ... I'm January. Mama, they're not going to let me come home!"

A hand appeared and broke the link.

# FIFTEEN

I'd never seen Rey so angry.

"Okay," he said with a cold smile. "It's time to screw those wads to the floor. Let's go public, plaster the channels with Julie's face and the details of what she's been through."

"They'll probably just hurt her more," I said. "Give her full punishment, destroy her."

"Not if there's a big enough outcry—"

The message flag appeared again, but this time it included a cross and Virginia faded in, looking apologetic.

"I'm terribly sorry," she said. "Julie was melting down so I reached for her and my hand strayed into the lasers. I probably scared you out of your wits."

"Something like that," I said. "What's going on?"

"The kids finally have their punishment dates, but Julie may not go home until she gets a ruling on the complaint filed by that guard."

Rey smiled, faux and nasty—a campaign is sounding better as the seconds tick along. I was about to say yes when another screen appeared, this one filled with Alex.

"I just cleared time on my schedule. Why don't you come in?"

"They're going to punish my daughter, and then ship her back to jail. Talking to you is going to help ... how?"

"That isn't what has her in a twist," he said.

"Oh, for God's sakes, what could be worse than that?"

"She saw your house on the market. Is she being disowned?"

"Oh, for God's *other* sakes, put her on."

"I would," Virginia said, "except this isn't the kind of thing you do over the computer, right?"

* * * *

Alex furnished his office with antique Craftsman style furniture, and he covered his walls with Cezanne and Picasso. I smiled a hello and chose a corner of the couch, rehearsed what I was going to say.

*It's time for a couple new rules, young lady. First, if you make a shit situation worse you get no support from me. Second, if you hit me again you pay for college.*

Julie padded in, sat closer to me than I expected, and a moment later her head was in my lap. She reached back, found my hands, draped them over her face and flooded them with tears.

"So ... when's your day?" I said.

"January seventeen. I'm sorry."

"And when's Rick's?"

"December nine. I'm sorry, mama."

I shot Alex a look. "Do those bastard cavity wads know that December nine is Tuesday of finals week?"

"I've told them," he said. "They won't budge."

"So how will he cope with school?"

"It's called an accelerated study plan."

"Wow. That's just so compassionate. Here, kid, have some more pressure until we're ready to kick the shit out of you—"

"Mama?"

The dry sand in her voice wiped away any new rules. "Yes, love?"

"Where will we live?"

"Where we've always lived," I said.

"You mean, you didn't..."

"I took it off the market when your sister moved in."

"When my ... who?"

"You know, the coffee mogul?"

"The what?"

"Kari. Your cellmate."

"Oh."

"You'll have to fight her for closet space. And the dog. They're in love."

Julie imploded and crawled into herself. "I'm sorry, mom. I was totally out of control. It was just ... so unfair."

I had one of those replies, adult words about life not being fair and sometimes you just have to suck it up, but she pulled away, squared her shoulders and looked at Alex.

"I broke one of the big rules," she said. "It's a thing in our family that you don't hit, and I knew it, and I went all grandma anyway."

"Grandma?" Alex said.

"My mother," I said. "When I was seventeen, I went out with my boyfriend—"

"The infamous Michael Gordon. Mom's first convenience," Julie said.

"Yes, the infamous Michael. And I came home seriously drunk. Plowed flat. The next morning, my mother hit me with my bedside lamp and gave me a concussion. So I laid down a rule when Julie's father and I were first married."

"But you let Julie have self-defense training," he said.

"That was about self-control," I said. "And we all need that. I certainly did, especially after..."

"After what?" Alex said.

I heaved in internal sigh—me and my big mouth—and made Julie turn and look at me. "Before we got married, Mike and I found a quiet spot on the beach, and ... I got half as naked as you, love. That's part of what rips at me, knowing millions of people do what you did, every day, and no one's the wiser."

"Do you want to be punished for that?" Alex said

"Has my daughter deserved any of what's come her way? Would she and Rick have started an outbreak? No. The worst they could have done was make a baby."

I wasn't about to go on. If I spilled about the punishment I did deserve, I'd certainly get it, right when Julie needed me.

"It's okay, mom. I'm not mad at you or anything. I just feel like shit."

She snuggled close and we spent the rest of the session not saying much, just quietly holding on.

* * * *

While we sat, another conversation took place that I didn't hear, but I have the truth.

Her Honor smiled at the old man and tried to fend off the heartbreak. The strokes had been hard on him, despite medicine's best, and it hurt to seem him like this. He'd been such a force in her life, the kind of mentor people dream of and few seldom meet. Not just lessons in law, but lessons in men, love, fly fishing, child rearing, tennis, finding a good mechanic, lawn care.

Despite the nature of the meeting, it felt good to be back in his office, with its rich paneling and rows of books, the pictures of his family still in the same places on his desk.

"Hello, Christo," she said.

"How are you, dear?" he wheezed in a reedy voice.

"As well as age and a fresh knee surgery allow," she said. "I was hoping you could explain something to me, a ruling you made on a sentence that I passed." She opened a computer file and set it in front of him.

"What's the problem?" he said as he squinted at the document.

"I imposed a standard sentence, one we've used for years, and then you had the defendant rearrested."

"Why would I do that?"

"Because a member of the Ventura Civil Guard filed a back-channel report."

"But ... there are no other signatures on this file. None of us can act alone on such motions. We have to rule as a body, after due consideration." He focused on her and for a moment he was the man she'd known—barrel chested and powerful. "You know that."

"Yes, Christo, I do. So what happened?"

He smiled at her, and she started at the vague light in his eyes.

"You haven't aged a day," he said. "Just as beautiful as always, Helen. So beautiful."

Her Honor tried to stop the sharp hiss of her breath. Helen was the girl in the black picture frame, there in the exact middle of his desk.

"I'm so proud of what you've grown into, Little Fire. Such a wonderful glow. Do you need anything more?"

> *Oh, God, please, what do I say? Tell me what to say.*

She moved around the desk, leaned over and kissed him. "That's all I need ... grandpa. As usual, your answers help me see."

"Well then, you get out there and give them what-for."

"Yes, sir. Always."

"That's my granddaughter. On top, all the way!"

She sobbed as her car drove away from the immense old house, and back in her chambers she opened a link to an obscure branch of the justice ministry. The clerk recognized her and smiled.

"How can I help you, ma'am?"

"I need to fill out a five-thirty-one."

Form 531 compels a judge or prosecutor to undergo a mental evaluation. Only another judge can file the form, and if you do, you'd better pray you're right.

"On who?" the clerk asked.

"Christo Vafiadis," she said.

"You mean..."

"Yes, the Chief Justice of the Provincial Supreme Court."

The clerk became all business. "Yes, ma'am. What reason do you have for the request?"

"I just talked with him about a serious breach of due process on his part, and the incident has slipped his mind completely. He also thought I was Helen, his granddaughter."

"Slips like, I made one just the other day," the clerk said. "Got a couple of my nephews mixed up."

"I'd agree with you, except that Helen was my best friend, and she drowned at age sixteen on a rafting trip. Thirty-six years ago."

* * * *

One week later.

Rey looked nervous to the point of being sick.

I felt the same way.

Did we have a few minutes to talk?

Of course. Er, the conference room's open, right?

And then I realized Her Honor was just as nervous as we were. Still, it was hard to breathe, having that authority focus on me.

"I'm not sure how to put this, Ms. Wilson. I took two weeks off for knee surgery, and then my husband and I took a three-week vacation, the first one we've had in years. Then

I got back to chambers and heard about your daughter. I'd have done something much sooner if I'd known."

Having her in that room, divested of bench and robe, was so surreal that I was tempted to smile and offer cookies. I fought off the urge as best I could.

"I'd appreciate you letting my daughter come home. And I'm sure she would, too," I said.

"No timeframes," she replied, "but I promise I'm doing everything I can."

I nodded and she focused on Rey.

"You've been feeding the muck channels about Christopher Coughlin. I want to give you some information."

We were sick in different ways by the time she finished, but we were also our professional selves.

"There has to be a way to preserve the old man's reputation," Rey said as he paced the room.

"I'd love it if you could," Her Honor said, "but in six months he probably won't know or care. Besides, the facts are hard to escape."

The med exam had tested positive for the early stages of Alzheimer's, Type 3—aggressive, untreatable, irreversible. The honorable judge was now on limited duty, his clerks were checking everything he did, and he was set to retire by mid-June of the coming year.

But that was only the end of the story. It began when Christo Vafiadis, a brilliant legal mind and charismatic soul, had been championed for the Provincial Supreme Court by Moira Coughlin, Christopher's grandmother. Along the way, he'd become golfing and tennis buddies with Moira's son, Peter, and then godfather to young Christopher, Christo's namesake.

And so young Christopher had received a complaint from a civil guard who'd once worked for him as a "foreman," and taken it to his godfather, knowing the old man was mostly a short circuit. Computer logs showed Coughlin asking for a meeting with him a day before Julie's second arrest order was handed down.

"Bastard," I muttered.

"Excuse me?" Her Honor said.

"I can only think of Coughlin as a bastard," I said as my cheeks caught fire. "It's hard to avoid the term."

"I prefer cavity wad, myself," Her Honor said. "Using his godfather's mental state to engineer a wife? I am deeply sorry for that, Ms. Wilson."

"Why?" I said.

"Because Christopher has been evil from day one. He grew up in a family that uses power ruthlessly—a grandmother who destroyed anyone who got in her way, an arrogant father who did the same, and all of it under the guise of leadership. Take charge and do what needs to be done, regardless of who suffers.

"Christopher ... it's almost like he's wired for that disease. He's a sociopath. When he was in high school—this boarding school in New England—he built a still and sold booze. Thing is, he paid a couple classmates to buy all the parts and do all the work. They got caught, of course, and when they tried to blame Christopher, there was no evidence. He'd paid cash for everything.

"I only found that out because I used to work with Chris's dad, and I heard them talking about it. Christopher actually boasted that the two boys who'd lost their educations were just drudge class, social climbers, and that he'd made enough to pay for school the next year. But do you know what was really appalling? Peter smiled, patted his son on the back."

"I'm not sure what to say," I stammered.

"And then ... that little shit tried to blackmail me," she said. "He marched up to me one day and told me I was his date for a courtship ball."

"You mean, a marriage dance?" Rey asked.

"Exactly. You don't just dance with who brung ya, you marry them as well, but Chris had been turned down by everyone he'd asked. So, after I'd stopped laughing at him, he told me that he'd go public with my working class roots, see to it that no one ever socialized with me or gave me a job. I laughed more and told him to try. What I should have done is report his slimy little ass, but I didn't, and I regret that. So you have my apology. I should have stopped that little shit a long time ago."

"One question," Rey said. "Shouldn't the FIS be hearing all this before we do?"

"No. I'll tell them, but only after we shine a bit more sunlight on the maggot."

Rey and I pulled an all-nighter, polishing the sunshine until it gleamed and damned. We spun the old man as the victim of a predator, and in the morning Rey fed the channels with a savage glee.

Then we went back to waiting.

... it's true that the Federation Master Charter doesn't address free speech or protections against cruel and unusual punishment. But we are trying to rebuild from Panama to the Arctic Circle, and right now we only have time for the essentials, and that means safety and jobs, creating something like a functioning society ... In other words, starvation trumps the refinements.

Now, I've listened to hundreds of messages and read dozens of online posts by people concerned about those missing protections, and I understand the concerns. But the Master Charter has provisions for being amended, just like the old constitutions in all the old countries, and future generations can add provisions as they see fit.

—Excerpt from a broadcast interview given by Gail McAdams, delegate to the Toronto and Mexico City Charter Conventions, omissions mine.

# SIXTEEN

I passed the time by learning to shuffle a deck of cards and play rummy. I've seen old vids of people working magic with a deck, and I'm nowhere near magic, but the game is fun and my daughter was impressed with my new ancient skill.

So I taught her the rules and she smeared me all over the table, but it was fun to sit in that cavernous room and play, chatter about whatever, and watch Coughlin browbeat his lawyers.

The FIS arrested him four days after our latest exposé, but not because of anything we'd done. A routine audit of his corporate computer system had found a government eyeball, a more sophisticated version of the one I'd used, far faster and almost impossible to detect.

Coughlin yelled that he was being framed, but that claim was a bit hard to swallow because the classified software had been uploaded from his personal machine, one he carried at all times. A federation judge revoked his travel credentials and set bail at five hundred million credits. To really drive the point home, he also required Coughlin to pay twenty percent of the bail amount instead of the usual ten in order to secure his freedom. Coughlin didn't have a spare hundred million floating around, so he fumed at his lawyers and we smiled.

I also took Jim for a walk on the beach.

"Nicely done," I said.

"Er, I did something right?"

"Coughlin's computer."

"What about it?" he said.

"Oh, don't play innocent with me. It's not like I'll tell."

"Tell who? Tell what?"

"The eyeball? The one the government found buried in his company system? It was uploaded from his personal computer. You didn't stash it during that meeting and set it to upload?"

He rounded on me with instant fury. "No. I did not." A second later his anger became a smile. "But I'll buy whoever did that a drink."

I believed him, and I still do.

* * * *

Knowing Coughlin was in jail and Her Honor was trying to make something happen gave the rhythm a new energy, almost a euphoria. I started work at four in the morning because it gave me time to visit Julie in the afternoons and teach Kari the joys of cooking with real food instead of processed soy.

I drank less.

The guilt shut its mouth.

We'd get through this, be fine.

That carried me through the end of October and a routine day. I breezed into the kitchen, looked out at the backyard and froze. A flimsy structure stood by the side of the pool, violet cloth and skinny poles rippling and bending in the afternoon breeze—a sunning tent.

Decades earlier, the start of an outbreak had been traced to a couple in a sunning tent, and since then they'd been built with transmitters that alerted the guards whenever they were occupied. I stomped outside, tore open the flap and my mixed motives came off sabbatical, ignited by the sight of a lush young body, sound asleep, washed in violet light.

"Happy Halloween." Kari gave me a sly smile. I settled in beside her and she purred as I rubbed her neck.

"Some costume," I said.

"Make quite the impression on the kiddos, wouldn't it?"

I paused, then took the risk, gently let the romantic energy flow her way, let my hand stray down to her hips, back up her spine. Her skin was marvelous, pure silk, and she purred some more.

I'd flirted with a gender-specific classmate after my first marriage blew away, but the idea drowned with my parents, and then Jim's quietly adamant love had buried the remains. Or so I'd thought. I wasn't sure why the shimmering little attraction was there again—a cold mother, a distant father, loneliness, stress, I was born that way—and I wasn't feeling analytical.

I let more of the energy go, let the stroking turn sensual, down her legs. If things progressed, well, the civils would be hard pressed to find the critical residue.

Then she twined a hand with mine and I felt the tears.

"Sorry if this was ... wrong," she said between sobs. "I put it up because ... it's like there's a piece of me they can't have when I'm here."

"No worries, dear. You own your body, not them, right?"

She nodded. "When I was confined to the house, this thing was a refuge, you know?"

The old Beach Boys song about being in my room skittered through my head, and I reached over and cupped her cheek. "Please be honest with me, dear. Is being here hard for you?"

"No. I ... it's like I don't have to hide around you. Does that make sense?"

"Perfect sense," I said. "I used to hide from my mom."

"This was like revenge, too," she said.

"On who?"

"My jizzhead boyfriend. Whenever I'm in here, I think, 'You wanted this and you'll never have it.' I just sort of toss it into the universe, you know? Sometimes I want to take pictures of myself this way, track him down online and send them, remind him of what he'll never get."

I knew not to talk, just wait and keep the hands gentle and patient. This one was malleable.

She sat up and wiped her eyes. "His parents smuggled him home, after he did his five days."

My mixed motives imploded and caught fire. "Oh, my God! He skated? Where'd he go?"

"Venezuela, probably. He was from there. Chickenshit bastard son of a raving jizz-head bitch."

"You know that emasculated him, right?" I said. "For the rest of his life, he has no balls."

"That's what my dad said. Me, I hope the ulcers kill him slowly."

"Good thought, dear. But if you ever find him, open a link and I'll help you tear off the real ones. Slowly."

We giggled and she slipped into her clothes—modest underthings, a brown peasant skirt and white blouse—hesitated, then opened her arms, still unsure if she deserved the hug. My motives burned to ash and blew over the horizon. They've never returned.

* * * *

Late November.

I almost let the link go. I was so sick of the 'answer this or else' tone that paying fines sounded like a good hobby. Except this flag had no attitude and different colors, green and gold and ... *school-oh-crap-what-now?*

The static data grid showed that Wilson, Julie L. had earned top marks in all her courses. Three weeks before the end of term. That called for a hug, so I showed up for visiting hours and gave her my best. We joined the latte line and saw Kari talking to a woman in a government business cloak. Kari shrugged, as though she was mulling an idea. The woman smiled and I heard her say, "Think about it and link me if you're interested. No pressure." She walked away with a cheery smile, saw Julie and smiled some more.

"What was that about?" I said in my mom voice, the one that makes a response not voluntary.

"She's, uh, fed social services," Kari said.

"Oh." The rest stuck in my throat.

"I can make a ton of money if I do enough images," she said.

In other words, a career in porn. The AIDS epidemic didn't kill that industry and nothing ever will. Instead, the government took it over and formed a well-regulated militia of beautiful bodies, an outlet for anyone too frightened by the virus to reach out to the living. It's also a sweet revenue stream, one we justify by wasting the money on AIDS research.

But porn requires a constant supply of fresh meat, so the government prowls for new talent. In return for your services, you get a cut of every image viewed or sold. Problem is, roughly a third of the militia ends up on death row.

"She said I'd sail right through the auditions—"

"Kari—"

"Oh, don't worry, mom. I said no."

* * * *

Later in November

The words 'holiday meal' and 'jail' just don't fit, like they come from parts of the universe that never quite meshed.

And what do you wear to a meal in jail? I tried on my entire closet before poaching some of Julie's baggy hemps.

That seemed like a nice bit of solidarity, until I realized my cloak would cover everything and it didn't matter.

But I had fun on the drive there, fantasizing about what I'd do if I met Coughlin. Spilling coffee on his crotch seemed the most viable option, one I could get away with, and one I laughed off because this was jail, after all.

Through the search machine, claim check in my pocket, and the guard actually smiled.

"Dinner's in the visiting area tonight," he said. "Got it all fixed up for you."

Did he sneer as he said that last? No matter, eating with families sounded better than a meal with a bunch of depressed women. The kid hugged me and we chatted about this and that as we inched through the food line and a guard motioned us to one of the few pairs of open seats.

Right next to Christopher Coughlin. He sat across from a woman who looked remarkably like him. More fortunate in the chin department, but aside from that, God hated her.

I turned to Julie and smiled. "This is going to be fun. Follow my lead."

I marched to the table, nodded at the guard standing close by, gave the woman my best smile.

"Well, this is a surprise! I'm Bev Wilson." I extended a hand and she shook it. "You must be family, you two look so much alike. Say, did Chris tell you he's the reason my daughter's still in jail? Oh, this is Julie, by the way."

"Hi," Julie said with a wave.

> *And dear God, can you please send me a camera? This is priceless.*

"Did he tell you he tried to buy her? Offered us a half million. Do you think that was fair? We don't have much experience with arranged marriages."

Her face twisted into the kind of look only the rich can achieve. It comes when they're forced to mingle with people beneath them. And maybe see themselves.

I sat and poured cream into my coffee. "So, Chris, any wiser?" I said.

No reply.

"Wonderful, isn't it, Chris? Having people jack your life around?"

He shot to his feet and glared at me with cold fury, a move that started two guards in our direction and caused his guest to shrink by at least a third.

"I don't know how you did this to me," he said as gravy ran down what passed for a chin, "but you are playing far above your level and you will regret it."

I smiled at the guard. "I believe he just threatened me. Probably my daughter, too."

"I believe you're correct."

The guard took Coughlin's left hand in a come-along grip, but that didn't shut him up.

"My investigators are closing in on you," he snarled as they pushed him away. "I'm going to have your ass, young lady."

"Let me know when you want it," Julie said with a smile. "I'll make sure it's ready to shit on you."

That was enough for Coughlin's guest. She beat a hasty retreat and Julie shook her head.

"So ill mannered. Please pass the salt, mom?"

"Certainly, dear."

"Oh, and happy Harvest Fest."

"It's been rather nice so far, hasn't it?"

# SEVENTEEN

"Good morning. Today is December eight—"

I slammed my fist into the top of the computer, and out of pure routine I reached for the headset, a gift from Alex. Therapy at home.

"Okay," I sighed. "Start where I left off."

My world became a cell—three walls painted in ochers and yellows, clear thick acrylic for the fourth. No privacy here, just a bed, sink, and toilet, molded out of something shiny.

A man dressed in a suit and a boy dressed in a coverall sat playing chess.

"That isn't right," I groaned. "Rick likes backgammon. Why can't you remember that?"

The game board changed and a soothing voice filled my ears.

"Sorry, ma'am. Your daughter's boyfriend will undoubtedly grow nervous during the last hours of waiting, but his supporter is trained to keep him calm and help him express his emotions."

"Good luck with that," I said. "He can barely ask for the salt."

"Guards will arrive a few minutes before the appointed time." It must have been the appointed time, because four guards with identically blank faces appeared. "This gives Rick time to get ready for what follows."

The simulated boy stood, took a deep breath, unzipped the coverall.

"The guards will allow the prisoner to—"

The headset flew across the room.

* * * *

December Nine.

Rick felt oddly calm as he watched Alex pull into the driveway. The horrible thing was now, reality, time to go.

*Okay,* he thought. *By the numbers. A quick kiss for mom, a hug for dad, out the door, hold still while he cuffs you to the armrest.* It was fascinating, seeing how they'd modified the car door for the occasion.

"Lot nicer than a prison van," he wheezed.

"Yes," Alex said. "Far more comfortable, and a better class of company."

"Yeah. If we're in an accident, you're not under orders to kill me."

* * * *

"Mama? They say they'll let us wait. Together. Tonight."

*Wonderful. Another chance for Randy to practice his aim.*

That, and I'd never seen her so frightened.

"We can ... do, like ... in Virginia's office."

"Want me to come now, sweetie?"

She rallied, fought back to herself. "No. I'll just study. I'm okay if I can just study."

"Well, that's nice for you," I said, "but what am I supposed to do?"

At least it brought up a giggle.

I have no conscious memory of what I did that day. The logs say I gathered marketing data for the god of clothing, but in my mind, that day began when I paid for a fast trip home, tried to eat a salad and found myself in the shower instead, pounding the floor while the spray stung my back and shoulders. I was glad we'd invested in granite.

* * * *

8:31 p.m.

The door with the rough cross was open and I peered in to find Julie with her head on Virginia's lap. The thought struck again, the same one I'd had when I'd seen them together in the back of that jail van: As a pair they looked like refugees, survivors who know that hands and breath are all they truly have, and those can be lost in an instant.

Virginia's computer chimed, and she put on her visor to keep the intruder from seeing us.

"What is it, Johnston?" She listened and her eyes narrowed. "Really? ... You think that's wise? ... You better be right."

"Right about what?"

I fought back a tide of panic, because my mind had cast this evening in stone. Everything at the prison would be entirely routine, swift and flawless. Rick would receive minimal pain. I'd hold on to Julie and be the strongest of mothers, pull her through, and God himself wouldn't dare change my plan.

Virginia ignored me in favor of Julie. "The good doctor has a proposition."

"No," I said. "Not tonight, whatever it is, and that's final."

Julie reached for the headset and Virginia batted her hand away. "Look at me, girl. You will say no if you aren't comfortable with this, clear?"

"Comfortable with what?" I growled.

"I want to," Julie said, but she bit her lip and started to put on her game face. Her right hand quivered as she pinched the bridge of her nose, her left twisted and tugged at her ring.

Virginia hesitated, then held out the visor. Julie clipped the spidery thing to her ear, and it hit me. They were letting her talk to ... *oh, hell no—*

"Hey, Goof!" She smiled and her breathing slowed.

I beat on the panic with everything I had.

"And I'm sorry, too," Julie said. "...Of course I can forgive you. ... Oh, don't be a snarf. We can't talk face to face, and this is working just fine. I feel quite forgiven. ... You want to talk to everyone? Sure."

She pressed a button on the headset.

Silence.

Everyone staring at each other.

Julie finally rolled her eyes and said, "Earth to Rick. We can't stand the noise, so please shut up some more."

"Oh. Uh, hi. Um ... uh, I wanted you to know it's not horrible here, okay?"

*Tell me that tomorrow*, I thought. *Please say it tomorrow.*

"And ... I wanted you to know I'm okay, that everything will be okay. That sounds lame, but it's the best I can do, and ... it'll be okay, Julie. You'll be alright."

My daughter smiled. "Thanks, Goof. You will be, too."

The smile grew warmer, she bit her lip—one of her happy gestures—and the visor went blank. That wonderful five-minute rule.

I reached for her and she caught my hands, looked at the bruises left over from my shower, rubbed them gently.

"You loved him, didn't you?"

"I still do," I said.

* * * *

9:57 p.m.

Diane Westmoreland sat on a bed. The recovery area was like any of the hospitals she'd seen as a doctor's wife—humming with the quiet energy of people going about their day and waiting to cope with something dreadful.

They'd wheel her son through that door in a few minutes, work on him behind that shimmering electronic curtain, and until then she was determined to pray for him, mentally wrap her arms around him, anything, but she would *not* escape to some corner of her mind. She would stay present for her son.

In her view, she hadn't done much in life—a decent mate but a complete dilettante as an artist, and now she was a failed mother. What else could she be? She was *here*, waiting while they ... she wrenched her mind away from herself and back to Rick by digging fingernails into her palms.

*Odd*, she thought. *My nails feel just like the edge of my favorite palette knife.*

She heard its familiar scrape on canvas, the creak of her easel, Miles Davis in the background, all wrapped in that delicious haze of creativity and paint fumes.

Rick walked by, almost pulsating with that secretive kid energy—something big had happened.

"Hold it, Tiger," she said.

He stopped, toed the floor, blushed.

"Spill it," she said.

"Um ... I did it." His hands shook.

"Did what?"

"Julie."

The palette knife froze. "What about Julie?"

"I ... kissed her." He rallied himself and looked her in the eye. "Did I screw up?"

"Did you ask her permission?"

"Yeah. Well, sort of. I mean, not with words, but ... you know. It was..."

"Body language," Di said.

"Yeah."

"Was someone else there?"

Rick nodded. "Julie's mom."

"Was it okay with her?"

He blushed, that sharp instinctive reaction. "She sort of caught us, but she was happy about it."

"Then yes, sweet boy, you did it right. Except it's scary, isn't it? You let your guard down."

"Yeah."

"And I'm proud of you for doing that."

Rick drew a deep, stuttering breath, shot her one of those pleased puppy smiles, as though he'd discovered infatuation and kissing on levels no one ever had or ever would.

*Ms. Westmoreland?*

Di fought back the giggle and did her duty. "But you've also set yourself up for loss, right? First romances don't last, and they can cut deep."

Rick nodded. "I thought about that. A lot. I'll ... I'll take it. The risk. It's worth it."

*Ma'am? Ms. Westmoreland?*

Di came back to now and saw the caregiver, standing with that detached compassion and holding a tray.

"We should stop the bleeding, ma'am."

He motioned at her hands and Diane saw the crescents of blood oozing around her nails. Yes, stop the bleeding. She was a doctor's wife, after all. Can't be leaking a biohazard, can we?

"Move," she said.

"But ma'am—"

She swiped at the tray and sent it half way across the room.

"Get out of my husband's way."

She somehow managed to help him sit on the bed and not smear too much blood on his shirt. His hands shook. "They'll bring him ... here. He's ... fine. In a while."

Diane knew he couldn't feel her touch, but she stroked his neck and kissed him, vaguely aware of familiar noises a few feet away—soft shoes, the squeak of wheels.

"Really, it's okay," Scott wheezed. "He'll be here ... they just need to..."

A voice drifted out from behind the shimmering curtain. "Okay, on three. One ... two ... three."

Di heard the rustle of cloth and a heavy thud as the caregivers shifted Rick off the gurney.

"But it's done now, lover," she said. "And they were lenient, weren't they? He had a great report so they cut it back, right?"

"Sev ... seventy."

She heard the patter and rush of water against flesh, the soft rhythm of hands applying soap.

"He ... said he'd come back. Keep Julie out of here."

Di tightened her grip on her husband and reached into a pocket. She knew he hated patches—he was easily the worst patient—so she palmed one, stroked his hand and rubbed his wrist. It would take longer, but he hadn't noticed.

"That's all he could talk about. That damned girl."

"They won't let him take Julie's place, lover. Don't worry about that."

"I will never stop taking it to court. I don't care if that little bitch is ninety before she finishes. I'll..." The drug hit home and cleared Scott's eyes. "Holy God, Diane. What they did ... Jesus."

"What do you mean? They cut his punishment by seventy percent, right?"

"No. They *gave him*—"

"Excuse me, but you can see your son now." The caregiver was all smiles.

Di struggled to absorb that horrible fact and the bed rolling toward them. They'd wrapped her son in a blanket.

His hair had grown to the point of mild chaos and it was still wet. She leaned over and kissed. He groaned and stirred, groaned again. The prison doctor inserted a sedative cartridge into a machine with practiced swiftness, entered a code, pressed a button.

"Mom?"

"It's over, sweetheart. Sleep now."

Rick was out cold a second later. The caregivers wheeled in two more beds. Di found the patches again, applied another to her husband, one to herself.

* * * *

10:22 p.m.

Julie listened as Alex spoke.

"He spouted that crap about taking my place, right?" she said. "I will not let that happen."

She handed the com back to Virginia with a growl and curled up on the couch.

"He better not try to take my place. I'll strangle him if he does. I don't care how long it takes. I'll rip his ears off and strangle him."

Without batting an eye, Virginia reached into her bag, produced a carafe, and a glorious aroma filled the room—Spanish style hot chocolate, rich with spices.

Julie loves the stuff, so she drank it by rote—staring into space while she downed half a mug—and a moment later she slumped into me.

"No worries, dear," Virginia said. "It's one of the doctor's old recipes."

"You spiked it?" I whispered.

"You don't need to whisper." She lit up a computer screen and touched an icon. "Hi, Steve. Young Ms. Wilson is ready for a night in the infirmary."

I kissed my inert daughter and wished her sweet dreams. Virginia escorted me out and handed me the carafe.

"Take this. You deserve a few sweet dreams, too."

* * * *

In the quiet of two a.m., Virginia sat on the side of her bed and listened to her husband snore. It was still the cutest snore in the world, but she barely heard it, pressing her mind elsewhere, praying.

God, she said, that young lady is asking why. Why the plague, why was she so stupid, why all this pain? I'll tell her the truth—that you don't answer that question, not really. It comes down to trust.

I know that.

I believe that.

I'll tell her that.

I hate that.

To the core of my soul, I hate it.

I want to give the girl more.

Why can't I give her more?

Why can't you just step in?

She's just a child!

And yes, I know.

We all are.

She wept then, silent tears that shook the bed. Alex stirred and reached for her.

"The Wilson girl?" he said. She managed a nod between the sobs. "And you've had the 'why' conversation with her."

"Some. The rest is coming" she said. "It always does."

Alex hugged her. He knew how she felt about the "why" answers, and he waited, gave her the room to speak.

"I keep telling God I want to give her more, you know, my usual rant." She fell silent for a moment, then clambered over the bed and straddled her mate, pinned his arms and looked him in the eye.

"I'm it, Johnston. I'm the 'more.'"

She recalled a conversation they'd had before she became a chaplain. A terrified kid would ask her for support during that day at the prison, those heinous five minutes. Could she do that, help the kid, and help the system hurt that kid? They'd know she was the one who walked them into that room. They'd hear her voice during the pain. Could she straddle black and white like that?"

"I don't know," she'd replied. "I guess so. If I'm called. I hope."

So now she felt a familiar mix of emotion play over her face—frightened surrender.

"Has she asked you to be there for her?" Alex said.

"No."

"But you'll offer," he said.

"You know me so well," she chuckled. "Thing is, I'm scared she'll say yes. Okay, fine, I'm *terrified* she'll say yes, and I'm going to do it anyway."

He pulled her close. "If you really are the 'more,' then you'll get what you need. You know that."

"I don't doubt that for second. But ... frightening."

She leaned into him, and for the first time in years, he rocked her to sleep.

* * * *

Julie wears handcuffs. I know because Guard One did it, or perhaps Guard Two, and they have no faces but they need none. After all, it's just handcuffing. Who needs a face for that?

It's also *time*. You can't fool me. I'm the mom. I know.

"Walk in cuffs or dance," Guard One says.

Julie smiles, the cuffs dissolve and who needs a face for that? She steps into One's arms and the pair spins out of the holding cell.

And then I'm in the hall. This makes perfect sense because Two cuts in, then One takes over, graceful and courteous, effortless dancers all, sweeping their way to another door.

The wrong door.

It's horrible behind there.

"May I?" I say. After all, Julie waltzes me to the door in the mornings, but/and/so I'm determined to spin her away from here—one-two-three, two-two-three.

Music would just ruin the moment.

"Mom!"

"What?"

"Hello!"

"What?"

"The dog?"

Harley. Right there all along, with his noble face and sad eyes.

"Come on, big fella!"

Julie kicks him, he curls into a perfect ball, they race toward ... God, no, wrong way. Wrong door. I race after them and overshoot, through the door, through the room, into my office and headlong into an Ansel Adams. The safety and glory of Yosemite, even with a storm closing in. This would be a perfect place except for the keening wind, high and piercing, the same terrified shriek that I'd heard when Jim almost ran over Harley one morning and STOP, DAMMIT! OR AT LEAST CHANGE PITCH—

I jolted awake, stopped screaming, looked at the clock, drank the chocolate.

# EIGHTEEN

Rick awoke to the strange weight of his parent's arms. The memory of the previous night—agony knifing through the fear—toyed with the edges of his mind, but something innate made him twist his focus away, grope for any thing, any place that was safer, or at least different.

He stretched a leg and his body screamed. He tried to stifle the groan but his parents jerked awake and before he could say anything, his father had pressed an analgesic to his neck and mom was holding on, saying he was safe, they were here, they could leave, he was free. At least she wasn't crying.

A gift box floated through the painkiller haze, and then he was laying down in the back of the car and mom's hand seemed to appear by magic, slip in with coffee and chunks of sweet roll, slices of apple, the gentle stroke on his neck that meant he was loved ...

He awoke hours later, reached around the seat and touched his mother's arm. She turned in a cloud of coffee breath and worried intensity.

"Do I ... need to say anything?" he asked.

Dad's expression softened. "No, you don't—"

"And your father would be incorrect." Mom used that tone, the one that said the males in the household were a pack of incoherent slobs. "Tell me your dreams."

Rick shrugged and glanced out the window while he gathered his courage. "My realistic dream ... medicine, I guess."

Dad chuckled. "So what's your unrealistic dream?"

"Play pro ball, retire before I get pathetic, join your practice. Thing is, I read somewhere that life only grants you one of your crazy dreams, and..."

He trailed off and mom tangled her fingers in his hair. "Crazy dream?"

Rick blushed. "Her."

"Julie?" mom said.

"Yeah. A first romance that, you know ... lasted."

Scott engaged the auto drive and swiveled around. "I want you to trust me on something, okay?"

"Uh, sure."

"All sorts of crazy dreams will come your way, and more than one will come true."

Rick nodded and accepted the kiss from his mom, then sat back and looked around. "So where are we going? This isn't the way home."

"We're moving on," Scott said.

Rick saw the expression on his father's face, knew what it meant. Dad was issuing a challenge.

They drove to a resort in the Sierras and nested in a small suite. As he tried to fall asleep that night, Rick heard the muffled noises from the other bedroom as his parents gave themselves to each other, stifled cries that rolled him over and twisted. Like most of the youngsters fresh from that recovery area, he buried his head under a pillow and wept for hours.

* * * *

The resort had a good snow base for early December. Scott and Rick rode to the top of the mountain and glided over to the day's first hill. They skied old style—no multiple edges or artificial intelligence to reshape the skis and get you back in balance when you fall apart.

Scott looked at Rick with those doctor's eyes. "What do you do before you start a run?" he said.

"Decide on your fall line, how you're going to do the first turn," Rick said.

"And then what?"

"Cut the turn."

"And then?"

"Shift your weight to the other ski, carve the next turn. Why are you asking—"

"While you're doing all that, what else is going on?"

"Well..." Rick hesitated, unsure of what his father wanted. "You stay flexible so the bumps don't knock you over, keep your feet under you, look ahead, be ready for what comes, enjoy the ride ... pick yourself up when you bite it."

Scott smiled—couldn't have said that better myself—then he motioned down the hill. Move on.

Rick pushed off and he followed, gliding through playful snow flurries and early sun, the icy clean smell of fresh snow. They reached a fork. To the right lay intermediate terrain—a groomed hill. To the left lay an expert's run—deep powder over moguls, the kind of run that demands skill, stamina, nerve, but mostly desire.

Rick veered toward the intermediate run, and Scott chided himself for a fool. Did he really expect his son to bounce back in a couple days? Besides, it was their first run. Let the muscles warm up and all that, a gospel he'd preached since day one.

Rick paused at the top of the run, then slipped into a tuck—chest almost on his knees, arms forward, shins jammed into the fronts of his boots—and disappeared. Scott did his best to keep up, carving long fast turns while Rick flew around slower skiers, turning only when the hill forced him, and by the end of the run Scott reckoned he was going fifty, maybe sixty miles an hour.

Rick sent a huge plume of snow flying as he stopped. Scott caught up, panting, and they glided to the lift.

"That was great," Rick said. "Let's go left next time."

Scott enjoyed the wave of relief—his son hadn't lost that fire—but he wanted to make sure of one thing. "You don't have to prove anything," he said.

Rick's eyes carried no smile. "Maybe not to you."

# NINETEEN

I heard a thump from upstairs and found Kari packing a bag.

"Going somewhere?" I asked.

"My aunt," she sighed. "Up in Tiburon. Dad and me. On a trip."

"That kind of aunt, huh?"

"She was nice when she found out, but now I can just feel the lectures, you know? All wound up and ready to go."

"I'm sure it won't be that way."

She gave me a look and a kiss. "You're so sweet."

I followed her out to the street, and one of those German cars swept up, the kind of car I'd expect a pilot to drive. I got a half smile from Kari's dad and they swept off.

*Oh, how fun. Christmas in an empty house. At least I'll have work.*

* * * *

Rey beamed at his seventeen employees.

"And to make sure you take a real break," he threw me a sidelong glance, "I'm firewalling the company's net at five today, and it won't be available until January. Go home, relax, enjoy your families."

*Yes, sir. I'll do that. In lockup. Merry bleeping Christmas to you, too.*

I told myself it could be worse, it had been worse. I'd spent the holiday alone for three years after my parents died. Not that I'd had to. Plenty of people had offered hospitality; I'd just used the day to hunker down with some good wine.

*So maybe the quiet will do you good, Beverly Anne. Learn to meditate. Go for walks after you visit the kid.*

The idea germinated and took root. A walk in the morning, face time with Julie, dance the flail, have some wine, read something fluffy, sleep with no cares. I was madly in love with my plan by the time I got home, and a spinach salad was the perfect start. Until the computer interrupted—visitors at the door, virus free and so on.

Will Selcraig and my sister-in-law stood with their arms draped over a huddled figure. The figure wore ... Jen's clothes?

I screamed.

Then I wrapped my arms around Julie and carried her inside. She peered around, frightened and bewildered.

"Did you hear it?" she said.

"Hear what?"

"My locator."

"Loc ... what?"

"This." She pulled back her hair to show the bump, the one that had been raw and red on the day Alex had taken us to lunch. It was healed now, barely discernible with her hair grown back.

"It beeped," she said. "When I came through the door. I'm a prisoner here."

* * * *

A mere tracking device (the same kind they use on animals) couldn't dent my joy. I raised my glass and said, "To Will, for working a miracle."

He shook his head. "Thanks, but it was Her Honor. She threatened the supremes with eternal damnation if they didn't fix things."

"Oh, don't be modest," Jen said. "You drew up the appeal."

"But she had the juice to drive an emergency ruling. I couldn't have done that," he said.

Something passed between them then, an affectionate glance that didn't register because I was too focused on the kid. She spent the rest of the evening wandering the house in a daze, touching things as though she'd never seen them before.

The next morning I found her by the back door, her hand on the latch and that bewildered fear spewing its choking fog. I put my hand on hers, pushed the latch and nudged her outside.

"You don't ... mind?" she said.

"No, sweetie. I don't."

"Can I ... play with the dog?"

Harley was about to crawl out of his fur, he was so happy, and I barked, "Oh, for God's sakes, Julie—" then I realized I couldn't take that tone, speak truth in that way. She couldn't hear it.

"Of course you can," I said. "I think he'd love it."

* * * *

Three days before Christmas, the computer chirped and Jen faded in.

"Heyya, sister dear. Any plans for Christmas Eve?"

"Not really," I said. "But what about Christmas day?"

"Oh, I'm having dinner with a friend and his kids."

I burst into laughter. I couldn't help it. "You're trying so hard to be nonchalant," I finally managed to say, "and it isn't working. How long have you been dating this guy?

"Well, he ... we ... for a while," she huffed.

"What's his name?"

"Since you're being such a dwinger about it, I'm not going to tell you."

"Aw, come on."

"Nope."

"Please?"

"Focus," she barked. "Christmas Eve plans, or I withhold all baked goods." Since losing her husband, Jen had become a master at pastries. "And besides, I want to check up on my niece."

The laughter became tears that I choked back, and still I don't know why. We'd leaked on each other often enough.

"Sweet of you," I wheezed.

We made plans to cook, drink wine, eat too much and stay up late. As we ended the link, I heard a soccer ball thud against the house. Julie flew around the pool with Harley in tow, but I saw no joy. The laps had that manic edge, the trapped-animal feel I'd seen during that run on the beach with Virginia. All those centuries ago.

She ran until she couldn't, sagged to the concrete, stared into nothing while the dog licked her face.

* * * *

The holiday spirit caught me by surprise. I'd reveled in it when I was young, mostly because it was the only time the Consevs achieved a vague semblance of love, but that glow had slipped away with time. Christmas was just a chance to shop and a nice day off.

So we were busy cooking when something like my daughter breezed into the kitchen.

"Mom says you're abandoning us tomorrow," she said.

Jen misread the voice, put her hands on Julie's shoulders. "No sweetie. I'll cancel those plans..." She finally saw the mischief in her niece's eyes.

Julie snorted. "A friend and *his* kids? That only means one thing."

"What's that?"

"They're still in diapers. He only wants you for your diaper changing skills."

"One of them is your age, and the other is almost done with college."

"And they're still in diapers?"

Jen narrowed her eyes and the cheer stole in, unexpected and sweet as we got tipsy, laughed at old holopix and stuffed ourselves. It got even better the next afternoon, watching Jen achieve the perfect lather.

"Okay, you heat this one for twenty minutes, but only ten on the stuffing or you'll dry it out. Oh, and the ... all you have to do is toss the salad, the dressing's in the fridge door ... no, it's on the second shelf in the yellow bowl ... oh, figure it out! I'm late!"

I put my hands on her shoulders and kissed a cheek. "Jennifer dear, have a wonderful time. If you think about us even once, you will go to hell."

"And if you dry out my stuffing, you'll be waiting for me."

She blew out the door, driven by nerves and a gale of laughter. The exotic car pulled away, we finished wiping our eyes, and Julie took my hand.

"She's doomed, isn't she?"

I nodded. "Nerves like that, she'll be married in six months. A year, tops—" I realized where the conversation had gone and gave her hand a squeeze. "You okay with this?"

She smiled. "Yeah. It makes life seem ... normal, you know?"

She pulled me into the family room and sat me on the couch, hustled into the kitchen and returned with a glass of wine.

"It's only two o'clock, sweetheart," I said.

"So? Sun's over the yardarm somewhere in the galaxy."

I sipped. It was a marvelous white, a viognier, just dry enough and nicely effervescent. Julie curled up next to me and leaned in.

"I'm glad this'll be a quiet day, mom. It's just so loud in there, people shouting all the time. I asked Virginia why, and she said nobody wants to think, you know? And I can see why."

I cringed a little. "I'm glad you're up for quiet, because I hadn't planned to do more than ... visit. You. In there. Today."

She leaned into me and curled into a ball. "That's okay," she croaked. "Quiet's good."

The computer spoke up five seconds later, and Julie whimpered, "Nooo." Through the windows I saw braids and nervous posture, Ke'andra standing with a hot dish in her hands and her eyes brimming.

"Can I apologize?" she said. "Please? I mean, I know you probably don't want me around and I don't blame you, but I at least want to say I'm sorry."

"Mom? Pull her through the door. If I reach outside, they'll..."

I pulled. The girls stared at the floor and bit lips, then Kee sort of threw the dish at me and wrapped Julie in a hug.

"I should have come to see you," she said. "I just ... I didn't want you to see me cry."

"Kee—"

"I figured you were already hurt enough, and I didn't know what to do. I'm sorry, okay? I'm sorry."

"Keeeaaannndraaa—"

"I should have been stronger, and I'm pissed at my slob ass for being so mad at first—"

"KE'ANDRA!"

She stopped, sniffed, looked at Julie with nervous eyes. Julie buried her face in Kee's shoulder.

I stood with the dish (a gumbo that promised heat), enjoyed the happy silence and wondered what to do next. I was about to head for the kitchen when footsteps clumped on the porch. The door opened, Kari dropped her bag and glowered into her visor.

"Where do you think I am? And you can tell her that if she wants to talk to me like that, she can let them do it to her first, then she can ask her jizz-head questions."

She yanked off her visor off and snapped it closed.

"Have I learned my fucking lesson," she muttered. Then she noticed us with a start. "Oh. Uh ... hi. Sorry."

Julie half dragged Ke'andra across the floor and latched on to Kari. A bewildered Kee  reached around them and started to make it a group hug, stopped, then joined in when Julie grabbed an arm.

"Kee, this is Kari. Our new seester."

Ke'andra and Jules had declared themselves 'seesters' at age six, and like blood relatives they'd bickered and loved their way through homework and dances, soccer and getting their periods, boys and would they always be this cup size?

"Uh, that's nice," Kee said. "How'd you meet?"

"Lockup," Julie said.

I couldn't see Ke'andra's face, but Kari giggled.

"Oh, come on, Kee. Don't get all perspirational," Julie said. "We only become ax murderers on Christmas after dinner. So when do we eat, mom? I'm starving and feeling weird urges."

I glowered at them. "We eat after you set the table, make sure your aunt's stuffing is thoroughly dry, spill the salad dressing all over the counter, and do it all with a high degree of elegance and taste."

Ke'andra snorted. "Guess we starve, Jules."

A moment later she'd snatched the gumbo out of my hands and scuttled to the kitchen with Julie in tow. Kari started after them and I stopped her, looked, saw the flares in those blue eyes.

"I'm sorry, dear," I said.

She shrugged, bit her lip, then started for the kitchen.

"Don't you want to hang up your cloak?" I said. It was a pretty thing, off-white linen with lace around the collar. "It'd be a shame to get food all over it."

She toed the floor. "I'm not ... dressed very well."

"And we are?" I was in my gardening clothes, Julie was dressed for Harley Ball, Ke'andra sported lime green shoes and a bright orange shirt to go with her old hemps.

"But..."

"Sweetheart, you're a sister. That's more than enough for Ke'andra," I said.

She shrugged out of the cloak and I saw why she was nervous. A sleeveless blouse and shorts above the knee could be misread. By a number of people. Mostly male. They'd drink her in before labeling her a slut and turning her into mind candy.

"Did you travel like that?" I said. Even with a cloak, you dress modestly when you travel or risk a chat with the guards. With her record, the chat could have turned into another stint behind heavy doors.

"Don't worry," she snorted. "I got a private seat. I don't have any money left, but it was worth it."

And then I saw. I put my hands on her shoulders, found her eyes, smiled into them.

"Good for you, girl." I fingered the blouse.

"Um, sure," she said. "What are you..."

"They don't own you," I said. "Under that cloak, your thumb is up and you're wagging it at them as hard as you can, right?"

She blushed—that gesture is something only a drudge would use during an angry drunk—then her eyes shrieked, another flicker of rage that faded into cold ash.

"Hello!" Julie called from the kitchen. "Those who slack off wash many dishes!"

The girl snapped to and shot me a weak half grin. Her eyes darted—left, right, left—and she waggled her thumb.

* * * *

We decided to dress for dinner. I loaned Ke'andra some of my clothes, and she served her gumbo as a first course.

Julie thumped Kari's back and handed her more water.

"Sorry," Kari wheezed. "Never had anything this spicy for Christmas before."

"I figured that a gumbo hot enough to fuse rocks would add a unique dimension to the holiday menu," Kee said. "And I wanted to apologize for being a moronic poultry poop."

"A what?" Kari wheezed.

"A stupid chickenshit," Kee replied. "It's also a test of character. If your eyes don't melt, it means you've been good and Santa will bring you something really nice. So we all know Julius here passed the test."

"I did?"

"Of course. Santa brought me."

Julie's head hit the table.

"So what did Santa bring you, seester Kari?"

"School. A place in New Hampshire that specializes in ... people like me." Kari blushed, hot with the shame that I assumed came from not being on the curve, not fitting in. "I start early next month."

"School?" Ke'andra scrunched her face. "You must've been waaay bad."

Everything stopped.

Julie rested her chin on her hands and shot Kee a nasty look. "Well done, seester."

Ke'andra started at puzzled. Reached stiff. Tumbled headlong into horrified.

"Oh. Oh, my God." She reached across the table for Kari's hands. "I'm so sorry. Oh, my God, that was so *stupid* of me."

Kari's mouth twisted and she glared at a far wall.

"I'm sure it'll be great." Ke'andra was nearly in tears. "Um, what kind of school is it?"

Veteran fighters know how to use their weaknesses, and Kari was an obvious veteran.

"It's a school for dyslexics," she said with forced brightness.

Ke'andra shrank. "I didn't mean to..."

I let the silence thicken and the eyes concentrate on elsewhere for a moment, then I snorted out a laugh.

"Well done, Kari. You're the first person I've ever seen reduce Kee to silence."

Kari burst out laughing. "It was fun watching you squirm."

And so we giggled through dinner. I served the girls wine. Kari and I rolled our eyes when the talk veered to soccer and who should play what this year (Walters had gained a *ton* of weight and Bennett was married and pregnant). The stuffing wouldn't send us to hell.

I got up to start the coffee and whip the cream. For once I did it perfectly, and as I dished up the first slice of pie Julie's voice drifted into the kitchen.

"So, Kee, what did Santa bring you?"

"More voice lessons." As though voice lessons were as common as breakfast.

Everything stopped again.

"*More* voice lessons?" Julie sounded incredulous. "Since when do we willingly study anything?"

"Well, since last August. I was going to tell you, but—"

"Oooh. Sing for me."

I had a hunch about Ke'andra's voice, so I hustled in with the dessert. She stood, shivered, and began to cry.

"It's January eighteenth, right?" she said.

Julie nodded.

"Okay, then. Here's one for ... then."

She took herself in hand, closed her eyes, and filled the room with a gentle flood of sound.

*"Sister..."*

She drew the first notes out, let them dance.

*"Keep your lamp trimmin' and a burnin'*
*"Keep your lamp trimmin' and burnin'*
*"I said keep that lamp a-trimmin' and a-*
*burnin'*
*"This world most done*
*"This world most done."*

She colored each pass differently, shaded them as she built to a crescendo that rattled my chest.

We gawped at her, and I finally said, "It was you."

"Me what?"

I told her about standing in the hall outside the choir room. "You're the one they don't have to worry about drowning, right?"

She blushed. "Well ... Rayner has to close the doors because all the other teachers get mad. And really, I'll sound better at the spring concert. I'm working on controlling this thing." She pointed at her throat. "Rayner calls it the wooly mammoth. Can you pass the cream, please?"

Kari passed the small pitcher, and as she did a silver bracelet peeked out from under her sleeve. Kee gave it a gentle touch.

"Whoa! You definitely pass my gumbo test."

It was a pretty piece—braided Celtic knot work done in white gold, with an oval setting of rose quartz. Vague alarms began to ring when I saw it. Something wanted to tumble, click in, but I couldn't make the connection.

Julie reached over and touched it. "Oh. Is that it? They are pretty."

"Care to fill me in?" Kee said.

Kari drew a ragged breath. "Well, when you're ... done, when you wake up in the morning, they give you one. It's a reminder to keep your head on straight. A jeweler makes them because ... sorry."

Something raw scorched those eyes, and I reached for her hands. "It's okay. You don't need to say anything more."

"And nothing will leave this house," Kee said. I believed her.

Kari smiled at us and took another breath. "No, it'll help to get this out. The jeweler makes them in memory of a brother. Who ... died."

"They'll give me one, mom. Er, sorry, I thought you knew."

"No worries, dear," I said. "I've just seen one somewhere before, and I'm trying to remember where."

That, and it was time to steer the conversation into the light.

"Kari, dear, when do you start school?"

"The second. We need to find an apartment and get me all oriented. I can't believe how much—"

"Oh, my God." Julie was pale. "Oh, no. No. NO!"

"What?" I said. "What's wrong?"

"The bracelet. Your bracelet."

"What about it?" Kari said.

"Virginia wears one."

# TWENTY

"You ... *you*?" I said.

Virginia took my hand as the waves lapped at our feet and the wind ruined my hair.

"Yes, me. Thirty-two years ago." She traced the design of her bracelet with an index finger. "Third one that jeweler ever made. So does this erode your trust in me?"

"I'm not sure I've ever trusted you," I said.

That didn't rattle her at all. "May I ask why?"

"I grew up in a Consev church."

"But I've never—"

"Don't get me wrong," I said. "I appreciate what you're doing for Julie, but they raise shame to high art. Why would I want them near my daughter?"

"I've never been a Consev, dear."

"I didn't even know what shame was until I went to see this grief counselor after my parents died. She saw a lot of it in me, and I had to look up the word, what it meant. I was that clueless."

"And you've spent years trying to fix yourself."

She spoke as much to herself as me, and I had no reply. It's hard to admit you don't feel fixable, that the flaws are too deep, too fundamental.

"Can I ask how your folks died?" she said.

"They went for a romantic cruise on an old square rigger. Built in the early twentieth century and supposedly restored. Damn thing sank without warning."

"And why would God let that happen?" she said.

I snorted. "That question barely registers with me. I'd rather know why God's followers can be such a pile of cavities. And I'm also old enough to answer that question. And recognize my lousy metaphor."

She chuckled. "If it helps, I don't have all the answers. Don't think we need them all, either. Just enough of them."

"You mean, you don't rail at God about what happened to you? You didn't ask why? You still don't?"

"Of course I did. But eventually I realized I'd know why." She looked at me for a long moment. "And that doesn't help much, does it?"

"Not a bit."

"Wouldn't have helped me, either," she said.

"So how'd you land in your mess?"

"When I was a junior in college, a friend invited me to spend a long weekend houseboating on Lake Shasta. And she brought along a brother, this handsome, dark guy. He was funny and smart and a little dangerous—raced motorcycles, the kind that go two hundred miles an hour. And he was beautiful, Bev. Just gorgeous. The perfect target.

"I played it shy-but-interested, made sure he accidentally saw me getting into my bathing suit. The rest was easy. I invited him for the day's last swim and dropped my suit on the deck. The look on his face as I dove in ... so intoxicating. I was young, I was hot, daddy was rich, I was untouchable."

"Daddy was rich?"

"I was a McFadden, Bev."

One of the old families. So rich and connected nothing can really dent them.

"We were all asleep when a guard boat came alongside. One of the park rangers had been on shore doing a wildlife study, trying to document some rare nocturnal field mouse, if you can believe it. She heard our voices and looked over as I was dropping my drawers, filmed it and turned it over.

"I almost laughed at them. I figured our lawyer would show up, take me home, and daddy would glare at me for an hour."

"No?" I said.

"They said they loved me, and it was time for me to grow up."

"So, you spend however long trying to scream, and then you find God," I said.

Virginia shook her head. "How, why, would a loving God let me go through *that*? No, I walked out of that prison, and ... we'd always gone to church, right? But only because it was a thing you did. So when I left the prison, the idea of God just went poof."

"But then it came back," I said.

She chuckled. "But then I married Chauncey Alexander Phillips Johnston the Fourth and had two amazing boys. Tim and Mike."

"You changed diapers and found God? I certainly didn't."

"Well, I did, in a way." She took a deep breath. "When Tim was seven he came down with a raging headache and a fever—just awful. They didn't know what was wrong, so they had him in an isolation bubble. We sat there holding his hands through those gloves.

"Alex looked at me and said, 'If Timmy dies, what will I tell Mike?' My giant of a man was just lost, Bev, almost helpless. So I prayed. Alex had gone to sleep. I leaned against the bubble and something broke, just slid away, and I begged God to spare my son. I told him I wasn't asking for me, but for Alex."

"And?" I said.

"What else? Timmy recovered, the doctors had no clue as to why, we took him home the next day."

"And that did the trick."

"Are you crazy? God would put me through all that, and then turn around and heal my son? I wasn't having any of it. But..." She looked at me out of the corner of her eye and a sly smile creased her face.

I took the bait. "But?"

"I started screaming. At God. Every dirty name in the book. And when I was done, I found myself listening. And that was it. God whispered when I was ready to listen. That took a decade, by the way."

We walked in silence for a while, the gulls crying on the breeze and my old bitterness surfacing.

"And now here you are, back in the middle of your nightmare," I said. "And I *do not* want you there, which means I don't want you here."

"Oh, please." She rounded on me. "My nightmare ended thirty-two years ago. This is about Julie surviving hers. And because I want that to happen, I'm not going away. I've signed on as her primary support."

I looked at her and sighed. "What I'm about to learn next will probably yark, right?"

"Probably. I'll be in charge of her during her day at the prison, from the time she arrives until she walks into that room."

"No," I said. "Sweetie ... just, no."

"Oh, yes. Bev."

"Why?"

"Because I'm a fine alternative to the screws who'd otherwise do the job."

"Have you told Julie about this?" I said.

"Not yet. I don't want her fighting me on it. She'll be worse than you."

* * * *

I told myself I wasn't lying to Julie by hiding what Virginia had done, just sheltering her from more stress and pain.

My conscience quit sneering after a few days.

Or maybe it just died of exhaustion.

I reveled in a peaceful morning, then heard the excited chatter from the girls' room. I peeked in, saw them packing Kari's bags, and being a dialed in and veteran mom, I said, "What the hell do you think you're doing?"

"School?" Kari shot back, hackles up instantly. "I need to leave early and all that?"

"Oh," I wheezed as my butt hit the end of the bed. "I thought you'd be here for ... longer." I leaked for a bit, and then said, "Okay, I'll come clean. I'm a bit upset."

Julie snorted. "We never would have guessed that, mom."

Kari just glowered at me.

"I was going to offer you a job," I said. "As my assistant."

I'd found room in the budget for another one, mostly by giving myself a pay cut. And don't accuse me of nobility.

"You'd have made gallons of coffee and crunched more gallons of numbers," I said, "but it's a step up from making coffee on a part-time basis."

I got a smile and kiss. "You really are sweet."

I told myself to stop leaking, put on a smile, help pack. School was light years better than a career in the porn industry. Or working for me.

The ride was quiet, her house another elaborate pile, just closer to the ocean.

"Sorry I couldn't mom you some more," I sniffled.

In other words, my mixed motives and I had been a bitch, but I couldn't find a way to apologize for something she may not have seen.

"I'm not sure I have ... wings, or whatever," she snuffled back. "But I'll try, okay?"

"Do you think I could talk with your dad? We didn't exactly start well."

"Yeah, I know. He isn't home, but he feels the same way, and that time will come."

"Okay, then. If you ever get disgusted with the winters back there, we have this dog, and this pool, and this bratty younger sister who'd love to have you around."

She giggled. "I'll link when I can read better than a nine-year-old."

A long hug, and I told myself not to feel guilty about more tears as she took her bags out of the back and lugged them up to a gate, pressed her hand on a reader. I watched her trudge up the driveway. She wasn't even my child and I still didn't want to let go, in part because she'd blown through my life all too quickly, and I knew I'd never see her again.

* * * *

Annie Waldenburg appeared the next day with a fresh batch of chocolate chip cookies. I showed her to the kitchen and poured coffee.

"Large news, Bev. I'm moving."

I caught my breath. My neighbor of two decades? She couldn't. I'd just lost a daughter. I needed her. Who else was going to take care of me?

"Why?" I said, fighting down a spike of panic. "And where?"

"The house is too much for me, and the memories are heavy, you know? Sometimes I still see Al, laying there on that couch with my grandson tugging at his arm. 'Grandpa, grandpa, wake up...'" She faded into the memory, shook herself free. "Seems real as day, sometimes. I've bought a smaller place up north, where I can smell the pine trees and I don't have to worry about so many damn weeds."

"But..." I stumbled to halt.

"I know this is abrupt, but hell, you can always come visit. It's a pretty place."

"When are you leaving?" I said.

"Tomorrow. The buyers want to move quick, but you'll like them. They're young military, just like you were, and they seem real nice. You get to be me now, the resident grand dame." She didn't bother pronouncing my new title in French.

Julie shuffled in. Annie looked at her, a quick flash of expression, and Julie tried to turn away as Annie stood and caught her arm.

"Don't you run away, girl. I saw the guards leaving with you and your young man. I take it the outcome wasn't good?"

"We were stupid," Julie said with a shrug.

"So you're facing a trip to prison?"

"Yeah. Sorry."

Annie dispensed one of those grandmotherly hugs. "Now you listen, girl. You don't need forgiveness from me, but you can have some anyway. And you knew full well that you couldn't go putting us all at risk, right?" Julie nodded, her face dark. "I'm not happy you got caught, but dammit, girl, I'm glad the safeguards are there, and you know why."

Julie flared and tried to pull away but Annie grabbed her other arm.

"Now you just hush a second. You're a strong girl, a smart girl. You'll learn your lesson won't you? Of course you will. You'll see this through and you'll be smarter for it. You'll have a good life, you won't make that mistake again, and that's a good thing. Maybe the best thing." Annie's eyes glittered, steely and righteous. "Maybe the only thing. Now you come visit when you're done," she said. "I have to keep packing up. Honestly, the junk you've got after forty years."

Her next hug ignored the stiff body language and she slipped out.

# TWENTY-ONE

January.

"Scared?" I asked.

Julie tried to chuckle. "I don't know why. It's just school, right? I'm five weeks ahead of everyone else, right?"

She'd insisted on studying through the winter break. It was her refuge, like Kari's sunning tent. So on that morning I had words, wise and parental: She'd been through more in the past four months than most of her classmates would ever experience. The world was bound to look different. She'd probably feel out of place.

I stood those words up and polished them. And then I said, "Ke'andra will be there."

"Rick, too. Um, it's okay if I talk to him?"

"That's up to you."

The car pulled in and Ke'andra was there, nervous and happy, clad bright purple, hand in hand with Charlie.

"Mama, I'm not sure if I can talk to Rick—"

Kee ripped open the door and dove into Julie's lap. "WILSON! I'm sick of eating lunch without you and Rayner needs you in choir. I have this stupid essay to write for music history and..." The tears exploded. She pulled Julie close, held on for a long silence, and then, "Everything's going to be okay." Another long silence, and she held up an index finger. "One for all."

Julie touched her finger to Ke'andra's. "And all for one."

"Blood sisters."

"And boy do we stink."

I rolled my eyes. Soccer. Again. It had to be.

"You'll be late," I said.

"Exactly," Ke'eandra barked. "No more tardy marks on your permanent record, you idiot jock. Move that slob ass of yours instantly!"

She pulled Julie out of the car and slammed the door. I felt so parental and wise as I seized the moment and drove away.

* * * *

A week later, Rick stood outside the choir room in the noise and rush between classes. Julie came out with Ke'andra and gave him a tentative smile. He approached, offered a hand.

"KNOCK IT OFF!"

He turned and groaned. Schwitter was at it again. The stupid oaf had someone backed into a corner, a younger boy livid with anger and fear. The runt was doing what you're supposed to, yelling and standing his ground, but for Schwitter that kind of response was like blood for a shark—snackie time—and he poked at the smaller kid, goading him to do it, sucker, swing that fist.

Even worse, Julie was half way to the lumbering slob, and she had that gleam in her eyes. He started after her, his heart clenching.

"Hey, cavity wad," she barked as she planted her feet.

Rick's heart stopped as Schwitter whirled, amazed that a girl would be so stupid—

The kick had a certain beauty—a dancer's grace, the ferocity of a diving hawk. A beat-up cross trainer disappeared into the flabby expanse of the idiot's groin. He hit the ground and vomited.

* * * *

The unrepentant girl blew rage at the universe and all the contents thereof.

"Should've ripped his ear off. Stupid thumb wagger's had it coming for years. Hope he enjoys his tour of the factory floor, and I *do not* care what Connery does. He can suspend me and put it in my report."

*And I hope you enjoy your full-strength tour of the punishment system.*

The words were poised, like runners in their starting blocks, but she stormed out of the room with a curt, "I'm gonna go study."

Jen looked at me and said, "Maybe I should live here for a while. Not leave her alone during the day."

"I don't know," I growled. "Maybe it'd serve her right. Jesus H., Jen. She knows they'll ruin her. Alex has told her, I've told her, Will has told her. It's like she's..."

"Determined to let them?" Jen said. "Because she deserves it?"

"Yeah," I croaked. "And you know what? I'm done. I give up. She wants to compost her life, fine."

The next morning didn't help. For some reason I found myself joining in the exercise video, a ritual started by Julie and shunned by me. The kid was almost buoyant as we stretched and bent and tortured ourselves.

"Nine days, and I am free, free, free," she said, "and it's my senior year of soccer. We are *so* gonna own the league."

I cringed. Nine days, and she was already as psyched up as she'd be for a big game.

"I'm so gonna laugh at them," she muttered. "The whole time. Wads won't beat me."

All I could do was shake my head and glare at the holographic workout queen.

"Come ON!" it said. "LUNGE and DOWN and UP REAL SLOW, COUNT and FIVE and FEEL THAT BURN!"

The com gave a quiet *dweedle*, Will's tone. He was probably linking Jen, so Julie said, "I'll get it," and made a beeline for the kitchen before Jen could react.

"Little poop," Jen growled. "Don't you stop, Beverly. You need this."

"COME ON! TOUCH THE FLOOR AND HOLD..."

I obeyed, glad no one could see.

"... EIGHT AND NINE AND—"

Julie shrieked, a knot of curses and fear. I covered the distance to the kitchen in giant strides and shoved myself between her and the hovering image of our lawyer.

"Tell me," I barked.

"They've stayed the execution, Bev."

* * * *

"Okay," I said. "She found an issue she could raise and the courts thought it was worth their time. I'm obviously happy for her. Where the hell did that bitch *find* an issue?"

Condemned inmates have three appeals, sped along by a phalanx of computers that look for procedural errors and holes in the evidence. Once that third appeal is done, so is the inmate. Out here, they call it death by software.

If the courts wanted to consider another issue, then someone had screwed up. Some idiot clerk had entered data incorrectly and my daughter was the victim, her life on hold until a half-wit drudge corrected the mistake. The rage bubbled, choked my sane voices. Jim was going to teach me how to make bombs. So help me God, he'd show me how—

"The condemned woman had a baby," Will said. "She wanted more time to nurture the child."

I tried to rub my temples, push the rage to a safe distance.

"I thought the bitch had to give it away," I said.

Will looked at me.

"Well?" I said.

"She has a name, you know. A history, a life, an education, a family that loves her."

"And I don't give a shiny new wad. How'd she use her baby as leverage?"

"She gave it to her parents and nobody caught on to what was happening. They brought the child to visit."

"And nobody thought to stop her?"

"This doesn't happen very often. Nobody noticed."

Julie reached for my hand. "So now how long before I go up there?"

"I don't know. I'm working on that. But don't worry. It's not like you'll spend the next year under house arrest."

* * * *

A week later, my computer spat out that generic beep, but I opened the link because I wanted this conversation, welcomed it with a sense of relief and something more.

"Hi. Again," he said. "I'd like to apologize for our first conversation."

"Me, too," I said. *And you can ask me out any time.*

"I've been pretty emotional since Kari's arrest, but that's no excuse," he said.

"Well, I've been the same way since my daughter's arrest, and we're only human." *But if you need to atone for your sins, ask me out.*

"Thank you," he said. "I'm Leif, by the way."

"And I'm Bev." *Come on, do it. Even if it's just coffee.*

"I was wondering," he said.

*And I'm not. I'm sure I'll love your favorite place.*

"How's Kari? I haven't heard from her in a while, and—"

"What do you mean?" I said. "She's at school, right?"

"What school?" he asked.

"In New Hampshire. Learning to read. The school you found."

"I never found a school."

"But ... I dropped her off. At your house."

"When?"

"Last Tuesday."

"I was home, and she was never there. Where'd you drop her off?"

"She scanned her palm ... oh, God, you don't have a gate, do you?"

"No. We don't. Where was this place?"

"On Gillard," I said.

He closed his eyes and groaned. "Social services."

Federation Social Services runs a number of elegant houses that double as sets for video and image shoots. The sleek militia lives there, earns doctorates in poise and makeup, physical fitness and the art of fake seduction. The locations are supposed to be a secret, but any local knows what they are. A dozen beautiful people in the same house? Dead giveaway.

"I'm sorry," I said. "I really thought I was taking her home."

He closed his eyes and broke the link without replying.

I kept the news to myself yet again. Julie didn't need it.

* * * *

The next day, my ex opened a link from Tyler McGowan.

"Sir," Jim said.

"My office as soon as possible."

"Do I need my lawyer?"

"Yes."

Jim was surprised at how calm he felt. His assistant would take over his job, the savings would go to Julie. A couple students would move the rest into storage.

They met that afternoon. Ty stood and didn't smile.

"I have orders for you, Major Wilson. You will transport yourself to the Glendale Hills correctional facility on the day of your daughter's punishment. The uniform of the day will be dress blues. While at the prison you will, without fail, support your daughter in any way possible, within the rules and norms of the prison at all times. After your daughter is released, you will put in your retirement papers. You can retire honorably, but you are relieved of all duties other than your daughter's day at the prison. Your career is over. Any questions?"

Jim thought for a moment. "Is that all, sir?"

Ty looked weary. And sad. "Yes. It is."

Jim shot to attention, but instead of focusing just over Ty's head he met his eyes and fought back tears.

"Thank you, colonel."

* * * *

And, just to make the month complete.

"How come they haven't ruled?" Julie asked.

"Because the computers can't handle this one," Will said. "A panel of judges has to consider it."

"How long does that take?" I asked.

"Nine months, usually, but—"

"What do you mean, NINE MONTHS?" I stepped between Julie and the computer again as Will held up his hands.

"Ease down, Bev. I've petitioned for what we call emergency relief."

My mind conjured an ambulance, roaring up our driveway and disgorging a dozen judges, gray-haired and wise (when they're sober), robes flapping and arms full of books as they race into the house. I couldn't help the laughter.

"Uh, sorry. Did I say something funny?" Will asked.

"No," I finally said. "The system does it for you, like that movie routine where the guy steps in shit, tries to clean it off and ends up smeared from head to toe before he gives up."

The block of crystals and acrylic smacked against the window over the sink, bounced off the counter and hit the floor, rebooted and signaled that it was ready.

Much to his credit, Will forgave that one, and what came after.

SACRAMENTO — The provincial legislature today passed the so-called "Non-Fatal Punishment" law by a wide margin.

Minor opposition to the bill came from members of the Green Party, who claimed the punishments would cause extreme emotional and physical pain. Senator Moira Coughlin, who authored the bill, stifled the dissent by using a computer model to demonstrate how the protocol would render the inmates unconscious with the same speed as the fatal system.

"They'll black out, they'll wake up, and hopefully they'll have learned the big lesson, that sexuality is there for marriage, so keep it in check until then," Coughlin said.

"None of us wants to go back to the old days, to having stacks of bodies under the Eiffel Tower, to watching San Diego burn. This simply builds on the Midwest statute. It's another layer of protection against that damnable virus," she said.

—From the News Bites web of the Sacramento Bee, omissions mine.

# TWENTY-TWO

February.

"Ms. Wilson, I'd ... can I invite Julie? To the prom, I mean?"

"Are you sure that's wise? I don't think God even knows when she'll be done."

"Yeah, but I'd like to do something hopeful. If it's okay with you. And ... if she wants to go."

"You don't need my permission, Rick. Your childhood ended in that pool. You may not be an adult yet, but you're not a kid, okay?"

"Uh, yes. Ma'am. Thanks, I..." He slumped into a chair, smacked—almost terrified—by that tiny bit of grace.

* * * *

The message arrived a few days later, and it was clear, despite the legalese.

The civilian oversight board had received an advisory from a former board member. I could guess who that was. The board had debated his concerns, found them valid, and contacted three members of the Provincial Supreme Court. After considering the issues in a special session, those three members, listed hereunder, had ruled.

Will told me the special session was probably a multi-beverage lunch, but still legal. And no, they weren't required to tell me they were meeting to dissect my life.

The ruling took one paragraph:

> We find that Wilson, Beverly A. failed to adequately supervise Wilson, Julie L., thereby furnishing Wilson, Julie L. the opportunity to

> commit a Class B sexuality offense. Therefore, Wilson, Beverly A. is compelled to appear at the Glendale Hills correctional facility at the appointed time and witness the punishment of Wilson, Julie L.

Failure to comply would result in a loss of everything I owned and two years in prison.

Will filed motions with the Federation courts.

I filed it away under More Shit Julie Didn't Need to Know, and the quiet voice reminded me that I deserved much more.

# TWENTY-THREE

March.

Julie stayed mostly in her room, studying with a dogged ferocity. Soccer tryouts were over and the team was building chemistry, solidifying without her.

"Don't worry, bud," Ke'andra said. "I'll come over after practice and fill you in."

"And UCLA will be so impressed," Julie croaked. She'd wanted to play soccer in the Rose Bowl since she was eight, and now that dream lay crumpled.

"Aw, come on, Jules. You'll be out there playing. Garner is good, but she isn't you. Everybody knows that."

Julie shrugged and broke the link.

I baked a pie that evening and listened to the chatter tumbling in from the family room.

"One over the sine equals the cosine," Ke'andra said. "I get that. But really, you need a prom dress, bud."

"Ke'andra Marie..."

"Seriously, Jules. Make Mop Head invite you to the dance. Because you *are* going."

Julie sighed. "He already has. He's even taking lessons."

"He ... him? Okay, concrete proof of God's existence."

"It'll be fun to watch him squirm."

"Exactly."

"But it's stupid to fly money on a dress I'll never wear."

"You'll wear it."

"Maybe. I'll think on it," Julie said.

A couple days later, Jen watched as niece and canine did battle around the pool.

"JULIE LYNNE!" My daughter skidded to a stop, wide-eyed. "I'm feeling optimistic. Let's get you a prom dress."

Julie glared at her. "*Et tu, Brute*?"

The result was a gorgeous off-white thing, shimmering in the full-sized holo screen at work. Julie twirled and smiled.

"Like it?"

"You look amazing, hon."

The smile morphed into something other. "Rick ... promised we'd be the first ones on the floor. It won't happen, will it?"

No. It wouldn't. And we knew it. But I was the mom. This was my job.

"When's the dance?" I said.

"May nineteen."

"Then you could easily be free to go. And if you can, I'll go with you and laugh while Rick tries to be three feet tall, despite the lessons. And if you can't, then we'll play cards or watch vids or cry, play with the dog, whatever. Now Julie?"

"Yeah?"

"Hang that thing up and go do those lunges or squats or whatever ladylike thing you do. And then, I think you should show me your skills at making a Panang curry."

"How hot?"

"The back of my head should melt."

"Soy-based chicken-like substance or beef-like substance?" She was giggling. I'd shoveled the bovine excrement and she was smiling. It was my job.

"Beef," I said.

She held up a finger, pressed it against her screen, and by design our primary means of communication cut us off when she tried to use a simple gesture to express love.

* * * *

The file arrived without warning and caught Jim by surprise. He didn't think the Civil Guard released disciplinary reports, but there it was, sent by Assistant Commissioner Tyler McGowan in accordance with some statute, and written in that corn-mush prose they teach to middle-school kids.

A routine audit of crime-scene videos had found actionable misconduct by Pavel Jankovic during the arrest of Wilson, Julie L. The infractions were clear. He'd fired a stunning dart even though he was in no danger of harm, and he'd shot from a distance of three feet. At that range, he was expected to hit Julie's upper chest or shoulder. Not her left breast.

He'd also taken his sweet time retrieving her from the pool (they can only let you drown if they know you've got the virus) and in the process he'd made insulting remarks about the military, a line he shouldn't have crossed, even though the detainee had.

After that, he'd dragged the dazed girl and her terrified boyfriend out to the patrol car without letting them dress.

When asked what motived his behavior, Jankovic refused to answer.

The Civil Guard gave him a choice. He could leave or stay on as a prison screw at reduced pay and a reduced pension. He'd chosen to stay on, and been assigned to another position.

We thought nothing of that, but it led to an event. I wasn't present for this conversation, but again I have the essence, the truth.

"Good morning, mister Jankovic. Welcome." The boss probably extended a hand, smiled and ran down the list of what was expected. Most bosses do.

Jankovic probably nodded and smiled through the litany. Most new employees do. And then, because you like to make a good first impression, he probably smiled and said, "I have something to show you."

# TWENTY-FOUR

April.

The eighteenth isn't just Velasquez Day. We do more than celebrate the man who brought the North and Central American countries together for mutual survival, then gave power back to a civilian government. And never mind all that icky slaughtering of anyone who got in his way. For us it's Emergency Relief Day, a personal holiday, a fine excuse for a long walk on the beach.

* * * *

I bit my tongue to keep from laughing. Rick was holding Julie in The Exact Right Way, just far enough to avoid improper contact.

"Okay," he said, "step and slide—"

*Dweedle* .

We all flinched, sharp and involuntary.

I accepted the link.

Julie reached for Rick's hand.

Will faded in. "Julie, we have a decision," he said. "The convict will be allowed to nurture her child for another two weeks, until the boy turns one."

"So when do I go up there?"

"June seven."

Julie looked bewildered. At first I wondered why, but then the date began to sink in and my lungs gritted.

"But ... it can't happen then," she said. "They have to change it."

"I don't think we have a choice," Will said.

"They can't do it then. Mom? Tell him they can't."

I lunged for the computer. "THAT'S THE DAY SHE GRADUATES!" Will didn't say anything, just looked sick. "FUCK YOU AND YOUR SYSTEM, WILL!"

The computer left a gouge in the paint.

Bewildered and nauseated, I lifted my daughter off the floor and rolled her into my lap. I didn't say I was sorry. For all its breadth and depth, the English language falls flat when it comes to apologizing. You can acquire a vocabulary of ten thousand words or more, yet only a few of those words express remorse or sympathy. After repeated use, *sorry* and its pathetic cousins lose their power.

Rick left without a word. I held on in that choking silence until the computer chirped and Alex faded in.

"I've just cleared time on my schedule," he said. "Virginia will come get you."

* * * *

Julie shuffled in and sagged onto the couch.

"Come on," Alex said at last. "You can find the words."

No response. She chewed her lip and stared into the distance.

Alex leaned forward. "Julie, I need you to look at me."

She complied and her eyes blackened, gleamed. She shot to her feet and bolted from the office, banging the door wide as she went. She was half way across the waiting room when Jim came in. She stopped, eyed him, tried to shrug past. He blocked her way.

Julie's hands went from still to blur, claws raking at her father's eyes. He flinched and jerked his head away; she broke into a fighting crouch—balls of her feet, balanced, ready—another blur.

He parried the kick with his left arm, a deft smear of motion. Julie recovered her balance, changed her stance, kicked again, punched a split second later. Neither blow landed and she sprang away, regained her footing and launched another volley—kicking and punching at knees and eyes.

She fought like a trapped wolverine. He fought like a Hollywood Zen master, calm and intent, the same expression he has when he's reading. And his hands were so fluid, their motions so spare as they fended off the blows.

It was hypnotic, this ballet of rage and self-preservation, and I realized I was sitting entranced, watching instead of being a parent. I was half way out of my chair when Alex took my arm.

"Let him do this," he said. "He'll do it well."

And he did, slapping the blows away, not a trace of anger, simply waiting until rage twisted into hysteria and she threw herself at him, tried to drive her forehead into his face. He ducked the blow, wrapped her in his arms and hung on until the rage became tears. His first, then hers.

* * * *

I didn't bother sleeping that night. Instead I gave Julie a sedative, eased her back into oblivion when she stirred, paced the floor.

A bit after three in the morning, I linked Virginia and left a terse message. I needed to talk. Really talk. Downstairs, coffee, and I stared at nothing until the computer chirped at five.

"When someone links in at three a.m.," Virginia said, "I know to link back. Especially when it's you."

"Let's walk," I said. "On the beach."

We started off in silence, and then Virginia took my hand.

"Tell me, Bev. Honestly. What was his name?"

"Let's just call him Evan," I said.

About my height, muscled and Nordic, laughing blue eyes and sandy hair, confident and outgoing, not too much arrogance.

I met him after my parents died. I'd lost two quarters of school—six months of talking to lawyers, selling my childhood home, putting the money into a trust and depleting mom's wine cellar. I'd rented a nice apartment far off campus and returned to Stanford heart sore, when I wasn't numb.

Evan breezed into one of my communications seminars, a small group of students delving into I don't remember what, and afterward he offered to buy me lunch.

"No, thanks. I'm busy."

"Some other time, then," he said as he breezed away.

He never pushed, never happened to show up at my regular haunts or adjust his schedule to coincide with mine. He just smiled.

I ignored him. I didn't have the resources for more. But toward the end of the term, on a late spring day, I found myself walking with him after class.

"I'm starving," he said. "Want to grab lunch? No pressure."

I reminded myself that some people do just want to be friends, and something unraveled, froze me in place. He looked at me, a bit worried.

"Actually, I'd like to go someplace wild," I said. "Feel like heading for the coast?"

He bought lunch and dinner; I bought the wine. We drove his car onto the bullet train with seconds to spare, and an hour later we pulled into the Point Lobos reserve and found a secluded spot where the wind sang in the trees and the ocean chattered against the rocks below. For some reason, the place was empty. I still can't fathom that.

I used my wrap as a blanket, and as we ate and got mildly drunk I blabbered about my parents and their single-minded pursuits of wine and neurosurgery. I only stopped when I realized I was crying.

He dug his fingers into my neck and shoulders. He had warm hands, strong like my father's.

"I can't imagine how much that hurts," he said.

I snorted through my tears, derisive and sharp. "Then why did I feel like celebrating after they broke the news? Why did I feel so free?"

"Probably normal," he said. "You get a shock like that and your emotions are all over the map. I mean, you grieved, right? You're crying now."

"I guess so."

"Well, then, the renowned Evan, world's wisest listening ear, thinks you can forgive yourself for that one."

"Thanks." I managed a giggle through the tears.

The sun was warm, the air lazy and rich with pine and the sea. He kept working at my knotted muscles until I stood and unbuttoned my blouse.

"Uh ... Bev?"

I shrugged it off.

"Oh, hey..."

My bra followed.

"Wait a sec," he said. "Just ... wait..."

I'd worn dress shorts, and I shivered as they slid down my thighs. I'd never known cloth could feel that way.

"Bev, please..."

I bent over as I slid out of my panties, and the reaction was exactly what I wanted—that gasp. I turned around, a leggy brunette who sort of liked her face and thought she needed bigger boobs. Evan looked at me with a mix of lust and terror.

"What're you doing?"

I knelt in front of him, put my hands on my knees and let him stare. "It's okay," I said. "No one will know. I ... I guess I want to be held."

He rose to his knees and took my hands. He wasn't obeying the training and walking away.

"You don't need to get naked for that. I'll gladly—"

I leaned forward and kissed him. "I didn't say I just wanted to be held."

I kissed him again and the world exploded—his clothes scattering, me pushing him down, an insane peak of grief and lust. I faded back into myself slowly, spent and drifting.

"Oh, my God," he said. "You ... you did baby stuff, right?"

I drifted toward his voice. "Yes," I sighed. "In the ladies, after we got off the train."

"Oh, Jesus, it doesn't matter. We're dead—"

"No! Stop!" I took his face in my hands. "We're not dead. We're ... not. And no one's ever going to know what happened." I kissed him, again. "Hold me? Please?"

We awoke still tangled, still alone, no guards except the birds and waves. I reached for him, kissed, fondled.

"If I'm going to get zapped for this," he said as he rolled me over, "it may as well be for all the right reasons."

He swept me away again, his arms rigid, ecstasy and loathing in his eyes.

"Holy mother," he said as he rolled off. "I can't believe we're this stupid. Jesus, God, who are you?"

"Evan, relax. No one will know."

He stood, groped for his clothes and dressed without a word. We drove home in silence, and after the car pulled up to my place I looked over to see him slumped in his seat, trying to wrap his mind around the loss of his virginity and the possible end of his life.

"You don't need to be afraid," I said. "Look, if you want we can go the courthouse, enjoy each other for as long as—"

"Just get out, okay? Just ... leave."

"But ... Evan, I feel real again. Like I can breathe. And this wasn't just about getting naked. Would you feel better ... can I say thank you?"

He didn't look at me, probably couldn't look at me, and another something came unraveled. I clambered out of the car and leaned in through the door.

"You know what, Evan? To hell with them. And their laws. I've seen enough death. It doesn't scare me anymore, so *fuck them*. They aren't going to keep me from living."

He shook his head and wheezed. "You ... you're crazy, you know that? You'll get us both killed."

"NO—I—WON'T!"

He didn't look at me, just leaned his head against the door and muttered, "Oh, God, oh, God, oh, Jesus, God, Jesus, God..."

I finally shook my head. "It's okay, Evan. You can run away now."

* * * *

I felt so calm as I put my hands on Virginia's shoulders. "And it's okay. You can report me. I feel just ... so much peace about what will happen."

She gave me a look. "How about I let God punish me for not reporting you and we'll call it good?"

"But ... I set the stage, Virginia. For all this."

Another look, worse this time. "Really?"

"Oh, come on. You know full well that nobody can hide what they really believe, and that's what we pass on to our kids. Julie's been soaking in my beliefs for her entire life. She must have seen to *hell with them* in God knows how many ways—off-hand remarks, body language, whatever. So what chance did she have?"

"Feel better now?"

"I guess. A little."

"Good. Because you're never telling Julie this story. Got it?"

I felt the lightness confession can bring, the laughter starting to bubble. "Yes, ma'am."

"Good. Now don't you have a job or something?"

* * * *

Rey handed me a mocha. I sipped, wished it was alcohol, let my mind drift until I caught him studying me.

"So what has you scared? Aside from the obvious, I mean."

"The waiting. Sitting there while the clock unwinds." I shuddered and barely heard his reply.

"I'll wait with you. I can be there until a few minutes beforehand."

Those words took a while to sink in. "You'll what?"

"Support you. We can play cards or something. They'll loan you a deck."

My voice came from elsewhere. "We like to play rummy. How do you know they'll let us play cards?"

He gave me the gentlest of smiles. "Because I've been there before. The place holds no mystery for me, Bev."

I heard but I didn't hear, the realities behind his words deflected by the fear drizzling through my mind. I heard myself saying, "... ask you to do that for me. You're my boss, for pity's sakes."

"But you've done something pretty amazing for me," he replied.

"I have?"

He held out a computer. "Sign this."

Automatic reaction—thumb to the pad, laser flash on my retina—then reality kicked in.

"What did I just sign?" I scrolled up the document, saw the name on the contract, and even though I tried, I couldn't smile.

"He bought it?"

"All of it. Says he wants to use it in Europe, too," Rey said.

"That means..."

"A budget increase of forty percent."

"So what took the *yutz* so long?"

"He consulted people in Britain and France to see how well his product would play there. Then he had to arrange for more factory space, and that meant more financing and you know how that goes. He figures to grow his business by three hundred percent in the next five years."

"So for now, we're heroes," I said.

He shrugged. "We both know that comes and goes. But this helps smooth over the bumps." He held out his computer again, and this time I authorized a deposit into my account. Thanks to Paolo Recchi's ambitions, I'd just banked six figures in creds.

"We did it," I said. "The classic advertising coup. Small shop scores major client. I should feel joy, Rey."

"Why, because an egotistical runt from Simi Valley wants to become one of the world's bloated rich? Not much room for joy there. I keep trying to tell Paul that it's only money, that it won't give him what he thinks it will, but he's hell-bent."

"You mean ... you know him? Personally? It isn't Paolo?"

"He's my nephew, Bev. The Paolo bit's an affectation."

"I've been badmouthing family since he showed up?"

Rey chuckled. "We all do. He deserves it."

A light dawned, one of those realizations you wish wouldn't come. "So, how many nephews do you have?"

"One."

"Oh, God..."

"That's what drives him, Bev, why he's so determined to build an empire."

I stared at Rey, slack jawed and mute. He chuckled. "I know it's a lot to deal with."

"Yeah."

"So go home and spend the afternoon pampering yourself."

"But I—"

"Now. Or you're fired."

He meant it.

# TWENTY-FIVE

May.

Charlie Parker wafted and the palette knife scraped until Rick walked by.

"Hold it, Tiger."

He ignored her. She followed him into his room.

"Didn't you hear me? I was talking to you."

No reply.

"Your father and I have heard from a half-dozen college recruiters," she said. "You're ignoring their links. You've set up a firewall."

Hard eyes, but still no reply.

"The least you can do is be courteous," she said. "They're offering you a free education and a chance—"

"I've told you what I'm doing."

"Teaching English in Botswana isn't a career path, kiddo. It's—"

"Then don't do it. You stay here and paint. That's been such a great career path for you."

"But Richard, this is your dream—"

"I don't give a shit."

Di saw the bewildered despair, knew she couldn't help him replace those dreams. That was his journey and he was in no mood to start. She fumbled for the right word or gesture or ... thing as another thought stole in, icy in its clarity: She was alone with someone who frightened her.

She fled.

* * * *

The almost-woman set the bowl of popcorn between us and flopped next to me on the couch.

"Are you sure this is a good idea?" I said.

"It'll be fine, mom."

The 'please wait' icon stopped spinning and a black screen appeared. A spot lit an empty stage. Ke'andra stepped into the light and filled the room with that hurricane of a voice.

*I looked over Jordan and what did I see...*

Julie tensed.

*A band of angels comin' after me, comin' for*
*to carry me home."*

The frightened girl curled into a ball and filled my lap, buried her head in my shoulder while I barked at the display to stop.

"She's singing for me," Julie said.

"I know. Why don't we watch this later?"

The almost-woman came back, that budding adult gravity.

"No, mom. That's not it. Look, I don't mean to be a drama bitch, but ... I've known this for a while now. I just ... I'm sure of this."

"Sure of what?"

"They're going to screw up and kill me."

* * * *

Prom night.

Two kids in sweaty workout clothes, sitting by the pool.

"May I have the pleasure of a dance?" Rick used the old speech.

Julie stared into the void.

TORONTO—The Federation High Court today refused to hear challenges to Midwest's controversial capital punishment law, but the court took the unprecedented step of issuing a brief statement about that law.

On behalf of the court, Chief Justice Emil Ancelin wrote, "The plague still poses a grave threat to this federation, and any measure to curb it should be allowed reasonable use and a chance to succeed...

"This court will consider challenges to the Midwest law only after data shows the law is not effective. Arguments that the method of punishment is cruel will not be considered because the Master Charter extends no such protections. Also, the principle behind the statute, that the punishment should fit the crime, has been established in law since Henry VIII of England.

"As the cliché goes, desperate times often call for desperate measures ... and when we compare our situation to that of citizens living in the countries of the Middle East, where the death penalty is applied swiftly and without regard for social or economic status, it is clear that using the ultimate sanction against sexuality crimes can help ensure a functioning society.

—From a *New York Times Online* story, omissions mine

# TWENTY-SIX

So.

Just what in the blue fuck do you wear while they torture your child?

That's the kind of question you ponder while the box of old papers shatters your closet mirror.

Jen raced in at the sound of breaking glass and lifted me off my feet.

"I want to know something," I said.

"What's that?"

"The execution is supposed to be painless. Instant oblivion, death a second later. We'd revolt if it wasn't. So why will my daughter suffer?"

Julie had stepped out of the house with her shoulders squared, buoyed by a quiet rendition of "Amazing Grace" from Kee and the calm that arrives when the thing you fear becomes now. I'd received no such gift.

Jen tightened her grip. "I don't know, sister-mine."

"Why do I have to wait until eleven to go up there? What difference does four hours make?"

My nightshirt lifted and I felt the astringent tingle of a patch. "This is a gift," Jen said. "Sleep now."

She woke me at nine by ripping off the sedative and applying a wake-up. "Two things. First, Coughlin was just sentenced to three years in prison. He's been stripped of his business and he gets to 'invest'—tee hee—fifty million in upgrades and fines."

"I refuse to care, Jen. I'd celebrate on any other day, but—"

"And I also just heard from my wretched younger sibling. We can go up to the prison any time. He's sending a car for us and driving himself."

Her Honor had pulled some strings. I didn't care why, just packed sweats and cross trainers, prodded along by Evan's face, with its dance of lust and fear, the feel of his cock, the voice wondering who was I?

* * * *

They confiscate your handbag and everything in your pockets. You'll get it when you leave.

You step through the machine with your hands up. It's a lot nicer than the manual option.

You sign a simple agreement to obey all guards and stay calm while visiting: ________________________

You shake your head because that single sentence will make you docile—*Jesus, God, who are you?*—and where is your child's father? He was supposed to meet us.

The disinfectant stench in the next room leaves you reeling, and your child's report may or may not help.

> I, Ronald Holderman, Superintendent of the Ventura Regional Justice Center, do swear that Wilson, Julie L committed no infractions during nearly four months of confinement. But I do note the aforementioned inmate skipped lunch on three occasions.

*And that will be enough right there,* I thought.

I looked around for guards, didn't see any, and I was almost ready to throw the computer when Jen caught my arm and made me keep reading.

We, the undersigned, do swear that Julie L. Wilson has shown a consistent pattern of maturity and growth under adverse and unjust circumstances. She completed her final year of high school almost two months ahead of her class, and has on several occasions taken full responsibility for her crime. For those reasons, we recommended the full measure of lenience. We would also like to remind the concerned parties that if they review other prisoner summaries, they will see that no similar recommendation has ever been made.'

Daniel J. Connery, senior educator.

C. Alexander Johnston, MD

I almost smiled.

* * * *

Another door buzzes open and you get the body slam hug from your child, a smile from her chaplain.

"What does the N.C.P. on your coverall mean?" I said.

"Non-capital punishment," Julie replied. "There's a joke for you."

"Er, what's funny about that?" Jen said.

Julie used that level gravity. "The system is old. It's broken. They're going to kill me tonight. Let's go see the garden." She stepped between Jen and me, seized our hands, led us to a door and addressed a guard.

"Day prisoner Wilson requesting the garden for herself and two family members."

The guard glanced at us and did nothing.

"The chaplain in charge just heard the day prisoner make a legal request," Virginia growled from behind us.

The guard eyed us and eventually pressed a button. The fresh air alone was beautiful. Virginia led us down a path, around a building, into a copse of trees, and we weren't in prison anymore. I'll give the garden that much.

You wander from setting to setting, surrounded by hillocks and trees that hide the prison and its walls, mute the traffic whirring by. We walked in the quiet of rustling leaves and squabbling birds, the scents of pine and wildflowers. Water trickled from fountains and gravel crunched underfoot.

Each setting has a theme—rhodies here, desert grasses next, an English cottage garden, and one that stopped me cold—a rock garden with bonsai. Serene little masterpieces.

"Well, hello there."

We yelped and jerked around, saw the smiling old woman, eyes crackling with laughter and something deeper, wiser.

"You must be Julie, yes."

"And you must be Mrs. Watanabe," Julie said.

"Mrs. Watanabe, my ass. Call me Sachi, yes."

I came back to my body. Sachi had that effect.

Julie grinned. "Do you remember Kari Edstrom? She talked a lot about you—"

"Oh! I hope she had at least *one* good thing to say about me. She's doing well, yes?"

"Yep. Going to school back east."

I bit my tongue and told myself Julie didn't need the truth. Especially today. I even managed to smile while Sachi walked us to the next setting, a plain vegetable garden, and we found ourselves pulling weeds from long rows of sweet corn. After a few minutes, Sachi took my arm as though we were oldest friends and walked me back to the rock garden. We sat on a simple bench made of three granite slabs, and she smiled up at me.

"I gave the inmates a simple order for this setting," she said. "I told them to make it peaceful, yes, because everyone needs a place to breathe, to let things go."

That was enough. I spilled everything I'd hidden—the nasty conversation with Rick all those months ago, my having to watch Julie's punishment. It was harder to talk about Kari's new job than it was to let Evan into the wild, even harder to admit I'd slapped my daughter.

We shared a long silence before warm wrinkles found my right hand.

"Good," she said. "Now you can take care of Julie, yes. It's almost lunch, so you should probably go. They're quite punctual around here."

"Why'd you start all this?" I said as we walked back to the vegetable patch.

A shadow darted through the eyes, tugged at the smile. "I tell people this place needed to smell better, but the real reason is that I lost a grandniece here, yes. She's still the youngest person the province has ever killed, and they botched it. She suffered. So I had to do something beautiful, yes, bring forgiveness, or the anger would have killed me.

"Now you might think I'm a lunatic, but my family and I will pray for you tonight. And, we're going to meet again, yes. I just know this, okay? So until we do, you take good care, and don't you worry about Kari, yes."

I walked away knowing the old lady was right.

And where the hell was Jim?

* * * *

You can't see the death house—sorry, the *Physical Punishment Unit*—from the main road in town. It's on the far side of the grounds, surrounded by its own fence. But it's one story and red brick, like the other buildings, and probably designed by the same drones responsible for airports.

And it's such a strange place for lunch. The cafeteria seats a dozen people, just day prisoners and their families, people just looking to survive, but the ceiling has a pepper gas canister anyway.

We noshed on a spinach salad, sliced meats and a good bread. Smiles and chatter flashed around me but I couldn't taste a thing and he may have been my ex, but I really needed him, *dammit where was he?*

"Coffee," I heard myself say, and an efficient young man with perhaps six months to live served me a steaming mug on a tray with cream and sugar. As he set it down, I was paralyzed by the sudden fear that if I did pick up the mug I wouldn't remember what to do with it.

As we finished the meal, Virginia studied us for a moment. "How would you like to spend the afternoon doing some volunteer work?"

"What kind?" Julie said.

"Care packages for Guatemala."

"Guatemala?" I spluttered.

"Geez, mom, the earthquake?"

"What earthquake?"

"The one last week? You know, flattened half the country?"

"Well, sooorrryyy. I had better things to think about."

Julie looked mystified. "Like what?"

"Like you."

"Oh."

We traipsed off to a warehouse by the garden, except I'm not wired for rote work. I tried to find a rhythm—socks, pants, diapers, baby formula—but my mind wandered, straight into the Golden State Academy gym and the milling bodies, the shuffle of feet on risers and the orchestra tuning up. I felt the excitement of parents getting ready to watch their children hit that milestone, saw the smiles and cameras everywhere, the parade of gowns and mortarboards, the boring commencement address—

"Oh, yes, sugar."

The inmate dragged me back to now.

“From what I see, your mom will be the world's best grandmother, so you be sure and push that along, give her some gray hairs, a few diapers to change."

I waited, watched.

Julie kept working and didn't reply.

* * * *

Class B prisoners get to pick their evening meals, just like the condemned.

We dined in that tiny cafeteria on grilled salmon, roasted small potatoes and snow peas sautéed in wine, if you can believe it. I could have sworn I'd have to eat pizza.

"Where's dad?"

"I don't know, sweetheart."

Despite the question and the feeling of being half naked because Jim wasn't there, we filled the room with chatter—how small Harley had been as a puppy, that time on the gravi-coaster where Jen lost a hat, then found it in a flower bed half way across the park from the ride.

I didn't see Virginia stand, but I heard the sudden quiet. She offered a hand to Julie and helped her to her feet. At first I wondered why, then I fought back the panic as a guard entered. She was the type who can leave you feeling mothered or kill you with just a glance.

"Hi, Julie," she said with a smile. "My name is Linda. It's time to start the first protocol, so do you remember the rule?"

"Help me through or put me through," Julie stammered. "Choice is ... mine." She looked at me, swallowed hard and turned gray. "Mama..."

I cut loose with my best hug. "Love you, forgive you, see you in the morning. Promise."

"I want to say goodbye to dad."

"I will move heaven and earth for that," Virginia said. "That's another promise. Now, can you follow me? Trust me?"

She lifted Julie's chin, caught the eyes, got a nervous nod. The door clicked behind them.

7:03 p.m.

# TWENTY-SEVEN

7:02 p.m.

The provincial executioner accepted a cup of tea. She wore the standard drab uniform and her gray hair in its usual tight bun.

"Two things," the warden said. "First, are you sure you're okay with pushing the button tonight? You look like you haven't slept in a week."

"I'll be fine, Grace," the matron replied. "Like I said, I've thought about this long and hard. Besides, who else do you have?"

"I can do it."

"And who will take your place? We've rehearsed with you in the room, and if you're not there it'll throw everybody off. Grace ... I ... the last thing I want is for something to go wrong tonight."

Grace looked at her again. "And that leads us to item two. I'm going to show you something that may change your mind." She told her computer to play the video from Jankovic, whoever that was, and up came the visiting area of the Ventura Justice Center. They watched impassively as Julie threw the computer at me, then the floor, and I slapped her, under those shafts of light.

"Who gave this to you?" the executioner asked.

"That new guard. He got demoted for the way he handled our young Ms. Wilson's arrest, but someone gave him this little souvenir when he left."

The women looked at each other for a moment. They didn't exchange nods. It was more a mutual understanding.

"I need to go look the system over," the matron said.

The warden nodded. "Thank you. I know this is hard."

The matron crossed the grounds, unable to shake the nagging voice that said something was off. Maybe not wrong or broken, but skewed.

A young guard let her into the alcove, and she tried to laugh at the voice. They'd tested everything during rehearsals that afternoon and the numbers had come up good and strong, so why the spike of angst? She chided herself for worrying, barked at herself that everything looked fine, and then she barked at the guard.

"Here." She handed him a neatly folded piece of clothing. "Have the non-fatal crew give this to the Wilson girl. Tell them she can wear it the whole time."

# TWENTY-EIGHT

7:12 p.m.

We escaped to the simple bench in front of the bonsai. I'm not sure how or why, or even if it was important, but the little trees had me muttering into the air.

"You're unbelievable. You stick me with the First Church of Incurable Wads, you make me an orphan, give Coughlin to the world ... and here I am anyway. Asking. Be with my daughter? Please?"

"Amen," Jen said in the same near whisper, and a moment later she clutched at my hand. "What are they doing to her? What's this protocol?"

"They scan her and draw some blood," I said. "They use the scans to adjust the 'apparatus'—don't you just love that term?—so it fits her, and they use the blood to formulate drugs for after. They also use it to..."

"Don't you choke this back, Beverly Anne. Please."

"They use it to calculate just how much she can take. Maximize the pain with no permanent physical damage."

"So what happens after that?" Jen said.

"She takes a whirlpool bath, nice and soothing, except there's hair remover in the water. Then she gets to spend an hour with her counterpart."

"Oh, God." Jen looked appropriately sick.

"Now, now. How else can you understand the full extent of your offense? You simply *must* have a chat with the person who'll die while you're trying to scream louder. It's *the* thing to do this season."

"And after this friendly little visit?"

"She and Virginia sit, I guess. Talk, wait, play cards or pray, watch Julie's spirit die ... I don't know."

I couldn't say more, didn't want to say more, just let the wind and birdsong wash around me, any kind of peace until I had to pay for being a mom. I made myself breathe, slowly and deeply—one breath, two—then boots crunched on gravel and a guard strode up to us.

"Come with me," he said.

"Did I do something wrong?" I said.

"Don't know. Warden wants to talk with you. Right now."

I burst out laughing, a manic peal that brought tears to my eyes.

"It's Coughlin. It has to be. He and his wad cronies have found another way to get back at me or Julie. Probably both of us."

Jen didn't reply—what could she have said?—and we and followed the guard back to the death house.

"Excuse me," Jen said to him, "but may I ask a question?"

"Sure."

"Has anyone heard anything about Julie's father? He was supposed to be here hours ago."

"What's his name, ma'am?"

Jen told him and he used his handheld. "Says here there's a Jim Wilson visiting a Julie Wilson in the PPU. He's marked as a special."

"What's that mean?" Jen asked.

"He's connected to a high-up. Someone big wanted him let in."

At least Julie got her chance at a good-bye.

"One more question?" Jen said.

"Certainly, ma'am."

"Will my niece receive any mercy?"

"Don't have that information, ma'am. System only tells you once the punishment starts."

We turned a corner, out of the garden and onto the concrete that led to the death house.

"By the way," I muttered at the sky, "you may be as much a wad as your followers, I mean, they are created in your image, right? But could you be ours? Mine? Just this once? Please?"

As the building loomed, I had the quiet sensation of being heard, just perhaps, there in the soft light of early evening.

* * * *

7:34 p.m.

Another door, another buzz, and the warden emerged, eyed us with that hard parental stare.

"I've been ordered to extend you every courtesy," she said. "You and Julie's father." The poor dear was choking on that one. "Your daughter wants to confess something, and chaplain Johnston thinks she'll be calmer if she does, so I'm giving you fifteen minutes. I'm also going to fill the corridor outside her cell with guards, and if you step so much as one thin millimeter out of line, you will become my guests."

* * * *

7:46 p.m.

The cell was just like the one in the simulations. The lights glared off the acrylic panel that faced the corridor, so all I saw was a pile of something on the bed until I stepped in and the tangle arms and legs became Jim and Julie.

The words escaped in a wild burst. "Oh, thank God! And just where in the vast expanse of ass-wad hell have you been?"

Father pulled daughter closer, kissed the top of her head and looked at me through exhausted eyes. His dress tunic was filthy and the left sleeve torn.

"Let's just borrow the old phrase and say film at eleven, okay? We have more important things to talk about."

He smiled at Julie. She bit her lip, tried to sit up, tried to make eye contact.

"It was my fault, mostly," she croaked. "He wanted to stop, but I took my shorts off, just ... stripped. Right in front him. And then I ... I took off his shorts. He wanted to stop, daddy, and I..."

She started to pull away but Jim pulled back, held on until she settled into him. His hands were large and still on her shoulders, welcoming and protective.

"I'll ... work," she said. "Keep the yard, cook or do dishes or whatever, clean the house—"

"Stop." Jim tried to lift her chin, catch her eyes.

"I mean, you can let me live at home that way, right?"

"No. I can't. I won't." He used a bit more force to lift the chin and catch her eyes. "You will do no such thing. We're going to take you home tomorrow. You're going to be our daughter and we'll be your parents. Just like always, okay?"

"I will?"

"Yes, sweetheart. Always."

I leaned around him and nodded to reaffirm that essential truth, saw the gash in his shirt and the blood around it. He caught my eye, shook his head and managed a wincing smile.

So we tried to reach through the thickening layers of fear with whatever scraps of love and grace we could find. Ke'andra would sing, we said. Harley would be delighted to have her back. We'd go for long walks on the beach, find the best South Asian restaurant, rent a cabin in the mountains.

And then Linda was standing at the cell door, looking at me. Our fifteen minutes were almost gone. She beckoned and I followed her out, down the corridor and away from the other guards.

"I'm retiring tomorrow," she said.

I stepped back, an involuntary flinch. "What does that have to do—"

She put a hand on my arm. "Hear me, please. I want to make you an offer."

"And that would be?"

"You write well. I've looked at your ads for at least fifteen, twenty years."

"How do you know that?" I said.

"They briefed us on you, and you know how to reach people, communicate." She hammered the last word into urgent syllables—com-MU-ni-CATE.

I nodded.

"I want—I need—to do at least one decent thing before I leave here. This place, it brutalizes everybody—prisoners, guards, visitors, families—and I need to know that I did more than just hurt frightened youngsters for twenty-five years."

"But what does that have to do—"

"I'll let you stay with your daughter until she goes through that door."

I remember the other side of the corridor coming into focus, blood roaring, the rush of my breath. Linda said something, flashed a reassuring half smile. I felt her lead me back to the cell, but I don't remember those eight or ten steps.

I do remember Julie hunching her shoulders and stepping out, but I couldn't remember why, only hear Linda saying it'd be okay as they cuffed her lightly and took her by the elbow. I watched them lead her around a corner, and then I was sitting next to Jim.

"Jesus, Bev, you look like you've seen the proverbial ghost," Jen said.

I looked at Linda. "She'll let me ... stay. Until. It's time."

Linda closed the cell door. "I would have finished at the top of my training class," she said. "Except I had asthma when I was a kid, and I couldn't run fast enough, so I ended up here. I have to know I was more than just a screw."

I raised my hand. "I'll do it," I said, "but only if they can stay with me."

Jim looked at her with hard eyes. "The warden has been ordered to extend every courtesy."

Linda smiled. "That's all the excuse I need."

Prison guards fight to balance authority and punishment with humanity and decency. Most of them fail. You can't rob people of their freedom without losing something inside yourself. Linda was trying to walk away with a scrap of humanity by giving me a chance to witness something that few outside the hermetic world of the prison had ever seen.

And then com-MU-ni-CATE.

I caught my breath, and then I asked one of those questions that had gnawed at me. "Tell me, when they trained you for this job, did they make you empathize?"

She nodded.

"Did they make you..."

Another nod. "We also felt the pain, but only for a second. And no, ma'am, that doesn't justify any of what will happen tonight. That's why I need your voice."

"This could bite you. Big fangs."

"Except I'll be off-continent in less than forty-eight hours. Can I get you a deck of cards?"

"Y-yes," I stammered. "Sure. And ... do you have any coffee?"

She smiled. "I knew you'd stand up."

* * * *

The cards were new, the coffee not bad. Jen managed to shuffle and glare at her brother.

"So, James Burton, you meet a bear with a grudge against dress uniforms?"

"Uh oh," he drew a pained breath, "my punishment name. Let's just say that I think we're going to have some interesting reading."

We keep journals here in the province of California. It's a mania with us. So much small history was lost during the chaos—the memories and stories passed between families and friends—that we're seemingly determined to make sure we never lose ours.

That's how we know the mind of Pavel Jankovic, from his journal. The rest we infer from the video captured by Jim's car.

* * * *

9:54 a.m.

The car stops. Jim gets out, opens the rear hatch, retrieves his dress blue tunic and starts to shrug it on.

"Ass wad military!

The gray streak drives him out of view.

Jim comes back into view, hunched over in a defensive fighting crouch. The streak is a man now, a prison guard bleeding heavily from a shattered nose. He swings the baton downward at Jim's head. Jim ducks under the blow, grabs the baton and arm, twists it around the guard's back. The pop as the bone breaks is distinctive and nauseating.

But it's also hypnotic, this other ballet of rage and the swift end of that rage. You can't see Jankovic reach for the stunner, but you see Jim kick it away. You can't see Jankovic reach for the knife, but sunlight flashes on the blade and

Jim clutches at the gash in his side. He gropes in the dirt, uses the baton once, twice, five times, then stumbles into the driver's seat, punches up a link and reports the incident to Tyler McGowan. His hands shake so badly he has to try four times before he can send Ty a copy of the video. He staggers around the car again, uses a pair of boxers from his overnight bag to stop the bleeding.

The camera shows the local civils and emergency techs going out of their way to be courteous. Jim shows them the gash, the bloodied uniform, explains why he's wearing it and he'll gladly talk but can he support his daughter first? Please?

Pavel Jankovic kept silent again, mostly because he spent a week in a coma before he died, but his journal said enough. One of his uncles had been sleeping off a drunk in a guard station on a May evening. In Minot.

Jankovic probably didn't know he was attacking the father of the girl who'd mouthed off. Jim was simply military, a target of opportunity, and the area wasn't covered by the prison's surveillance cameras.

* * * *

8:06 p.m.

Jim fell silent, tugged at a loose thread on his ruined tunic, came out of his reverie and started to shuffle the cards.

"Rummy, anyone—"

He stopped, looked out of the cell, then stood—not fast, not slow. Julie shuffled in and sagged into him, stayed there while Linda undid the cuffs. He winced as he picked her up and settled onto the bed, then he gave me that look—now what do we do?

I shrugged and saw the young father bursting through the door, sweeping his giggling toddler into a dance, the approving smile that said she was beautiful in that dress, the sheer weight of *daddy* in those exhausted eyes.

"It's okay to just be quiet," he said. "Just hide here, pretty girl."

"She was horrible," Julie wheezed. "Said if it wasn't for me, she could be spending time with her baby. Said I was just one last adolescent shithead. And she's right."

"No, she—"

"If it wasn't for me, she could've spent another two hours with her baby. Now she'll never see him again. They won't let him come back in."

* * * *

Time becomes important when the Civil Guard arrests a loved one. You count hours and minutes in ways you never have before. And in that cell, time became what I'd feared—an undefinable and invisible tyrant, moving at its petty pace, refusing any pleas for the mercy of speed. They have clocks in the corridor to keep the hors d'oeuvres from getting more nervous, and I shuffled the deck, dealt four hands of rummy and watched a minute tick by as Julie rallied herself and joined us. Jen took the first trick, another minute slid past, then Julie smiled and shook her head.

"Mom ... all that stuff about dying tonight? Really dumb. Sorry."

I chuckled.

Jim looked sick. "What?"

"Nothing, dad. Just me being stupid and scared, that's all."

So we talked and played rummy, gloated when luck favored us and moaned when it didn't.

And then it was 9:48.

I was busy cursing time for slipping away when another chaplain appeared. Iron gray hair, stocky and powerful. He smiled at Julie, then all of us. "Major Wilson? I need you to come with me, sir."

Father and daughter stood. He kissed Julie's forehead, a gentle caress, like he'd done since she was twenty minutes old.

She smiled, took his right hand in hers, made him point his index finger and count her freckles.

He leaned close and whispered. She looked up at him—really?

He nodded and smiled—yes, really—and he was gone.

# TWENTY-NINE

9:50 p.m.

Virginia rubbed patches onto my daughter's body.

I pretended to emcee a fashion show:

*Julie is nicely accessorized by an electrolyte on her neck and a heart protector on her chest. Both are in shades of blue that were* all *the rage at Milan this year—*

Maybe not.

Julie's hands shook as she zipped up the coverall, and her eyes flared and darted around the cell before they settled on me.

"Mom ... how can you be here? You won't watch, right? You can't watch. I don't want you seeing ... it. Me."

I eased her back onto the cot and kissed the forehead some more. "Don't you worry. I know what to do."

"You do?"

"I promise I do."

9:53 p.m.

Six guards appeared in the corridor, a different crew than the ones we'd seen, but just as drab. I wondered how a uniform could grant so much power and yet make a person so insignificant.

And then two of them came into the cell. One carried a piece of folded clothing, the other a tray with some kind of medical package. I made out the word 'sterile' in green letters.

The first guard unfolded the clothing and offered it to Julie as though it was a birthday gift. "Here. Maybe a bit small, but nice, huh?"

It was a tattered robe in a shade of pink, and Julie looked so bewildered.

"No," she said. "I can't wear anything. I was naked when we got caught."

"The warden can bend the rules," Linda said. "It's really okay."

Julie flared. "Rick didn't get to wear anything, Kari didn't, I'm not."

The screw with the robe flinched backward, bumped the guard behind her and upset the tray. The packet dropped to the floor. Linda picked it up and glared at Tweedles Dee and Dum until they left the cell, and then of all things she handed the packet to Julie.

I thought my daughter was remarkably calm as she tore the packet open and took out two slender gray cables, fittings on one end and plastic tubes on the other, gleaming with some greasy gel, and suddenly I wasn't afraid.

Since that first link from the guards so long ago, this part of the "protocol" had torn at me. Alex had tried to condition my daughter for this moment, shape her mind to hide away and survive, but not me. I'd had no prep. None of us had thought I'd be in that cell, so I welcomed the calm, almost bathed in it.

I kissed my daughter, said I'd be right outside, tried to look the Tweedles in the eye as we stepped out. They looked past me, ready to step in should anything go wrong with the "nestables."

Nestables. A term coined by, and used only in, the prison.

Soft as cotton, coated with all the right chemicals and ready for insertion into my daughter's body, just like anyone condemned to death for a sexuality offense. Oh, and they cost the taxpayers four thousand creds. Economies of scale and all that. You don't have many repeat customers.

Jen and I shuffled a few feet down the corridor. She groped for my hand and we leaned against each other, closed our eyes and sagged into the wall. I wish I could have closed my ears.

"It's easier if you start with the large one." Virginia's voice was calm and level, reassuring as it bounced along the walls. "Just go slow, you have plenty of time ... take a deep breath and try again ... there you go. Pull gently ... okay, ready for the next one?"

"It's cold."

"I know, dear, but that'll change in no time. Do you want me to steady your hands?"

The second insertion tube clattered to the floor with a cheery tick-tock. I shuddered and Jen squeezed my hand, then my shoulders, and I opened my eyes, told myself I could do this, *would* do this. All of it. I had to com-MU-ni-CATE.

I slid past Linda, buried my face in Julie's sopping hair and let God hear me scream while I inhaled the metallic reek of fear.

"Is it time?" came the leaden voice.

"It is," Linda said. "I need your hands."

I helped Julie put her hands behind her back, closed my eyes and heard the cuffs ratchet shut, opened them just as Linda hooked the leads to them, and then Julie pulled away from me. With a sudden flare of strength, she looked over at Virginia and said, "Let's go."

Before anyone could react, she brushed past the guards and started down the corridor. Virginia fell in behind her; the guards scrambled.

9:57 p.m.

I stood with my jaw hanging, heard the shuffle of Julie's cloth slippers and the hard raps of shoes, the hiss of the door. And then—I swear this is true, and so do Julie and

Virginia—I heard someone say, "Oh, you'll love eating there."

The shuffle of feet became rapid, random, frantic. I heard Virginia say, "Julie, I need you to look at *me*. Concentrate on *me*—"

The door hissed shut.

* * * *

9:58 p.m.

Eighty-five miles away, Ke'andra's hands shook as she tried to hold the starter to the wick. Diane Westmoreland reached out to help, but Charlie got there first and the candle flared to life. Kee grabbed Charlie's hand in a death grip, and she groped to her left for another hand, any hand. She found Rick's. He found his mother's. Di reached for her husband, and moment later all hands joined. They looked at Ke'andra, expectant and smiling.

"I can't do this," she said.

"But you already are," Di said. "Tears are a song all their own, aren't they?"

Kee took a sobbing breath and the first two notes flowed in a thick wave of sound, as elegant and rich as a fine red wine, despite the tears behind them.

"Sister..."

* * * *

9:59 p.m.

Sometimes, the gifts surprise you. Mine came as Linda walked us along.

> *So keep your lamp a trimmin' and a burnin'*
> *This world 'most done ...*

It came in the different key and slower tempo, and it was clear, as though I was standing with them.

* * * *

10:00 p.m.

The executioner watched as the door hissed open and the guards hustled in the main course. On the pretty side of plain—peaches-and-cream skin, wonderful eyes, hips meant for kids, a flat belly despite the one she'd had—and like her two young men she wore only white cotton slippers. That was the law, of course. Nekkid while you make the beast, nekkid while it devours you. Let the punishment fit the crime.

They didn't give her a chance to think, just hustled her in and got going. Out of pure reflex the matron flipped on the holoscreen.

Except she hadn't meant to do that.

For years she'd steeled herself against the possibility of seeing someone she knew on that screen, or even worse, through that mirror. Every time she'd played that scenario she'd concluded she was tough enough.

But now ... the terrified girl, balking as the chaplain nudged her toward the chair and helped ease her down.

The matron had never reckoned on seeing someone she loved in that screen, and she churned with self-loathing and ... calm. Maybe it was the erosion of her conscience or the death of compassion, but it was still her job and she was a pro, except for ...

"Dammit," she muttered to the wall. "They forgot to give her my robe."

* * * *

10:00 p.m.

Another door hissed open and we found ourselves in a room with cheery yellow walls and two neat rows of bright red plastic chairs.

The chairs faced a thick window that ran floor to ceiling, darkened electronically so we couldn't see what was happening on the other side.

Two of the chairs were occupied, one by a civil rights monitor, there to ensure Julie hadn't been beaten or otherwise mistreated before she was tortured. How anyone could make that determination with the screen darkened still eludes me. The other was an official witness for the courts, there to ensure the law got its meal. No one looked at us or spoke.

Jen wound her way through the chairs toward the recovery area. Linda gave me a weary nod and motioned.

"I have to tell you to sit there, please."

Jen stopped. "Huh? What's she saying, Bev?"

"I have to watch, Jen. I got a court order."

"They ... I'm staying."

She settled beside me as Linda pressed a button on the wall. The darkened pane began to clear but the audio came on instantly, glorious high-def sound—scuffling shoes and quiet voices shot through with Julie's quavering, terrified wheeze.

Just as the pane cleared, one of the screws casually flicked a remote control and a bright light cast Julie into sharp relief, blinded her and made her jam her eyes shut. She looked quite prim, like a little girl at a tea party, but then she had no choice. The straps held her that way. One around each wrist and upper arm, one around her ankles, another around her waist. And those eyes, shut so tightly.

A clock behind the chair counted not just the hours and minutes, but also the seconds, and it was now ten o'clock and forty-three seconds, forty-four, forty-five—well past any deadline. Nobody would try to stop the execution.

One of the guards pressed small wafers onto Julie's temples—superconductors, held in place by a gel that penetrates the skin and cuts the resistance to nothing. Another guard attached a wire to the disc on Julie's left side, but when the wire on the right didn't click into place, the guard used a handful of my daughter's hair to provide the needed leverage. A moment later a strap seemed to unfold itself from the chair back and wrap itself around Julie's forehead, but it was all so fast, so hard to take in, and then there was another strap around her chin and something pulling her head tight, into a rubber pad on the chair back.

"Oh, my God."

I don't remember speaking. Neither does Jen. But we remember the quiet, horrified words.

And it wasn't the sight of my daughter—trussed and helpless—it was the jarring contrast between her and the guards. She sat hyperventilating, wet and pasty in that shrill bluish light. Virginia knelt beside her, leaned in close, held her hand and whispered—two figurines in a swirling cloud of gray uniforms, the guards moving like wraiths around them, vague and formless, plugging Julie's body into the panel behind the chair, connecting her to the earth.

10:01:56 p.m.

Virginia leaned closer. I couldn't make out the words, but I heard a sad, fervent voice, the familiar cadence of prayer and the loving weight behind it. A yellow light flared on the panel, a guard touched Virginia's arm. She stood and said, "Where are the shadows, Julie? Find them. Let them take you away."

I knew what she meant. The staircase at home casts all sorts of shadows, and the child Julie had made them into her wonderland, her Narnia and Middle Earth, where everything always turned out well.

"No," Julie wheezed, and someone dropped a gray cotton hood over her face.

* * * *

10:01:56 p.m.

"You!"

The matron heard the icy voice and looked out. The main course was focused on the mirror, glaring with the fury Julie had seen earlier.

"You are going to have an interesting conversation with God, and I'll be there to share it. I don't care what he does to me, but I'm going to love watching what he does to you."

The matron started. In twelve years of doing society's darkest job, none of the condemned had said a word to her. It wasn't the voice, but the sheer novelty of receiving that rage. Mostly this job was routine—two jolts and bank the money—so a little variety was nice. She'd definitely give this evening more than one line in her diary.

The prisoner's eyes held steady for a frozen moment, then collapsed, as though she'd stirred a pile of embers for one final wave of heat and now the energy was gone, the eyes glassy and bewildered. Or maybe they could already see the long journey.

The hood descended, the guards stepped away, the warden looked at the mirror and gave a businesslike nod.

* * * *

10:01:57 p.m.

"Find the shadows, dear heart."

"No, no ... I can't," she wheezed.

"Yes, you can," Virginia said. "Right there."

"No ... mama? Mama?"

"Sweetie, I'm here. We're both here." My voice surprised me—confident and planted.

"MAMA?"

"I'm right here, honey—"

"OH, GOD, M—"

* * * *

10:02:07 p.m.

Just like she'd done since Julie was six, Annie Waldenburg pushed the button.

# THIRTY

10:02:07

I'd feared this moment.

Dreamed this moment.

It disappointed me.

Julie just sat up. No wild jerking, no hissing or buzzing, only a strangled, gurgling wheeze and tight muscles, a body frozen against the straps in that oh-so-correct posture.

Except for her hands, scrabbling at the arms of the chair as though she was groping for an elusive cross-stich needle.

10:02:10

"The Class B prisoner..."

*Wow! Still the same voice as my doorbell!*

"...has been scheduled to receive full punishment."

# THIRTY-ONE

I giggled.

We'd had that glowing report, and yet someone had arbitrarily decided to give my daughter sixty seconds of rank agony because lunch had given them gas or their shoes were too tight.

Something jerked at my right hand, and I heard the tick of shoes on the floor—Jen's?—vaguely registered someone vomiting. But that was distant, secondary, drowned by a screaming mind.

*Damn you/throw something/DO SOMETHING/SHE'S HELPLESS!*

But what? Scream? Cry? Hit Linda with a chair? Leave? I couldn't do any of those.

I sat, just as frozen as my daughter.

Mute and cowed, black with shame.

Unable to look away.

What you're seeing is so dispassionate, so calm and clinical. No hysterics, just your child's gurgling moan and the guards looking elsewhere with stolid faces.

10:02:13

Movement, swift and certain. Virginia stepped around a guard and approached the chair, knelt, closed her eyes, and then her whole body jerked as she seized Julie's left hand.

"No," she said through clenched teeth, her arm shaking as the current flowed to God knew where. "Not this one."

And then I wasn't giggling, wasn't helpless. I had words, and I had tears.

"I'm still here, sweetie," I said. "And I love you, just like always."

10:02:22

"Probably even more."

10:02:26

"Sounds crazy, huh, in a place like this?"

10:02:37

Julie sagged into the chair. I counted agonized, shallow breaths—one ... two ... three.

Then she screamed.

# THIRTY-TWO

10:02:43

The second wave arched my daughter's back...

*Such an elegant line. I should have Di sketch that.*

... the scream became that gurgling wheeze again and her thighs squeaked against the seat while her feet slapped the gray tiles.

The rest leaves me ashamed.

10:02:48

*I wonder if Rick did that, quivered that way?*

10:02:51

*I wonder if the counterpart's dead, and ... wow, somebody really mops this place. Spotless. And would you look at my shoes? How'd I scuff them?*

10:02:57

The gurgle stopped. Julie quivered from head to foot, her face pointed slightly up, the line of her back not so elegant.

# THIRTY-THREE

A mechanical arm swung from the back of the chair and pressed a sensor. The med screen on the wall lit up and displayed four horizontal lines, red at the bottom, then blue, green, and white.

And the white line wasn't straight, wasn't flat. Annie could see that, even with the warden and doctor huddled around the screen. Heart? No, that was green. White was the brain, a few random nerve endings still bravely carrying on.

Some bodies did that, struggled for life despite society's best efforts to the contrary. She thought of them as durable convicts.

*And do we have a solution for you, dearie.*

As the warden and doctor stepped away, Annie focused on the holo screen and did something for the first time. "I'm not sorry I called the guards, girl," she muttered. "Not for a minute."

She'd never spoken aloud in that alcove, never needed to. But now her words lined up and stood proud, where it mattered. She took a final sip of tea and put down the cup. The warden turned and faced the mirror.

* * * *

Guards moved toward my daughter.

"Bev?"

How interesting.

"Bev?"

I heard a rhythmic squelching, looked over to see Virginia walking through the ribbons of vomit, oblivious to them.

"What're you doing here?" I said as she reached for me. "Shouldn't you be talking to Julie?"

"It's over, dear."

"It ... oh."

She took one of my hands and led me toward the recovery area. I barely caught the yellow flash and the guards jerking back, away from the chair—

"Virginia?"

"What, dear?"

I took in the clock—10:03:51—as a convulsion rolled down Julie's body. Arms circled my neck, and I knew the refuge of wool against my face.

*NO. STAND UP. LOOK.* SEE.

In a final instant of clarity, I tried to give my daughter a true witness, someone other than a guard. Too many kids had shuffled down that hall with nobody to see or care, and I would not let my daughter's pain to go unseen. I had to com-MU-ni-CATE.

But I couldn't watch. I'm only human, and I did what I suppose most of us would do. I stood with my forehead on Virginia's shoulder and stared in mute fascination at the concrete floor.

*Next time, bring shoe polish—*

"Get out of my way."

The voice sounded through the speakers, and I saw Linda, fury in every crease, striding through the door, putting an old fashioned key into the side of the panel. Turning it.

The yellow light winked off again.

My daughter slumped again.

Her chest didn't move.

How ... interesting.

# THIRTY-FOUR

Caregivers don't have the right to help a Class B prisoner until the guards turn on a green light. They came anyway, flooded in and muscled the guards aside, a crusade of indignation and woman scorned.

Straps folded themselves back into the chair. An I.V. cuff circled Julie's right arm. The oxygen generator sealed itself to her face. She was no help at all as they moved her to the gurney. That was so unlike her.

And she was so tan. When had she spent time outside?

"Uh oh, this one's failing."

The voice sounded almost scared, and Virginia tugged, led, and I watched myself step out of prison and into nurture and safety. She led me past the holo curtain and I stopped, stared at the shimmering barrier, heard the voices on the other side.

"Alright, people, she's down. Lungs at zero."

"Start with five of Ultrox."

"Bastards."

[Silence.]

"Drugs on board."

[Silence.]

"Nothing yet.

"Do another five."

"It still isn't working. Less than twelve."

"Give her another ten. You can't be too aggressive with this stuff."

[Long silence.]

"Still nothing."

"Bev, dear, come on. They know what they're doing." The voice was familiar. A hand pulled at my arm.

The curtain shimmered.

"Julie, honey, can you cough for me, please?"

"Still below the bar."

"Come on, sweetie, wake up."

An alarm began a rapid beep.

How ... fascinating.

# THIRTY-FIVE

I know this: Christopher Coughlin sat alone in a bare cell, nothing but a mattress on the floor and a sink and toilet that hadn't been cleaned in a decade. They'd stashed him there because it was a short walk to the loading bay, where a hauler would take him to Glendale Hills the next morning.

I can imagine the dark voices, quiet whispers of a lost fortune and a name so blackened he'd never reclaim it. And the Wilson bitch was probably sound asleep by now, free to go home.

I know Coughlin saw the mattress and the torn seam around its top. He used his fingers to worry the stitching, loosen it, and as the cloth came away he found circular cord.

# THIRTY-SIX

"Come on, honey."

"Really, Bev, we need to let them take care of you."

Virginia tugged again, and I ... grew, towered over the shimmering barrier, pushed past it. I'd read the holy text—parents must wait outside the curtain—but it was just so natural, watching myself step through. I towered over the shape on the table, marveled at it—an ankle and foot on one end, chestnut hair on the other, people in between wearing those shimmery sterile clothes.

"Come on, honey."

"Poor thing. Those wads could've stopped at two."

"Or they could've not done it all."

"Okay, people, how long has she been down?"

"At least four minutes."

"Shit. This isn't working."

I loomed over the people and raised a fist.

# THIRTY-SEVEN

"What th' hell you doin' here, boy?"

The young guard bristled. "I'm on break."

"The hell you are, boy. You're guarding a single prisoner on sub-six, an' you got nothin' to do but sit in a chair and ignore him for eight hours. Didn't they tell you in training that you never leave anybody alone the night before he goes to prison? Didn't you hear the same thing from me two hours ago?"

"Didn't they tell you the rules for this job? I know what I got the right to—"

"Get your ass back down there *right now* or you'll be hauling trash and cleaning toilets for the remainder of your very short career. I make myself clear to you, boy? Move or I write you up."

Randy Few probably grumbled as he rode the elevator down to sublevel six. He'd worked hard, built his chest and arms until they were serious, man, developed a rep among the bad guys that made them obey when he talked. Yes, sir. And none of that seemed to matter. The senior wads always gave him the crap details, and all because of that holy woman complaining about the way he set the military brat into her place.

But he was tougher than the old guys. You could tell they was just waiting until that pension kicked in and they could go to Shasta Lake or wherever and catch fish until it was time for the diapers.

Things would change then. Nobody in a coverall would mouth off. Ever. Well, they'd try it once, then they'd starve due to high-grade jaw misfunction.

The elevator disgorged him onto the loading bay. He settled onto his chair, and from the cell he heard cloth ripping. Idiot was probably tearing his clothes off, he was so afraid of going up north. Served him right by all accounts, getting people killed when they was trying just to earn a wage, and the stupid rich bastard only got three years. Wasn't fair. Randy listened with maybe half an ear as things quieted down.

Then his hair stood on end.

That was one thing they told you in training—trust your gut—and the cell was way too quiet. He looked in just as the inmate looped a thin rope over a pipe. And the pipe was over the toilet. And the inmate was standing on the toilet.

Even Randy could figure that one out.

"Prisoner will stop!" he barked.

Coughlin ignored him. The video confirms it.

"I said knock it off and get down against that wall right now!"

In the video, Randy unlocks the cell just as Coughlin finishes securing the rope. He almost has his head in the noose—a clumsy slip knot—when Randy punches him in the gut with a baton.

# THIRTY-EIGHT

"BREATHE, DAMN YOU!"

I drove my right fist into Julie's side with everything I had...

"WAKE—UP!"

...registered stunned faces as I struck again.

"NOW! I DIDN'T SINK EIGHTEEN YEARS INTO YOU JUST TO HAVE THEM—"

Someone caught my fist and I was me again, five-foot-seven again, slouching toward middle age. And what the hell had I just done?

Who's that?/How'd she get in here?/Oh, God, it's her mom.

"Wait ... thirty ... forty-one ... here she goes. Good."

Julie's eyes fluttered, showed their whites, and what the hell *had* I just done?

I don't remember stepping out, just the yellow and blue of the curtain, the words 'Privacy, Please' shimmering just over it, the hospital smell, Virginia's hand on my arm.

"Julie, honey, can you cough?"

I heard two slow marches of air, a third, and then, "Good girl. Where's she at?"

"Ninety-nine."

Hoo, boy/ That one scared me/Okay, sweetie, let's get you clean.

"Come on, Bev."

Virginia tried yet again to move me, and a bath? That was my job. I'd swabbed every square millimeter of my daughter's body until she was old enough to do it herself. Privacy, my ass.

I wasn't as tall this time, but I still loomed. The shape lay on its right side while elbows bent and hands moved through a slime trail of bubbles and foam, fingers going deep into the scalp. The shape had always liked that, me rubbing the chemistry into her hair.

A spray of water drove away the foam, revealed a slender back, a toned waist, the flare of hips. Those hips would probably round a little, become that perfect bit more inviting, and then the shape would spend the rest of her life battling to keep them that way. Or she'd neuter them with layers of fat.

But for now they were beautiful, tan and white, and maybe they would nurture a child. I smiled at the idea until careful hands pulled gently on a slender gray—

The plunge left me reeling and motion sick.

*Oh, God, all that soap in her hair.*

"How'd she get in here again?"

*What if they run out of water?*

"Oh. Come on, dear. Let's go this way."

"You can't leave ... that," I pointed at the bubbles, "her scalp gets flaky."

"Don't worry, hon. I'll make sure that doesn't happen. I promise."

"And no product. She hates product."

"We know, hon. We know."

This hand led me to a side door and the musks of pine and sage, a quiet voice telling me I was brave.

I could only nod (I think) and take in the three-quarter moon and Orion's belt, shake as the night air chilled my sweat, wonder why shoe polish had ever mattered.

I heard a noise, off to my right, and my mind ticked an item off some list—the fusion generator outside the fence had shut down. I was the mom. That was important.

Tires crunched on gravel as a gray cargo van eased by and I was the mom. That van carried a dead body and I was the mom, I needed to com-MU-ni-CATE.

About that van.

The way it stopped at a gate.

Moved again.

Found the maglev strip.

Sped away.

"Ms. Wilson?"

"Huh? What?"

"Your daughter's ready."

"Ready? For what?"

* * * *

"Daddy? I'm here?" The shape sounded so surprised.

"Yes, beautiful. You're here. You're safe."

Given the size of its budget, you'd think the justice ministry could provide words for that occasion, a suggested vocabulary for parents and maybe some time to use it, but the doctor is quick with that sedative.

And please, fluorescent pink blankets? Ke'andra's color, not the shape's, and I was going to ream the bastards, saturate the muck channels with all the facts, dump the shame thick and fast. Com-MU-ni-CATE.

Virginia handed me a mug. I gulped half because my throat had never been so dry. The hot chocolate stole in like a welcome summer rain, and the shape's hair was wet against the mother's cheek. It smelled familiar, a wonderful old smell.

The dream of tires crunching on gravel lasted forever.

# THIRTY-NINE

The father let the car drive and the anger bleed away, slowly, safely. A gray hauler with barred windows came the other way, and he caught a flash of weak chin and proud eyes, the rigid posture of someone wearing pride, his only defense.

The father couldn't smile.

The mother sat in back and cradled the shape in her lap. Something niggled, griped about a whatsits in her handbag. It was important. It was nurture. You're the mom. Take care of it. She reached in, found a ring with a stylized soccer ball, and the shape stirred as the ring slid home.

"Mama?"

"Yes, love?"

"You were there. You watched."

They'd given the shape a long-term pain killer, a segmented patch. When one dose ran out, just rub the next segment. The mom rubbed, then stroked the shape's hair until sleep returned.

* * * *

Home.

To a yard covered with streamers and a poster on the door:

> WHO NEEDS AN APPENDIX?
> GET WELL, JULIE!
> WE MISSED YOU!
> WE LOVE YOU!

All the mother could think was, *Oh, God, the yard's a mess and they punctuated.*

The father lowered the shape onto the couch. The mother draped a blanket. A while later she rubbed cream into bruises on arms, ankles, that toned waist.

"Tell me, mom."

"Tell you what?"

"Why'd you watch?"

The shape fended my hand away from the patch and that was enough. She became light and shadow, cracked lips, a waterless voice and the thing I feared most—godforsaken eyes.

"Because they made me," I said. "I didn't tell you because things were awful enough. So now you tell me, sweetie. Did you find a place to hide? Did any of that work with Alex help?"

Julie twined her fingers with mine. "You called out to me."

"Yes, I did. I don' know how I found words, but—"

"I'm glad you did," she said.

"You are?"

"I tried to hide, use the words, all that stuff he told me to do ... I was too scared. But I heard you, and I knew what to do, where to hide."

"Where was that?"

"Your voice."

# FORTY

On that morning, wearing nothing while pitching a campaign would have been better than the smothering exhaustion and the roaring in my ears.

"And I'm telling you, Alex, she's worse now than when we brought her home," I said. "A lot worse."

"Does she talk about how she feels?" he said.

"No."

"Does she do anything physical, play with the dog?"

"He licks her face."

"Has she seen her friends? Have they been over?"

"They left a nice mess in our yard."

"How did she take that?" Alex said.

"She was asleep. And the last thing I needed was streamers on my fucking lawn."

"Bev?" He waited until I looked at him. "For now, this is normal. But link me if it goes on past next week. And Bev? Invite the friends."

I slumped against the counter and sipped at cold coffee. It was almost eleven and I still wasn't showered or dressed. I'd spent the past four nights sedating myself and waking up in a cold sweat after vivid, severe dreams. Then I'd awakened some more and held my daughter after her vivid, severe dreams. I could barely move, let alone deal with teens and their innate hysteria. Invite the friends.

I shook my head, started to warm up the coffee and heard footsteps creaking on the porch, then a soft thud. I jerked the door open, saw the yard clear of streamers, the sign gone from the door, a huge bouquet on the porch and a flash of sunlight on the blond mop. I groped for words, and the best I could do was, "You cleaned this up yourself?"

Rick walked back to the porch and stopped at the foot of the stairs.

"No, ma'am. Charlie and Kee helped." He motioned at the flowers. "For Julie. I didn't knock because I didn't want to wake anyone up."

Even in my splattered state, I could see he was dying to ride in on his war horse and rescue. I had no idea what to do with that.

"Thank you," I said. My mind lunged, fumbled for the smart action, the right words. "Now tell me something. How would you have felt if Julie showed up five days after you were done?"

He looked at me, weighing his words. "I woke up some nights and felt so alone, like nobody else could understand. But I was afraid to say anything."

"Why?"

His eyes took on that obsidian jail-gleam—the truth is crowning yet again. Gird thyself.

"Because you don't really understand unless you've been there. So Julie was the only one I could really talk to, and I didn't want her to understand."

Well, crap. What was I supposed to do with that? I'd just witnessed honesty and confession on the adult level—forgive me, reverend mother, except I haven't really sinned. I was groping for a reply when I felt a hand on my back and Julie pushed past me.

She eased onto the stairs. Rick hesitated, settled beside her, offered her a hand. She ignored it.

"I'm glad you're done," he said. "Glad you're home."

No reply, just a long, numb silence.

"It's okay," he finally said. "I'll go. Just ... I'm sorry. Please try to remember ... that, I guess." He started to stand.

"They took my body away," Julie said in a vacant wheeze.

Rick sat again. "I know."

He put a tentative hand on her shoulder and she started, as if seeing him for the first time.

"You're here," she said.

"I ... flowers."

"Why?" Her voice had gone even more flat.

"Because I..."

The fog lifted, replaced by something darker. "Why? Why are you here?"

Rick gathered himself. "Because. Because I love you, and so does Kee, Charlie, your family. I'm here ... dammit, because you're here. And don't worry, I get that you don't want to see me anymore. It's okay. I'll go."

It wasn't okay, but what choice did he have?

"What I did," Julie wheezed. "To you. My family."

"No. Stop. Alex taught us not to go there."

Julie faded away, then straightened and looked at him.

"You really would have taken my place? Let them do you again?"

He nodded, dead serious.

"Why? I'm just me."

"And I love just you. The way your pony tail bounces, that scrunchy look when you do math. The way you giggle. That's what really got me. It was never the big things, the soccer or whatever. You bite your lip when you keyboard. And you giggle."

Julie burst into tears, then a giggle came from behind and mowed them down. The emotions set up an odd rhythm—tears, giggle, tears, giggle, yin, yang, until the two melded into drenched laughter.

Rick waited until she reached something like calm, reached out to rub a shoulder or stroke a cheek, hesitated, put his hand down. "You should probably rest."

No reply again, but a comfortable silence, and Julie finally nudged Rick's shoulder with her head. That was one of their signals, her way of saying she was sorry.

"Of course you're forgiven," he said as he pulled the hair away from her face, saw the smudges under her eyes, still so vivid. "And you really should rest. Kee and Charles want to come over with pizza."

"You guys went out, right? After graduation? Charlie promised to make sure you went," Julie said.

"Kee thought it would taste funny without you. We all agreed."

Later, I learned that someone had asked Ke'andra why Julie was missing. She'd made up a quick lie about Julie's appendix blowing, then gone into the ladies and donated her appetite.

Rick stood, helped Julie stand and gimp over to me, then he picked up the flowers and offered them to her.

Her eyes grew wide and she shied away. "I don't ... I'm not..."

"Yes, you do deserve," he said.

"No."

"Yes. This is ... love, beauty, all the things that place isn't. You need to go here," he nodded at the flowers.

Julie reached out slowly, almost fearfully, took them and gave a tentative sniff. Yellow roses, orchids, curly willow branches, joyous and serene. I suspected Sachi was behind it.

"Thank you," she croaked.

Rick patted his heart with his fist. "Talk later?"

She nodded.

He turned to go, but she stopped him with a hug. "They took my heart away," she finally said.

Rick tightened his arms. "Share something Alex told me?" She nodded. "If they'd really taken your heart away, you wouldn't be here crying."

She pulled away and brushed at a tear. "Thanks."

"Now rest, okay? Sleep, play with the dog, go for walks, laugh at the dreams."

"I'll try."

Rick smiled, stepped off the porch, and that was goodbye for them. They had one failed try at a date a few weeks later, and years passed before I saw him again.

* * * *

Ke'andra and Charlie arrived as advertised, hands tangled while they balanced two large pizzas from Haggis & Company, their favorite joint.

I smiled through the noises of eating and the dream chatter of teens. Charlie was headed for engineering school in some place called the Palouse. Julie quietly admitted that maybe she could catch on at UCLA and get a scholarship. Ke'andra grudgingly agreed to give higher education a try, if she could sing.

I grudgingly told myself the friends had been good and I smelled bad. I was coming downstairs after my shower when I heard Julie say, "Do you think we could do that, fight back?"

"Julius Lynne, nothing your slob ass does will ever surprise me."

"I can see it now," Charlie said. "You'll become prime minister and usher in a wave of prosperity, then you'll get the chairs banned outright. And I'll be the power behind the throne, your gatekeeper, the most feared person in Ottawa."

Ke'andra snorted. "And you'll learn all that at engineering school?"

"Of course. Multivariant calculus is the key to life, the source of everything. It leaves you all-knowing."

Charlie would never shut up, and that was okay. I padded into my office to see if work had disintegrated, started scanning and ignoring just as a fist slammed into a chest.

"You'll be the most bruised, you don't shut up," Ke'andra said.

"Yes, ma'am."

I smiled. They were probably headed for the altar, they'd probably stay married forever, and that was a good reason to get got lost in some random neuron surfing, so I didn't hear anyone come in, just the hands on my shoulders and that elegant dark skin.

"Remember when you did this for me? I'd be sleeping over and have a bad dream."

I purred.

"Thanks. For being my second mom. I probably don't know how much I needed you."

"My slob ass, you mean?"

"Well, yeah."

I let the moment live, then said, "Is he really going to do it, Kee? Leave for wherever?"

"Looks like it," she said. "He's got a ticket for a couple days after his birthday."

"Does Julie know?"

Ke'andra shrugged.

"Do you think he'll tell her?"

She sighed. "I'm too scared to ask, he's so angry. And I hate to say this, but I have voice lessons so I kind of need to go."

"You? School?"

"If it's voice, it isn't school. It's joy. And the Julian one is dead on her feet. Sedate her or something?"

I shook my head. Teen hysteria indeed.

* * * *

Julie dozed away the afternoon, slid toward tears or laughter when she was awake but never quite got there. The visits had pried open the lid on her emotions, at least this round, and they simmered, just under the surface.

Jim and Jennifer bustled in at dinner time, loaded with takeout from our favorite South Asian place. They'd taken up residence since we'd come home, sleeping in my office or by the pool, worried about the husk on the couch and helpless to do anything except say they loved her.

So I wish I'd had my camera for what happened next—the look on Jim's face as Julie skidded into the kitchen on stocking feet and slammed into him.

"Brave hunter kill wild Chicken Vindaloo."

Jim spun her around. "Look who's entered the building," he said.

"Rick came over."

"And?"

"So did Kee and Charlie. They all basically told me to cut the bullshit and forgive myself."

Jim narrowed his eyes. "And?"

"We ate pizza."

Jim gave her his fake-nasty smile. "So you don't need dinner."

She returned the smile. "Sorry. Starving."

We dug in, talked about Jim's day, and Julie held up a hand.

"Wait. Just ... something. Big."

We held our collective breath.

"Aunty Jennifer dear, you drove up to—there with mom, right?"

"Yes," she said.

She narrowed her eyes, the prosecutor swooping in for the kill. "So how'd you get home?"

"Will took my car up and got me," she said, her face carefully neutral.

"Oh."

I bit my lip and waited.

"OHHH! He's the ... he's your..."

Jen blushed and smiled. Jim chuckled.

"Does he have the brotherly seal of approval?" Julie said.

"If I tried that with my sister, DNA really wouldn't help them identify my remains," Jim said.

"Wow. That's ... please pass the naan? Have you set a date?

"He hasn't proposed, Julie, and we're taking our time."

"Yeah, sure. What do you want us to wear? Have you picked out colors? What about a church?"

She grew ever more brittle as she yammered on, almost obsessed.

"Wow, a high-powered lawyer in the family. He'll be useful. Does he practice sports law? I may need an agent."

Rational sounds from a crumbling girl. It was like watching one of Hollywood's unstable doomsday machines—seams eroding, smoke wafting, the building around it shuddering and starting to crumble.

"Green. Mom and I both look good in green, okay? And make him buy you a rock. Like, ten carats. I mean, it's old-fashioned, but it says the right things and you're *really* worth it..."

We all pitched in with the dishes and started a game of Race 'Em, three-dimensional backgammon with timed moves.

"You'll do it, won't you? Awful bridesmaids' dresses as revenge on me ... DAD'S NOT VERY NICE!"

Jim finished making one of those lucky moves that devastate everyone else. Julie glowered as she rolled the dice and moved her pieces.

"So tell me, recruit Julie," Jim said. "Rick came over."

"Yep."

"And he called you on your bullshit. What did he say? Care to share?"

Julie looked at her father and a furious tangle invaded her face—fear, joy, grief, rage, and God-please-forgive-me-because-I-can't.

*Here it comes*, I thought. *How did Jim know to say that?*

"He ... said he loved me?" She shuddered and moaned, high and keening, almost airless. "How could he do that? Daddy..."

The first of the crying jags. Alex had warned us about them and given strict orders to let them happen. Jim lifted her out of her chair and settled her on the couch in the family room. Time crawled in a haze of shuddering sobs and Julie pounding her father's chest while I rubbed her feet.

She exhausted herself hours later, collapsed against her father and settled into what looked like sleep. Jim picked her up again and started for the stairs.

"Mama, can I have a dream patch? Please?"

"Of course, sweetheart." Not that they worked, but I retrieved them from my purse and found Jim rubbing his daughter's back and breathing, slow and deep, calming her.

"Dad?"

"Yeah?"

"Sorry I was so mad at you."

"You had good reason to be."

"I'm not so sure. I sort of think I understand now. Sometimes your heart, it reaches for things, doesn't it? I reached for something, just ... the wrong way."

Silenced by yet another curve from his daughter, he shook his head and smiled. I settled to the floor, rubbed in the patch and we held on until her breathing slowed.

# FORTY-ONE

I didn't care how late it was or how much wine it took, I was going to bed in an elevated mood. Or maybe insulated. Either way, screw that sleep hygiene crap.

Jim came in and sat at the table. "She's out for real," he said. "Jen's with her."

I poured him a glass and sat beside him. He offered a hand and I took it, renewed my acquaintance with the bumps and wrinkles on his fingers.

"I'm sorry, Bev. For everything—"

"Who was she?"

He looked at me for a long moment. "Head of the finance division," he sighed. "We worked on some accounting upgrades and ... flirted."

"Was it fun?"

"No. One date was more than enough."

"Really?"

"Let's just say she eats the male of species."

"Did you marry her? Screw her?"

He shuddered. "I said goodnight and drove away as fast as I could." He looked at me, level and direct. "And I'm sorry for that, Bev. I know we've apologized for the small stuff, the boredom, the fights, but I'm the one who ... why are you asking this now?"

"Because I need you to screw me until I'm raw."

The hand shook but the eyes were steady, intent. "Can you forgive me?" he said.

"Can you forgive yourself?" I replied.

"Fair enough. Can we do it better this time?"

"I will if you will," I said.

He looked at the clock, it was almost midnight. "They still have that all-night thing at the justice center, right?"

* * * *

In the stillness of early morning, the couple gave up on straightening their clothes, emerged from the car and walked arm in arm to the house. Without warning, he picked up his bride and carried her through the door.

They wasted no time on dreams.

Three days later, their daughter finally realized what they'd done.

# FORTY-TWO

Six months later.

Tyler McGowan hated Mondays, packed with more than the usual bovine croissants. And this pile reeked. He'd spend exactly three minutes scraping it off the department's shoe, then he'd take a pain reliever.

The scraggly piece of muscles and attitude leered as he and the lawyer entered the room.

*Fine* , Ty thought. *He gets two minutes.*

"You ever hear the one about shit rolling downhill?" Ty said.

Randall Few snorted. "Course I have. Gonna make it roll on you for this."

*Make that one minute.* Ty started the video, froze it after Randy had spit a dozen shells, glared at the stupid punk until he shrank.

"You see that woman there?" He pointed to Jen, frozen in prayer, sunflower shells on her blouse and in her hair. "She is one of the richest people in the country. And she is currently rolling all sorts of shit downhill. And I'm not about to let any of it hit me. You're welcome to take your firing to court, but if you do, I'll simply turn this video over to the prosecutor and bring you up on every charge we can find. We may even make some up."

The lawyer glared at her client and began to gather her coat and bag.

"You will turn in every last piece of gear we've issued to you," Ty said. "If we find a single loose thread or missing button, I will have your ass for theft. And for the rest of your life, if you so much as look at someone the wrong way, I will know about it and turn you into a puddle of goo."

Randall Darnell Few made his way to Alaska, found work on a crab boat of some kind, and on a rare night of calm weather, when everything should have gone smoothly, his right ankle caught in a length of heavy rope. A five hundred pound crab trap saved the gene pool from anything he may have left behind.

* * * *

Another two years gone.

The god of clothing is on his way to becoming an international force. I've had a miscarriage, sent Julie to college, and I'm frustrated. I've looked for ways to fight back, force the system into something like fairness, or perhaps self-awareness is a better term, but I've come up empty.

* * * *

The computer announced the name and I opened the door to Sela, one of Annie's daughters and Julie's favorite babysitter. The gawky teen had blossomed into a happily married woman on the computer end of the professional tier.

And even through the hugs and smiles I knew something was off.

"So, dear. What's new with you?" I said.

"Mom ... went to Salzburg for a Mozart festival, and her heart gave out. She died in her sleep."

I said all the usual things and meant them, even backed them with tears.

"Mom wanted you to have this." She handed me a rectangular package wrapped in the usual webbed hemp, and I knew from the feel it was some kind of book. I said more of the standard words, hugged Sela goodbye, promised to keep in touch.

A few days later I unwrapped the package, found a diary and a letter addressed to me.

Annie had always said she couldn't write worth a gnat's fart, and the letter confirmed it. It also made my nerves jangle in ways they hadn't since Julie's arrest.

> Dearest, Bev.
>
> I'm giving this to you because I wan't you to know that what I did I did out of love, not just for Julie—but for everyone—all of us. I think that you will understand and I hope that you wont think to badly of me. Remembar that I tried to give her my robe.
>
> —Annie

Give who a robe?

I opened the diary, found sickening contents recorded in a grade-school hand. The first entry didn't mention names, just a drunk executioner and an Asian girl who received five jolts. Some bodies just don't conduct electricity, so after Sachi's grandniece died horribly, they started with the electrolyte patches.

Most of the entries took a single terse line—date, gender, courage level, number of jolts, amount paid. I counted an average of twenty-eight executions and twenty snacks per year for almost fifteen years. The state paid her four thousand a death, a thousand per snack. A six-figure income and more than four hundred dead.

Julie, though, she rated four pages. I read them, reread the decision to give my daughter full punishment, and keenly aware of what power can do I contacted Will.

He filed all sorts of forms with the Federal Investigative Service. Big Uncle said thanks and we never heard anything more.

# FORTY-THREE

Another five years under my belt.

This book has provided marvelous therapy, a metric ton of hope since I received Annie's diary, but I just gave a draft to the reviewer I fear most. He's one of stranger twists in this this story, this reader, and so far he's behaving as expected, meaning he links in over the smallest detail.

"I wasn't an almost-man, Bev. I was a boy."

"You're making me look too noble, Bev. Julie, too."

"Am not."

"Are too."

And so on (I love arguing with him). But he hasn't reached the chapter that has me nervous.

* * * *

The link came on a Saturday.

"What are you doing?"

"Er, cooking—"

"Don't move. Don't you even twitch."

I defied the command by stirring a sauce and growing nervous. The sweet guy was still in residence, but the now-man carried layers of muscle and drive, a diamond toughness that sometimes intimidated my husband.

I had just enough time to register fury as he lifted me off my feet.

"Just what in the blue fuck are you thinking?" he said with quiet menace. "You've confessed to a capital crime in writing?"

"Don't worry—"

"Don't..." His eyes flooded. "They'll fry you. They're good at it."

"No. They can't."

The look on his face was one for the family archives. "And just how many stupid pills have you—"

"I checked with Will. There's a well-established defense for this kind of thing, and I won't even get arrested. Now will you please put me down?"

"What about Evan, or whatever his name is? What if they find him?"

"He's dead, Rick. He went back east to visit a friend, got into a fight in a bar and someone brained him with a chair. So if they charge me, I'll just smile and ask them to produce the witnesses and the physical evidence. Okay, that'll be Will's job, but he's ready to go. And that's only part of the defense, by the way."

That did nothing for the murderous glare. "What's the rest?"

"Your honor, that passage is simply a metaphor, my way of expressing the guilt that I'd heaped on myself over my daughter's failure. I've filed an affidavit with the court stating as much, and yes, the counseling helped. Can I breathe now?"

"No," he growled. "This crap about Julie being your victim, absorbing your attitudes about sex through osmosis or voodoo or whatever? Last time I checked, we screwed up all by ourselves."

I managed to snake a hand free and stroke a cheek. "I'm telling the truth about what I thought at that moment. Metaphorically, of course."

He deflated and lowered me to the floor. I took his hand and led him to the family room. We'd splurged on a new couch, another 1960s reproduction, a wonderful blob of a thing in charcoal fabric. He slumped into it.

"You're sure? About the confession?"

"Yes," I said as I slumped beside him. "Will vetted that chapter thirty-six ways to lunch."

He pulled his feet up and rested his head on his knees. "I'm still scared."

"That just means you're smarter than me."

We laughed long and hard, one of those celebrations of being human, and then he grew serious.

"You publishing this book, is it really fighting back? I mean, it may help, open a few eyes, make a few creds, but will it change things?"

"I only know one thing, Rick. I look at you, I think about the piles of shit Julie went through, and I have to scream. So that's what I'm doing. And I'm hoping. And it feels good."

* * * *

Changing the story became its own form of torture. Rick's version of the truth ran contrary to mine, and my wisdom. I struggled for a few days, then Virginia opened a link and gutted that struggle, made it childish and obsolete.

"I need to see you. Please? Right away?"

"Of course, dear, "I said. "What's wrong?" She looked like someone fresh out of, well, the chair.

"No. Not over a link. In private."

Her hands shook as she handed me the thick envelope.

My lungs clenched when I saw the spidery handwriting.

Chaplun
Ventura Regyonal Justis Ctr.

Annie. Again.

"I rearranged my office," Virginia said. "I'm so sorry."

"For what, dear?"

"I found that." She pointed at the envelope. "Behind my desk. It came on a busy day, and I meant to deal with it, but it fell behind my desk and I forgot about it. Until I saw it this morning. I ... read it."

She slumped into the couch, too obliterated to talk. I fished out a stack of papers and a memory bubble. The hard copy at the top of the stack made me sick. No bureaucratic language, no euphemisms.

> You may have been told that the new punishment law calls for Class B prisoners to receive a field anesthetic. In my opinion, that section is merely advisory. If you have qualms about not implementing it, see me in person and I'm sure we can find a beneficial arrangement.
>
> —Moira Coughlin

*A field ... OH, JESUS, GOD, A FIELD ANESTHETIC?*

They're a military tool. The medic applies a patch to a wounded soldier, then a jolt from a stunner. The drug reacts with the current and the medic has a good ten minutes to work without all that screaming.

In other words, my daughter was supposed to wink out, just like (we hope) the condemned. And so was every other terrified youngster.

I knelt beside Virginia and took her hands. "I know this is hard, love, but what did Coughlin mean by a beneficial arrangement?"

"Memory bubble," she whispered.

I plugged it in and found financial records. Coughlin had bribed two prison wardens, a couple dozen guards, and at least three officials higher up in the justice ministry. With campaign funds, of course.

And there was more, the provincial seal on a dozen files, overlaid by two shimmering words:

PROTECTED/VITAL

In the Province of Greater California, most records are public property, but not all. Some information is just plain private, such as family court records and medical data. And sometimes the powerful try to seal records quietly, bury some dirty secret. You can blow the whistle on most of those secrets unless they're considered "vital to the proper functioning of government."

Virginia could land in prison for merely possessing these files, and if I didn't report her, we'd share a cell for at least five years. I didn't care about me, but the idea of Virginia in a cell made me even more ill. Then her hand shot into my field of view and tapped one of the documents to open it. The "vital" secret was the original copy of Coughlin's offer of a bribe.

"Okay, I get it," I said. "She hid her crime by marking everything as a state secret. But hon, you need to be careful here. I don't want you getting hurt—"

The wreck had become a fury with razor eyes. "I don't care, Bev. People need to know what she did."

"Does Alex know—"

"He's a big boy. Now shut the hell up and stop trying to protect me."

I managed a nod and she tapped another file.

"Here's the punishment law." She scrolled down. "Here's the paragraph. It look advisory to you?"

> **14.18.23:** Prison officials will, without fail, provide an approved military field anesthetic to individuals subject to Class B punishments . Prison officials will do this at the appropriate time, and in a way that ensures immediate unconsciousness.

"I don't know what to say, Virginia," I wheezed.

"Does this affect your book in any way?"

"Of course," I spluttered.

"Then don't say anything, Bev. Write it down. I don't care what happens to me. Write it."

* * * *

Now another two years, almost.

Ke'andra leans in and speaks, words tripping over each other in their haste and urgency. She hugs me and I hug back, then I float down the hall, buoyant with hope. Oozing it. Filthy with the stuff.

I knock on my neighbor's door and almost jump up and down as I spill my good news. She looks at me with defeated eyes and says nothing. I tell myself to go in and comfort, be the mom and all that, she's only nineteen. But then the familiar voice sounds.

"All inmates to cells. Doors closing in sixty seconds."

I step quickly, sit on my bunk with my hands on my knees, prim and proper and ready for inspection, a little girl at a tea party.

The door slides closed.

—Transmitted from Maximum Security Level A of the Ventura Regional Justice Center.

# ACKNOWLEDGMENTS

Leta-Rose Scott deserves endless hugs for reading countless drafts of this book, all bad, and the screenplay that fueled it. If I could, I'd give her a new body. Sandy Zboyan and Tess Wiggins gave me a shove by wondering why I was so worried about the basic story line. The beautiful Michelle brought love, music, the time to write and the keen eye and fearless criticism every writer needs. Loreen La Penna, Claudia Weisz, Joannie Kervran Stangeland, Janet Miller, and Brian and Marilyn Wilcox, and John Murphy read drafts and gave encouragement and input. Michael Garrett kicked my butt firmly out of the first person, present tense (almost), and convinced me to cut the story in half. And last but definitely not least, Lisa Konick helped me find and unravel those last few kinks.

*Newjack*, by Ted Connover, showed me prisoners, guards, and how prisons dehumanize both. Jim's words to Julie at the prison sprang from Henri Nowen's *Return of the Prodigal Son*.

Deunan Berkeley showed me part of Julie's warrior spirit, Maggie across the street showed me more, and Dave Crosier provided shelter during the worst of storms. Beau stood guard and didn't snore while I started this book; now Gypsy has that duty.

Notice how often I used "give" and its relatives? I'm a lucky guy.

I also need to thank a few strangers, the sparks who collided and became this story. The first is a Ugandan girl who lost her parents to AIDS and broke down just as one of my sisters, Claudia Bratt, took her picture.

The second spark was an anonymous New York man who contracted the 3-DCR strain of AIDS. I didn't make that up; start your favorite search engine and learn more.

The third spark came from this place in Iraq called Abu Ghraib. I won't thank the prisoners who ran into a few of my country's degraded people—some of them may have been just as bad. But some weren't, and either way that doesn't excuse my countrymen.

Finally, I suppose I should thank the people behind that third spark, the steel of deceit that struck the flint of immature and warped soldiers: George W. Bush, Dick Cheney, Alberto Gonzales, John C. Yoo, Jay Bybee and the other members of what Garry Trudeau called "the torture crowd."

Nah.